MURDER ON
MADISON SQUARE

Center Point
Large Print

Also by Victoria Thompson and available from Center Point Large Print:

Murder in the Bowery
City of Lies
Murder on Union Square
City of Secrets
Murder on Trinity Place
City of Scoundrels
Murder on Pleasant Avenue
City of Schemes
Murder on Wall Street
City of Shadows

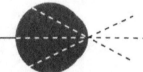

**This Large Print Book carries the
Seal of Approval of N.A.V.H.**

MURDER
on MADISON SQUARE

A Gaslight Mystery

Victoria Thompson

CENTER POINT LARGE PRINT
THORNDIKE, MAINE

This Center Point Large Print edition
is published in the year 2022 by arrangement with
Berkley, an imprint of Penguin Publishing Group,
a division of Penguin Random House LLC.

The text of this Large Print edition is unabridged.
In other aspects, this book may vary
from the original edition.
Printed in the United States of America
on permanent paper sourced using
environmentally responsible foresting methods.
Set in 16-point Times New Roman type.

ISBN: 978-1-63808-389-4

The Library of Congress has cataloged this record
under Library of Congress Control Number: 2022934781

MURDER ON
MADISON SQUARE

With thanks to my friend and colleague Timons Esaias, who relentlessly researched electric automobiles to find the information I needed for this book. No one works harder than a fellow writer who is looking for a good reason to procrastinate from his own work!

I

"A rich lady is here to see you," Maeve said with a mischievous grin. She had closed Frank's office door behind her when she came in so she could make this announcement in private.

"A rich lady?" Frank echoed with a grin of his own. "Is it my wife or my mother-in-law?"

"It's a *client*," she told him smugly.

"And how do you know she's rich?" he challenged. Maeve had begun her career as nanny to Frank's children, but over time, she had somehow managed to become part of his detective agency, too. Sometimes her detection skills astonished him, although he made sure not to let on.

She sighed in dismay at his question, which she must think demonstrated his lack of faith in her abilities. "Her clothes. She's new money, though."

Frank bit back another smile. "And how do you know that?"

Maeve's nose wrinkled as she considered. "She's not *comfortable*."

"What does that mean?"

"You know, the way Mrs. Decker is. No matter what happens, she's always so calm and sure of herself."

Ah yes, the confidence that comes from being

9

born with money and knowing you never had to worry about a thing. His mother-in-law had it in spades and so did his wife, Sarah. It had been bred into them for generations. Frank Malloy was new money, though. He would never have that confidence.

"All right, who is she and what does she want from us?"

Maeve reached across his desk and laid a calling card on top of the papers he'd been working on. It was engraved on high-quality paper. MRS. ALVIN BING. The address was an upscale neighborhood in the city. "She wouldn't tell me what she came for. She said it's private and she would only discuss it with you."

"Show her in, then." Frank laid the card down and straightened the papers on his desk. He stuffed them into a folder and set them aside.

"Do you, uh, need me to take notes?" Maeve asked hopefully. "Gino is still out."

Frank's partner, Gino Donatelli, had gone to deliver a final report to a client.

"If I need you, I'll call you," Frank said. Maybe Mrs. Bing had something to say that wasn't fit for Maeve's ears. "And don't worry, Miss Nosy, I'll tell you all about it when she leaves."

Maeve sniffed in derision at his teasing and went out to fetch Mrs. Bing.

Mrs. Bing appeared to be in her late thirties. She had never been a beauty, but she was a

10

handsome woman who benefitted from being dressed well. Very well, in fact. Maeve had been right about her clothes. Being married to Sarah had taught him how to spot the work of a fine dressmaker. But her fashionable attire could not disguise her worried expression. She was greatly distressed and trying her best not to show it.

Frank introduced himself and invited her to sit in one of the wooden, straight-backed client chairs. His office was intentionally utilitarian since he had the luxury of choosing which clients he wanted to represent, so he felt no need to impress anyone.

"How may I help you today, Mrs. Bing?" he asked when she didn't speak.

Her gloved hands clutched her purse tightly, as if she were afraid he might snatch it from her, and her eyes were tortured when she gazed at him across his desk. "Mr. Ottermeir suggested I see you."

"The attorney downstairs?" Frank asked. Ottermeir had never sent him any business before.

"Yes, he . . . Well, perhaps I should start at the beginning."

Frank nodded his encouragement.

"I wish to obtain a divorce from my husband."

"I see." He was very much afraid he did see. "I'm sure Mr. Ottermeir explained how difficult that will be."

11

"Yes, he . . . I understand that adultery is the only grounds for divorce in New York."

"That is my understanding as well."

Mrs. Bing closed her eyes for a moment, as if gathering her courage. "Mr. Ottermeir said that to obtain a divorce, I would need proof that Mr. Bing was . . . unfaithful."

"That's right, and as I'm sure he also told you, such proof is very difficult to get."

She drew an unsteady breath. "He also explained that in such cases, it's possible to, uh, trick a man into providing such proof."

Frank would need to have a talk with Mr. Ottermeir, if this was the kind of business he thought he could send up to him. "Did he tell you how that is usually done?"

"Yes." Obviously, she found the subject as distasteful as Frank did, but she said, "He said that there are, uh, young ladies who will assist in these matters, for a fee."

Frank leaned back in his chair and sighed. "So I am told. I'm sure Ottermeir also explained that the man in question is somehow lured to a hotel room and there he is met by a scantily clad young woman and a photographer who takes pictures of the woman embracing the man. These photographs are then used in court as proof of adultery in order to obtain a divorce."

"Yes," she said weakly. "That is exactly what he told me."

"And did he send you to me because he thought I could arrange for your husband to be caught in such a compromising position?"

Mrs. Bing was now mangling the purse she held in her lap as her hands gripped it ever more tightly. "He said . . ." She paused to swallow. "He said that many private detectives are able to arrange such things."

"I'm sure some are, but I'm afraid Ottermeir misled you if he suggested I am one of them."

Mrs. Bing blinked in surprise. "Oh."

"I'm sorry, Mrs. Bing. I can see you are, uh, distressed, and I understand that a woman might have many good reasons for wanting to divorce her husband, but New York State only recognizes one of them. Did Ottermeir suggest that you could move to another state where the laws are more accommodating?"

"He did mention that, but I don't . . . I can't just pick up and move to Indiana or the Dakotas. I . . . I don't have any money of my own, you see."

"You aren't likely to have any after your divorce either. I'm sure Ottermeir warned you that judges rarely grant wives a settlement or alimony."

"I've been poor all my life, Mr. Malloy, at least until I married Mr. Bing, so I'm not afraid of that. I just . . ." Her voice caught and she clapped a hand over her mouth as if to stifle a sob.

Frank jumped up and went to the door. "Maeve," he called. "Will you get Mrs. Bing a glass of water?"

"I'm so sorry," Mrs. Bing said, digging in her purse for a handkerchief.

"Don't be. I'm sure this is very difficult for you."

"And even more difficult now that I know you can't help me."

For a second, Frank had a twinge of regret. Rarely did he face a situation where his own moral code prevented him from helping someone in need. But maybe Mrs. Bing's problems were of her own making. She hadn't really told him why she wanted a divorce. For all he knew, she was the unfaithful one in the marriage.

Frank moved back to his chair behind the desk. "Did Ottermeir suggest a legal separation as an alternative?"

"He did, but . . . Mr. Bing would never agree to it. Even if he did, I . . . I fear he would insist on retaining custody of my daughter."

"Yes, the courts do usually grant the father custody of the children, since he is more likely to be able to provide for them."

"Mr. Bing is not Carrie's father," she said defensively. "This is a second marriage for both of us, you see, and . . ."

Maeve had appeared with the glass of water. She offered it to Mrs. Bing with a reassuring

14

smile. "Are you all right? Can I get you anything else?"

Mrs. Bing accepted the glass and gratefully took a sip. "Thank you, no, I'll be fine now."

Maeve gave Frank a hopeful look, but he shook his head and she slunk out with obvious reluctance. He needed to find out more about Mrs. Bing, if only to have something to placate Maeve with.

When the door clicked shut again, he said, "I can't help you stage an adultery scene, but if you are in a difficult situation, I may be able to help you some other way, especially if you are in danger. Is your husband violent, for instance?"

She sighed wearily. "No, not at all. He . . . he also provides well for me and my daughter."

"You said this is a second marriage for you both. How long have you been married?"

"Almost nine months."

Frank blinked in surprise. Nine months wasn't very long to decide a marriage wasn't working out, especially if Bing wasn't unfaithful and was a good provider. Many women would be more than satisfied with that, no matter what other bad habits Bing might have. What could he have done to send her out to find an attorney? "Perhaps if you told me the reason you wish to divorce your husband, I could—"

"Thank you for your time, Mr. Malloy," she said, rising so abruptly the water sloshed out of the glass she still held, splashing onto her glove. She hastily set the glass down on the edge of his desk. "I'm sorry to have bothered you."

"It's no bother, Mrs. Bing. I really would like to help you if I could."

She gave him a smile that was ghastly in its despair. "I appreciate that."

"Here," he said, snatching up one of his business cards from a holder on his desk. "Take this in case you change your mind, and don't hesitate to call on me if I can assist you."

She took the card, albeit reluctantly, slipping it into her bag along with the handkerchief she no longer needed. Then she headed for the door. He had to hurry to get ahead of her so he could open it for her. Then she scurried through the front office and out into the hallway without even glancing at Maeve.

When she was gone, Maeve gave him a chastening glare. "What did you do to her?"

"I had to tell her I couldn't help her."

"What on earth did she ask you to do?" Maeve knew he wasn't above bending the rules if that's what it took.

"She wants to get a divorce. Ottermeir told her I could set up a trap for her husband with some floozy and a photographer."

"Ottermeir? That shyster on the second floor?" she marveled.

"The very same."

"I'm surprised he doesn't have his own floozy and photographer on staff."

"So am I. I need to pay him a visit to discuss the kinds of work I'm willing to do."

"I should hope so. And in the meantime, what about poor Mrs. Bing? Did she tell you why she wants to divorce her husband?"

"She did not, although I did ask her outright. I told her I might be able to help her in some other way, but she just stormed out."

Maeve frowned. "She stormed out when you offered to help her?"

"Yes."

Maeve shook her head. "I find that hard to believe. What exactly did you say to her?"

"I . . ." He tried to remember. "I did tell her I'd like to help her. I asked if Bing was violent, and she said he wasn't."

"And you believed her?" she demanded.

"She wasn't upset by that question, so yes, I believed her. She also said he's a good provider, and apparently he is faithful, since she would have had to stage a scene with a floozy to prove he wasn't."

"He sounds like a prize."

"A lot of women would agree, but then . . ." He replayed the scene in his mind. "It was when I asked her to tell me why she wanted a divorce, if he wasn't guilty of the usual sins, that she jumped up and left."

"Oh my."

"Yes, oh my."

"Do you think she's the one who has a lover, and she didn't want to admit it?"

"That's one possibility."

"And I guess there are all kinds of reasons a woman might want to divorce her husband."

"I can think of a few," Frank said with a sad smile. "But New York State doesn't recognize most of them as valid."

"So, I guess you'd better be sure before you marry someone in New York, because you're in it for life."

"Yes, you are," Frank said, "unless you find someone with a floozy and a photographer."

"The poor woman," Sarah said that evening when Frank and Maeve had finished telling her and Gino about their mysterious visitor. Gino had come over for supper, and the four of them were sitting in the parlor now, relaxing after the children were in bed for the night. Frank's mother sat off in a corner, knitting by the light of an electric lamp, which was the one advantage she seemed to really enjoy now that her son was a millionaire.

"Why do you assume she's the injured party?" Gino asked. He and Maeve were sitting together on the love seat. Sarah noticed they were sitting a little closer than friends would sit, but not as close as lovers would sit. Maeve still wasn't ready to admit her feelings for him, although Gino had made his plain.

"Because the woman is always the injured party," Maeve informed him.

"Well, not always," Sarah felt obligated to say, "but very often she is."

Gino shrugged. "You're probably right, but she said he's rich and he doesn't have a mistress and he doesn't beat her."

"He doesn't sound all that bad, does he?" Sarah admitted. "But she said she'd been poor all of her life until she married him, and she's willing to give that up and be poor again to be rid of him. He must have done something that upset her terribly if she wants to divorce him after only nine months," Sarah said. "I'm not sure I'd even want to guess what that might be."

"And it doesn't even matter," Maeve said, "because she won't be able to get a divorce because of it."

"Maybe she'll find another detective who will help her stage the photographs," Gino said.

"Maybe she will," Sarah said sadly. "In any case, I hope she manages to get away from him if he's as bad as he must be."

The conversation turned to other topics then and after a while, Gino turned to Malloy and said, "Do you think this is a good time?"

"I don't think there will ever be a *good* time,"

Malloy said with a twinkle, "but you might as well tell them."

Maeve's puzzled expression reassured Sarah that she wasn't the only one mystified by this conversation. Gino reached into a pocket of his suit coat and pulled out a folded sheet of newsprint. "There's going to be an automobile show at Madison Square Garden starting this weekend." He spread out the paper to reveal an advertisement announcing the "First Annual Automobile Show." The Automobile Club of America was the sponsor.

Sarah hadn't known such a club existed. Perhaps this was a club Malloy might consider joining, since he had steadfastly resisted her father's efforts to get him to join the Knicker-bocker Club.

"What happens at an automobile show?" Maeve asked doubtfully.

"I'm not sure, since no one has ever had one before, but I'm guessing they show motorcars," Gino said with a grin. "Lots of them. More than a hundred different kinds."

"Why would you need to see a hundred different kinds of motorcars?" Maeve asked.

"So you'll know what kind is the best," Gino said.

"I thought you already decided that, and Mr. Malloy bought that one."

"They're making improvements in motorcars

all the time. It's a good idea to see what's new."

"Why?" Maeve was teasing him now, but he hadn't realized it yet.

"So you'll know which kind to buy the next time."

"The next time?" Sarah scoffed. "One automobile is all you'll ever need, I'm sure."

"Yes," Malloy said, playing along. "Why would I ever need another one?"

Gino was beaming now. Motorcars were one of his great loves, which was why he'd convinced Malloy to buy one in the first place. "Like I said, they're making improvements all the time. They'll get easier to start and easier to drive and someone will figure out how to make them more comfortable. You'll want a new one before you know it, mark my words."

"I'd just as soon not mark them," Malloy said with mock solemnity.

"But you want to go to the automobile show just as much as I do, and I think Mrs. Frank and Maeve will enjoy it, too."

"Just walking around Madison Square Garden and looking at motorcars?" Maeve said doubtfully.

"They'll have demonstrations, too. They have an indoor track for the motors to drive on and even a hill for them to climb. It will be interesting."

Plainly, Gino wanted Maeve to go, and just

as plainly, she wasn't particularly excited about it. But Gino was undeterred. "They even have motors that are easier for ladies to drive."

Maeve perked up at that. Gino had taught her to drive, but cranking the engine and changing the gears was physically difficult. "How much easier?"

"I'm sure someone will show you if you go to the automobile show."

Now she was intrigued, but still she turned to Sarah. Sarah surrendered with grace. "If you're really interested, I'll go along, too, although we'll probably be the only females there."

Sarah had to admit the automobile show was fun. Madison Square Garden had a stadium-like room with lots of seating around it for spectators. The automobiles were displayed in the center of the floor and a track ran around the display in an enormous oval. As Gino had told them, it even had an artificial hill so the motorcars could demonstrate their ability to meet any obstacle. Some of them performed better than others, much to the delight of the crowd and consternation of the owners.

During a break in the demonstrations, the four of them wandered down to the floor to stroll through the displays. Most of the automobiles looked little different in design from the carriages currently swarming the city streets and being pulled by horses. *Horseless carriage* was the perfect description for them. Creative designers had put the engines in various places, out of sight, and installed a steering tiller, pedals, and whatever other mechanisms each vehicle required. Sarah was quite impressed.

Malloy and Gino were having a great time discussing the various advantages of each type of vehicle with the men who were staffing each display. Sarah had learned that motorcars were built by hand and that over two hundred companies were making them in America. No wonder the company representatives were so eager to engage with potential customers. The small market for motorcars could hardly support so many manufacturers, so only the most successful would survive.

After a while, all the vehicles began to look alike, however, and Sarah was delighted to spot a bench. "Do you mind if I sit down for a while?" she asked Malloy. "You can look at the rest of the displays and come back for me."

"We can go back up into the stands, if you like," he said gallantly.

"What, and miss seeing all the rest of these motors?" she said with feigned amazement. "I wouldn't dream of spoiling your fun."

"Have mercy on her," Maeve advised. "She must be bored to death."

"Well, not to *death* exactly," Sarah hedged.

But Malloy had already turned his steps toward the bench, and since Sarah was holding his arm, she followed. A lady was already sitting on it, but there was plenty of room for Sarah.

"Excuse me, miss," he said. "Do you mind if my wife joins you?"

The lady had been looking rather forlorn, her gaze fixed on the floor and the brim of her stylish hat blocking any view of her face, and when she looked up at Malloy she gasped in surprise.

Not happy surprise either.

Her startled gaze darted over to where two men were discussing the merits of one of the motors on display, then back to Malloy. "Please don't let on that you know me," she whispered urgently.

"Of course," he whispered back, and then said to Sarah in a normal voice, "You can wait for us here, dear. We'll come back for you, or if you get bored, you can come and find us."

Mystified, Sarah played along. "I promise not to wander too far." She took her seat beside the woman, and Frank rejoined Gino and Maeve, who had been too interested in one of the motors to notice the exchange. Sarah turned to the lady. "I hope you don't mind my joining you. I'm afraid I chose my shoes more for style than comfort this morning, and they're letting me know it."

The lady was a bit flustered from her encounter with Malloy, but she smiled politely. "Not at all. I'm glad for the company."

"Did your husband drag you here today, too?" Sarah asked.

The lady's gaze again darted to the two men still deep in conversation. One was gesturing to various parts of the motor while the other looked on skeptically. "Uh, yes."

"Do you already own a motorcar? My husband bought one a few months ago and now he's obsessed with them." A slight exaggeration. Gino was the one obsessed.

"My husband owns a company that makes them," she said a bit reluctantly.

"Oh really? How interesting."

"Not really, and not very interesting," the lady said. "He's always complaining about how much money he's losing. I wonder if motorcars will ever catch on."

"My husband's partner strongly disagrees. He thinks they'll eventually replace horses completely."

The lady gave Sarah a sad smile. "I'm sure I don't know and would never dream of forming an opinion on the matter."

Sarah returned the smile and in a soft voice said, "I gathered that you know my husband. Are you a client?"

Her eyes widened and once again she glanced in the direction of the men, one of whom must be her husband. Sarah couldn't quite identify the expression in her eyes. It wasn't the emotion a woman displayed when she was afraid for her safety, but it was something very close to that. When she turned back to Sarah, she whispered, "I'm not really a client. He . . . Mr. Malloy couldn't help me. Please don't say anything in front of my husband."

Malloy had mentioned only one client he'd been unable to help. This lady must be the mysterious woman who had wanted a divorce she couldn't obtain. That would explain her eagerness to keep her visit to Malloy a secret. "Of course not. I'm surprised he couldn't help you, though. He's usually very resourceful. He used to be a police detective, you know."

"I . . . I didn't know, but this . . . this matter isn't one a detective can really help with."

Sarah knew better than to reveal her knowledge of the case, but she could see this woman was obviously in distress. Her soft heart demanded that she at least reach out to her with whatever compassion she could offer. "Can anyone help you? Perhaps a friend could offer some assistance."

The woman's grief was painful to behold. "Not unless a friend can change the laws of New York State."

Maeve was admiring the upholstery in one of the display motorcars when Frank approached her and Gino. "Don't look, but the lady on the bench with Sarah is Mrs. Bing," he told them.

"Who is Mrs. Bing?" Gino asked, looking anyway. Frank pinched his arm to make him stop.

"The lady who wanted a divorce," Maeve informed him.

Frank hadn't mentioned her name when telling them her story in a small attempt to protect her privacy. "She particularly asked me to pretend I had never met her, and you two should do the same."

"I *haven't* met her," Gino reminded him.

"Then act like it."

"Is her husband here?" Maeve asked.

"I expect so. When she saw me, she looked over at one of the displays. She was probably looking to see if he was watching her."

"Then we must meet him," Maeve said. "Do you know which display it was?"

"Yes, I do, but be discreet," Frank warned them.

Maeve batted her eyes at him in a parody of innocence. "Of course." She tucked her arm through Gino's and added, "Lead the way, Mr. Malloy."

They paused to look at several other displays before reaching their target. By the time they did, only one man remained. He was obviously the company representative whose job was to tout the advantages of their particular motorcar. Frank hoped he was Mr. Bing.

"Welcome," the man said, sticking out his hand for Frank to shake. "Alvin Bing."

Frank returned his smile and shook his hand. Bing was a handsome man of about fifty. His neatly cropped beard and lush, dark brown hair showed a few threads of silver, but he was still what Frank's mother would have called a fine figure of a man, tall and solidly built. "Frank Malloy. Is this your motor, Mr. Bing?"

"Yes, I own the company. Well, part of it anyway. Do you own an automobile, Mr. Malloy?"

"Yes, I do."

"Is this an electric?" Gino asked, having moved closer to examine the vehicle.

"Yes, it is. The finest one being made. The battery lasts for twenty-five miles between charges."

Gino was already shaking his head. "I did a lot of research before Mr. Malloy bought his motor, and we decided a gasoline-powered motor was the best."

"How can you say that?" Bing asked, his salesman's smile never faltering. "Everyone knows the internal explosion engine is dangerous, to say nothing of the hazards of cranking it to start. You can break a thumb or even an arm if the motor backfires while you're cranking it."

"Yes, but what do you do when the battery dies and you're miles from a charging station?" Gino replied smugly.

"You'll never be far from a charging station in the city," Bing countered.

"But what if you leave the city? With a gasoline-powered motor, you can get a can of gasoline at any pharmacy or general store. You'll never be stuck."

"Why would you want to leave the city? That's the only place with paved roads. No motor can go far on the mud tracks they call roads out in the country," Bing replied. "Almost eight thousand automobiles have been sold in the United States, and four thousand of them are right here in New York City. That should tell you what automobiles are made for."

No one could argue with that. Country roads were definitely unsuitable for automobiles.

Maeve wasn't going to be left out of the conversation, though. "Is it true electric motors are easier to start?"

"Oh yes, little lady. Driving an electric auto is so easy, I've taught my wife and both my daughters to do it. They're forever taking one of our autos out to shop or visit with friends."

Both his daughters. Mrs. Bing had mentioned only her daughter. Did Bing have a child of his own, too?

"Isn't that right, Carrie?" Bing called.

A young lady appeared from the other side of the automobile in the next display. She looked to be about fifteen and was remarkably pretty, with golden curls and bright blue eyes. Carrie, Frank remembered, was Mrs. Bing's daughter. He had a moment to study her as she walked over to join them. Sarah would have called her dress fussy, because of all the ruffles, but it was no doubt expensive. Her hat was ridiculous, which meant it was expensive as well. Her smile lit her face and she looked at Bing with what could only be called adoration. If Bing was cruel to his wife, he was obviously indulgent to his stepdaughter.

"Isn't what right?" she asked him.

"That I taught you to drive, and you have found driving an electric auto to be very easy."

"Oh yes," she told them. "You just push the lever and it starts right up. You have to remember to unplug it before driving away, though," she added with a becoming blush and a coquettish glance at Bing, who shook his head in mock despair. "But I can drive it by myself."

"So you can take your friends driving, and you don't have to worry about a chauffeur listening to your private conversations," Bing informed Maeve.

Maeve widened her eyes in feigned amazement. "You drive it all by yourself? Perhaps you'll show me how to start it."

Carrie escorted Maeve over and began to demonstrate. Bing turned to Gino. "I think you'll have to buy an electric motorcar for your wife."

Gino only smiled.

"Did you say you owned the company that makes these electric vehicles?" Frank asked.

"I'm a partner, yes. It seemed like a good investment. Automobiles are the future, Mr. Malloy."

"My father-in-law is convinced they'll never replace the horse, but I've been wondering if I should consider investing in them myself. Did you say there are four thousand of them in the city?"

"Yes, indeed. You see them everywhere now. Those gasoline engines won't catch on, though. They're too noisy and they scare horses. You also can't enclose the vehicle because of the fumes from the engine. I'm sure you've noticed how unpleasant it is to ride in an open vehicle during the winter."

Frank had definitely noticed it.

"Electric autos don't have fumes so they can have windows to protect the passengers, and they don't make any noise," Bing went on with a salesman's enthusiasm.

"What about steam?" Frank said just to keep Bing talking.

"Not very practical, I'm afraid. Imagine that you need to go somewhere and you have to wait a half hour or longer for the water in the engine to boil before your auto can move. And if you run out of water and there's none nearby . . ."

"But if you only drive in the city, won't there always be water nearby?" Frank said to be contrary.

31

"You've got me there, Mr. Malloy," Bing said, his salesman's demeanor never wavering. "But there's still the issue of waiting for it to boil."

"Yes, we never even considered steam, did we, Gino?"

"Not for a minute," Gino confirmed. "Even though it is the most popular type after electric."

Maeve and Carrie returned from examining the auto.

"He was right," Maeve said, apparently impressed. With Maeve, it was hard to know for sure since she was such a good liar. "It is very easy to start, and you don't even have to change gears. Changing gears is the worst part, I think," she confided.

"Do you drive, then?" Bing asked. He was eyeing Maeve with more interest than Frank found appropriate.

"Oh yes," she replied airily. "Mr. Donatelli taught me. I admit that cranking the engine is a challenge, but I've learned how to do it."

Bing gave her a smile, one that even Frank recognized as designed to be charming and a bit flirtatious. "You are a woman of many talents. I told him he would have to buy you an electric auto, but now I gather you are not his wife."

Maeve returned his flirtatious smile with one of her own. "Not yet, at least."

"Oh, Papa, you promised to buy me some ice cream," Carrie said suddenly, frowning at Maeve.

"Not now, Carrie," he said, giving her an impatient glance before turning his attention back to Maeve.

"I'm just concerned about how far I can drive on a battery charge," Maeve said, studiously ignoring Carrie. "Is it possible to carry an extra battery?"

"They're quite heavy, which adds to the weight of the vehicle, but I'm happy to report that Mr. Edison himself is working on a battery that will be lighter and will last even longer."

"I told you they're improving motorcars all the time," Gino reminded her.

Maeve ignored him, too. "How long until the new battery is ready, do you think?"

"Very soon, I'm sure. If you are interested, I would be happy to take you for a drive so you can see how easy it is," Bing said, warming to the topic. Frank wasn't sure if it was Maeve herself or the prospect of a sale that had Bing so interested, but plainly Carrie wasn't at all happy about it.

"Papa," she said sweetly, obviously having decided that whining wasn't the best tactic. She slipped her arm through his and looked up at him with those big blue eyes. "I'm sure these people would like to see the rest of the displays."

"Yes, we would," Gino confirmed, as if he was jealous of Bing's attention to Maeve.

"Thank you for the information, though,"

Maeve said. "I'm seriously considering an electric auto now."

"Please, take my card and let me know if I can help in any way." Bing handed one of his cards to Maeve and then, almost as an afterthought, to Gino and Frank as well.

Gino hustled Maeve away, but Frank took a moment to shake Bing's hand again. Bing had to extricate his arm from Carrie's grasp to do so.

Frank walked away, but he took a moment to look back, and was surprised to see that instead of chastening Carrie for her rudeness, he was giving her the same charming smile he'd given Maeve and patting her shoulder reassuringly.

How very odd.

II

"It is odd," Sarah agreed later when she and Malloy were back home and alone in their private parlor. She had told him about her conversation with Mrs. Bing, and he had told her about his observations. "If Mr. Bing is so impossible that his wife is desperate to divorce him, why does her daughter seem to have such a good relationship with him?"

"Well, from the way he flirted with Maeve, he obviously dotes on young ladies," Malloy said. He was resting his sock feet on a footstool and he wiggled his toes with apparent relief. He hadn't enjoyed walking around the displays any more than Sarah had.

"So he probably spoils the girl, but not the mother."

"And maybe Mrs. Bing resents this or at least disapproves."

Sarah frowned. "Most women would be thrilled to find a doting stepfather for their children."

"But some might be jealous," Malloy reminded her.

"Perhaps, although Mrs. Bing didn't seem like the type."

"Fortunately, it's none of our business since she's not a client."

"I'll try to remember that, although I did give Mrs. Bing my calling card and offered her some sympathy if she needed it."

"You are such a good person, my darling wife."

Sarah gave him a look. "Don't flatter me, Malloy. You know I'm hoping she'll call on me so I can find out more about what's going on."

"Just remember it's none of our business."

She smiled sweetly. "Of course."

Frank was wishing he'd decided to stay home as he made his way to his office building the following Tuesday. Election Day was always a crazy time in the city and the streets were clogged with men making themselves available to the ward heelers who collected voters to make the rounds of all the polls, earning a drink for each vote cast. Everyone was saying that McKinley would easily win a second term as president, which made Frank a bit sad because that meant his old friend Theodore Roosevelt would also be elected vice president. That dead-end job would render him invisible and powerless for the next four years, which was exactly what the New York politicians intended. Teddy had made too much trouble as governor of New York the past few years, and they'd seen nominating him for vice president as the perfect way to rid themselves of the annoying reformer.

"Extra! Extra!" the newsboy on the corner

shouted. "Millionaire gets run over by his own motorcar! Extra! Extra!"

As a millionaire who owned a motorcar himself, Frank couldn't resist a story like that. He dug a penny from his pocket to purchase the single sheet of newsprint the boy was selling. Others were also eager to read all about it, so Frank had to quickly step away to find a spot where he wouldn't be jostled and could scan the sheet.

There was no picture. The newspapers rarely printed photographs since the process was so expensive. Instead, they would have an engraving made of any available pictures and that would be printed, but this incident had happened late last night. They wouldn't have had time to make an engraving yet, although the story itself didn't really need one. A man described as a millionaire had been run over in the street and left to die. The driver had apparently fled, and no one professed to having witnessed the accident. Normally, the police would have simply located the owner of the automobile to identify the driver, but the vehicle turned out to be owned by the victim. The strangest part of the story, at least to Frank, was the identity of the victim: Alvin Bing.

His easy-to-drive auto had been driven over him.

Maeve was already at her desk, having escorted Frank's daughter, Catherine, to school earlier that morning. Gino was keeping her company when Frank entered the office.

"Did you see?" he asked, slapping the extra down on Maeve's desk.

Gino and Maeve leaned over to read it, their heads nearly touching over her desk.

"It's Bing!" Maeve said, having spotted the name first.

"He got run over by his own automobile?" Gino marveled. "He did say they were easy to start but not that they could drive themselves."

"I'm pretty sure it didn't drive itself," Frank said with a look to remind Gino he wasn't showing proper respect for the dead.

"But whoever was driving ran away," Maeve said, still reading. "And no one saw who it was."

"Not one *admitted* to seeing who it was," Frank corrected her.

"Where did it happen?" Gino asked, leaning over to see the story again.

"Just off Madison Square, it says," Maeve reported. "Do you suppose he was coming from the automobile show?"

"It's possible, depending on when the accident happened," Frank said. "The show was open until half past ten."

"Someone will probably remember if he was there that night," Gino said. "And who he was with, I suppose. That should make it easier for the police."

"Well, it's an ill wind that doesn't blow somebody some good," Maeve said, looking up with a smug expression. "Mrs. Bing won't need that divorce now, will she?"

The next afternoon, Sarah was enjoying her solitude. The children were still at school, and so was her mother-in-law, who accompanied their son, Brian, because he was deaf. Maeve and Malloy were at the office. The house was blissfully quiet.

She was reading the *World*, which announced in gigantic letters that McKinley had won reelection and would be taking Governor Theodore Roosevelt along with him to Washington City as his vice president. Sighing with regret that poor Theodore would soon virtually disappear from politics, she turned the page in hopes of finding more interesting news. There she saw a small article about Alvin Bing's mysterious death.

Unlike the extra that Malloy had brought home yesterday, this story featured a picture. The engraving couldn't possibly depict the real event. It showed the poor man lying in the street with one wheel of the automobile resting on his chest. Sarah shuddered to think this might have really happened, but quickly decided it was, like much of the so-called news, an exaggeration to make the story more sensational and sell more newspapers. She did, however, read the article, looking for any new information that might have been discovered overnight. She learned nothing new, though.

She had just finished the article when the doorbell rang. She wasn't expecting anyone, but her neighbor Mrs. Ellsworth often dropped by to chat. She heard her maid answer the bell and have a brief conversation with someone. Then she appeared in the doorway of the library where Sarah had been sitting.

"There's a lady here to see you, Mrs. Frank." She handed Sarah a calling card for Mrs. Alvin Bing.

Sarah managed not to reveal her surprise and asked Hattie to show her in and bring them some tea. By the time Hattie had escorted Mrs. Bing to the library where Sarah had been reading, Sarah had managed to school her expression to mild interest. She greeted her visitor warmly, offering her a seat by the fireplace, where a small blaze chased away the November chill.

"I was so sorry to read about your husband, Mrs. Bing," Sarah said when they were both comfortable.

"I . . . Yes, thank you." Although she was tastefully attired in black, Mrs. Bing didn't appear to have been grieving very much, although she did look a bit worried.

"I was just reading about it in the newspaper.

I don't suppose they have any idea how it happened, do they?"

"It was a . . . a horrible accident, I'm sure," Mrs. Bing said without much conviction.

"Of course it was," Sarah agreed. "I've asked my maid to bring us some tea, or would you prefer something else?"

"What? Oh no, tea is fine." She glanced around as if looking for something. "I don't suppose . . . I mean, is Mr. Malloy at home by any chance?"

"I'm sorry, he's not, but if you need to see him, he's probably in his office, and if he's not—"

"I can't go to his office," she said too quickly.

"But you said you'd been there before. I'm sure if you—"

"But I can't go *now*. I can't let anyone see me there. No one must know why I tried to hire Mr. Malloy."

"I'm afraid you didn't tell me why you tried to hire him either," Sarah said, managing not to lie about already knowing.

"I . . . I was seeking to divorce Mr. Bing," Mrs. Bing reluctantly admitted.

Sarah frowned in feigned confusion. "Private detectives don't handle divorces. Isn't that the business of attorneys?"

Mrs. Bing closed her eyes as if drawing on some depths of inner strength before replying. "I did see an attorney about the matter. He advised me to find a private detective to help me, uh, stage a scene that could be photographed to prove my husband was committing adultery."

Sarah didn't have to pretend to be shocked. Even knowing what Mrs. Bing was going to say didn't mitigate her disgust at the situation. "And I gather Mr. Malloy refused to help you."

"Yes, and I don't blame him. I can't imagine anything more distasteful."

Sarah could, but she didn't mention it. She was obviously more jaded than Mrs. Bing. "I guess I can understand why you wouldn't want anyone to know why you'd contacted Malloy. It would be quite embarrassing and—"

"It's not just embarrassing," Mrs. Bing said. "I wouldn't care about that, but the police . . ."

She closed her eyes again and drew an unsteady breath. She was, Sarah realized, near tears.

Fortunately, Hattie chose that moment to arrive with the tea, which gave Mrs. Bing a chance to compose herself. The tea probably also helped. When Sarah judged Mrs. Bing was calm again, she said, "I know the police must be very interested in finding out what happened to your husband."

"They have been rather . . . unpleasant," she admitted.

"I know they can be rude and—"

"It isn't their manners that upset me. They seem to think I had something to do with Mr. Bing's death. They practically accused me of it, in fact."

Sarah widened her eyes in surprise she didn't feel. "Why would they think that?"

"They were able to figure out that Mr. Bing had a companion with him the other night. That person obviously was driving when the auto ran over him."

"But if it was an accident . . ." Sarah offered.

"If it was an accident, why did the driver flee instead of getting help for Mr. Bing? At least that's the question they asked me. I had no answer, of course."

"Of course," Sarah said in complete sympathy.

"Then they started asking me questions about my marriage and was it happy and did Mr. Bing treat me well, things like that. Plainly, they thought I had run him over with the auto because I hated him."

"I see, and if they knew you had gone to an attorney about obtaining a divorce . . ."

"Yes, then they'd be sure I did it, since the attorney told me I didn't have any grounds for a divorce."

Sarah could have eased Mrs. Bing's mind by saying the police often lost interest in these cases if no reward was offered, but she wasn't sure about this particular case. The newspapers were often relentless when a rich man died under mysterious circumstances. By hinting at scandals, they could keep the story going for weeks and sell thousands of papers. Publicity was almost as good as money in motivating the police, too.

"Was there a particular reason you came to visit me today, Mrs. Bing? Not that I'm not happy to see you, but you did ask about my husband."

"Yes, I . . . I'm not sure if Mr. Malloy can help me with this, but you did say he used to be a police detective himself."

"That's true." Until an enormous inheritance had made it impossible for him to work for the New York City Police Department anymore.

"I was hoping . . . That is, I was wondering if he might give me some advice. He knows how the police work and what I can do to convince them I didn't kill Mr. Bing."

"But you're afraid to be seen going to his office," Sarah guessed.

"Yes. I'm terrified someone will find out why I went there the first time."

"I can't make you any promises, but I'll certainly tell Mr. Malloy why you wish to see him, and he may well have some advice for you."

"I'll pay him, of course, or hire him or whatever the arrangements usually are. May I call on you again to find out if he can help me? Since I can't go to his office, I mean."

"Oh no, that won't be necessary. Mr. Malloy and I will call on you at your home. We're friends, after all, and a condolence call would be the most natural thing in the world."

"Oh, Mrs. Malloy, how can I ever thank you?"

Sarah smiled. "Wait until I've been of some help to you, and then we'll worry about that."

Maeve checked the watch pinned to her lapel. She would have to leave the office soon to walk little Catherine home from Miss Spence's School for Girls. Having two jobs could be a little wearing, since she was responsible for Catherine and Brian in the morning and after school until bedtime and she worked in Mr. Malloy's office during the day. Maeve wouldn't have changed a thing, though. Not many girls like her—penniless orphans—ended up half so well off, and none of them got to work for a millionaire private investigator. Maeve was sure of that.

She looked up from her typing when the office door opened. A young woman of about twenty stepped in and looked around as if uncertain she was in the right place. A lot of people acted like that when they came into Mr. Malloy's office.

"May I help you?" Maeve said in her best professional secretary's voice.

The young woman looked around again. She was a nice-looking girl with dark hair artfully arranged. She wore a forest green walking suit that Maeve would have died for and a hat she didn't like at all. Everything about her said money, though. After a moment's hesitation, she said, "Is this Mr. Malloy's office?" She looked down at a card she held in her gloved hand. "Mr. Frank Malloy?"

"Yes, it is. Did you have an appointment?" Maeve knew she didn't. Maeve scheduled all the appointments.

"No, I . . ." She must have remembered herself. She straightened slightly and assumed a haughty expression. "I should like to see Mr. Malloy."

"May I tell him what it's about?" Maeve asked, not moving a muscle.

"It's . . . confidential."

To Maeve's great annoyance, Gino appeared in the doorway to his office. Naturally, the sound of a woman's voice would have drawn him. He looked particularly dapper today in his tailor-made suit with his coal black hair slicked back, and he was smiling his most charming smile.

"May I be of assistance?" he asked.

The young woman looked him over in surprise. "Are you Mr. Malloy?"

"I'm his partner, Gino Donatelli."

She didn't actually turn up her nose, but she might as well have. Maeve knew a moment of satisfaction. "My business is with Mr. Malloy."

"I'll see if he's available," Maeve said, rising at last. "May I tell him who wishes to see him?"

She hesitated for the briefest of moments and then said, "Miss Pearl Bing."

Maeve managed not to react, although she

could plainly hear Gino's slight gasp of surprise. She'd have to speak to him about that later.

Frank easily recognized Maeve's expression this time. "Who is it?" he asked before she could tease him. Plainly, someone interesting had come to call.

"Miss Pearl Bing."

"Pearl?"

Maeve shrugged. "She's around twenty, so maybe she's the other daughter."

That seemed logical. "Send her in, then."

"I'll *show* her in," Maeve said with a grin. "It will give her another chance to act superior."

She was gone before he could ask what on earth she meant by that. Then she escorted Miss Bing in and he understood completely. Miss Bing obviously disapproved of everything and everyone she had seen since entering the offices of Frank Malloy, Confidential Inquiries. She glanced at the chair Maeve indicated as if she was debating whether to dust it off before sitting on it, but after a moment, she surrendered with a sigh and sat down.

Frank had risen when she entered, but now he sat down, too. "Thank you, Miss Smith."

Maeve looked like she wanted to stick her tongue out at him for sending her out, but she left, closing the door softly behind her.

"What can I do for you, Miss Bing?" he asked.

Her dark gaze took in the room again and finally settled on Frank once more. He saw no change in her attitude. "Why did my stepmother come to see you?"

Frank didn't so much as blink. "Who is your stepmother?"

"Don't toy with me, Mr. Malloy. You know very well. Ethel Bing. Mrs. Alvin Bing."

Frank smiled benignly. "I should have guessed the last name would be the same as yours. Alvin Bing, eh? Is this the same gentleman who was killed in the automobile accident the other night?"

An emotion that might have been pain flickered over her lovely face, but it also might just have been annoyance. "I'm sure you know it is."

"I'm very sorry for your loss, Miss Bing."

His condolences forced her to thank him, although she was far from gracious. "You still haven't answered my question, Mr. Malloy. Why did my stepmother require your services?"

"Miss Bing, perhaps you noticed the lettering on my office door. The name of my firm is *Confidential* Inquiries. That means even if your stepmother had visited my office, as you seem to think, I couldn't tell you why or anything else that she shared with me in confidence."

That brought the color to her cheeks, which only enhanced her beauty. "But she had your business card on her desk. I . . . I found it there this morning."

Frank wondered if she'd found it because she'd been looking through her stepmother's things, but he couldn't ask her that. "Maybe it was the card I gave your father." He didn't know if he needed to protect Mrs. Bing's privacy, since she wasn't really a client, but he decided it couldn't hurt to do it anyway.

"My father?" Plainly, she resented Frank for mentioning him. "What business would my father have with a private detective?"

"I have no idea, but I met him at the automobile show last Saturday. He was trying to convince me to purchase one of his electric autos." Frank honestly couldn't remember if he'd given Bing one of his cards or not, but he certainly could have since he regularly did give his card to new acquaintances.

"Oh," Miss Bing said. "I had no idea you knew my father."

"How could you?" Frank asked amiably. "But I can hardly claim to know him. We only met that one time."

But she wasn't listening. She was looking around the room again and thinking. "What exactly does a private detective do?"

An interesting question. Frank settled back in his chair. "I help people when the police can't. Or won't."

"Could I hire you to, uh, help me?"

"Yes, if I agree to take your case."

49

She frowned at that. She probably wasn't used to being denied anything. "Can you help me prove my stepmother murdered my father?"

Frank needed a minute to recover from that shocking question. "Did she?"

"Of course she did."

Frank tried to look wise and unruffled. "If you have proof of it, you should tell the police. You don't need to hire a private investigator."

"The police are buffoons, and they aren't interested in anything I have to say."

Frank could believe that. "But if you have proof . . ."

"I don't have *proof,*" she admitted reluctantly. "Nothing that would convince the police, at least, but I know she did it. Who else would have wanted him dead?"

"I don't know, but why would *she* have wanted him dead?"

"Why does any woman want her husband dead? She probably wanted his money. Maybe she has a lover. That would be your job, to find out."

"And what if I found out someone else did it?"

She really frowned at that. "But you wouldn't, not if I hired you to find out she did it."

Frank supposed she could find a private detective to do just that, but he wasn't going to encourage her to look for one. "My fees are pretty high. Are you prepared to paythem?"

For the first time she looked uncertain. "How high are they?"

He named a daily rate that was twice as high as he normally charged, when he bothered to charge at all. "I usually ask for a week in advance," he added to increase the pain. He knew girls like her might receive an allowance, but they had no real money of their own.

"Is that, uh, typical?" she asked, clutching her purse more tightly.

"Fairly typical," he lied.

"I . . . I'll need to make arrangements."

"And I'll be happy to discuss the case in more detail when you return," Frank said.

She rose abruptly. "Thank you for your time, Mr. Malloy," she said, making it sound like she was chastening him instead.

"I'm happy to help, Miss Bing. I really was very sorry to hear about your father."

That emotion flickered across her face again, and then she left the office so quickly, he didn't even have time to get the door for her. She was gone by the time he reached the outer office.

"You have to learn to be nicer or we'll never have any clients," Maeve scolded him with a wicked grin.

"She wants to hire us to prove Mrs. Bing killed her husband."

"She actually said that?" Gino asked, having come out of his office.

"She actually said that. I told her we charge twice our usual rate, Maeve, in case she actually comes back to hire us."

"Do you think she will?" Maeve asked with interest.

"I hope not. I'd hate to have to admit I was just stringing her along."

"Yes," Maeve said with a knowing grin. "She is bound to take that badly."

"I hope you didn't agree to such a preposterous plan," Sarah said later when Malloy had told her about his visit from Pearl Bing. They were enjoying their private parlor, where the children couldn't overhear them talking about murder.

"No, I didn't agree to it. How can you even ask that?"

"Because I had to be sure. You see, I had a visit from Mrs. Bing today."

"Mrs. Bing? The wife?"

"She's a widow now, but yes. She believes the police think she killed her husband."

"Maybe we should tell Pearl that the police are willing to do her work for her and for free."

"Malloy, stop joking. None of this is funny."

"I'm not joking."

She glared at him.

"Well, maybe I'm joking a little."

"At any rate, Mrs. Bing obviously needs our help, and she's willing to hire you, too."

"If she did, I couldn't work for Pearl, although I'd probably have to give Pearl a reason."

"And somehow manage not to betray that you're working for her stepmother."

"Yes, that could be difficult. But I told her I charge a lot more than I really charge, so maybe she'll decide she can't afford to hire me."

"We can hope. I told Mrs. Bing that we would pay her a condolence call so you can tell her if you'll accept her as a client."

"That seems like a lot of trouble. Why doesn't she just come to my office?"

"Because she doesn't want anyone to connect you with her. She's afraid someone will find out she was trying to divorce her husband."

"Oh, I see, because that would give her a good reason for wanting him dead."

"Exactly. That's why I thought a social call would be a good solution, but now . . ."

"Now what?"

"Now I'm wondering how we explain to Pearl that we're paying a social call on her stepmother."

"I told her I met her father at the automobile show."

"Did you? Good! Then I can explain I met Mrs. Bing there as well, which has the added advantage of being the truth."

Malloy grinned his approval. "The truth is always preferable. It's so much easier to remember."

Frank came home for lunch the next day, and he and Sarah set out afterward for the Bing house. Mrs. Bing had given Sarah the address and they had even settled on a time. Frank had chosen to take his motorcar, even though it meant driving it himself. Gino usually drove when they went someplace together, but he wasn't going with them today. Besides, Frank enjoyed the motor much more when it was driven at a sensible speed, like five miles per hour, which Gino never did. The city had been right to make that the legal speed limit, although few drivers observed it.

In any case, it seemed appropriate to arrive at Bing's house in a motorcar.

A maid admitted them and showed them into the formal parlor, where Mrs. Bing waited alone. She rose to greet them. "Thank you so much for coming, Mrs. Malloy," she said for the maid's benefit. "And Mr. Malloy, what a nice surprise."

Sarah murmured her condolences until the maid had withdrawn and closed the door behind her. Mrs. Bing invited them to sit down on a love seat near the fireplace, and she took a chair opposite them. The room was tastefully furnished and free of the clutter that traditional parlors usually sported. Everything here appeared to be quite new. Frank remembered Mrs. Bing saying that she had been married to Mr. Bing for only about nine months. Could they have purchased and furnished the house at that time? Where had Bing lived before?

"I told Mr. Malloy everything, and he has agreed to accept you as a client, Mrs. Bing," Sarah was saying.

"That is a tremendous relief to me, Mr. Malloy. I don't know how to thank you."

"You can begin by telling me more about Mr. Bing, so I can figure out who else might have wanted to harm him," Frank said.

"Oh dear, where should I start?" She rubbed her temples with her fingertips, as if even thinking about it made her head hurt.

"Start with the night Mr. Bing died," Sarah suggested. "Do you know where he went that evening and who was with him?"

The question gave her a moment's pause, and Frank wondered why she hesitated, but she recovered quickly. "I can't know for certain, of course, but I believe he attended the automobile show that day. I know he was there in the morning, and I believe he intended to stay all day. He had been attending it every day, or so he said."

"Do you know if anyone was there with him?"

"I do not, although I observed when I was there on Saturday that he spoke with a great many people at the show, so any one of them might have been with him when he left."

"Did he mention any plans to meet anyone that evening after the show?"

"Oh no. I normally had no idea where he went or even exactly when he went out, which is why I can't even be sure he was at the show. He is . . . I mean, he *was* a very private person, and he seldom told me anything about his affairs."

"And yet you knew he wasn't unfaithful to you," Frank reminded her.

"I had no reason to believe he was, but now that I think about it, I often didn't know where he went or what he was doing. He belonged to a club, I think, and he would sometimes mention going there. He also went to the factory quite often, where they make the automobiles. He was fascinated by the process."

"But the factory would be closed in the evening, wouldn't it?" Frank asked.

"Oh yes, I suppose it would be, so he probably wasn't going there," Mrs. Bing said a bit uncertainly.

"But that night he indicated he would be attending the show, is that correct?"

"Yes, and I know he spent a lot of time there since it opened. Carrie and I were there with him the whole day on Saturday."

"I gathered he was trying to interest people in buying the autos his company builds," Frank said.

"Yes, and he doesn't think Will is a very good salesman."

"Who is Will?" Sarah asked, sparing Frank the trouble.

"Willard Warren. He's Mr. Bing's partner in the company. Will actually does all the work. I understand that he designs the automobiles and oversees all the building of the vehicles or whatever you call it. Mr. Bing just made an investment when Will needed more money."

"He'll probably know if Mr. Bing was at the show that night and who was with him," Frank said. "Do you have any idea how the company was doing?"

"What do you mean?" Mrs. Bing asked with a puzzled frown.

"I think he is asking if the company was making any profit," Sarah said with a reassuring smile. "He probably doesn't want to offend you by mentioning money."

"Oh, I don't think the company was doing well at all. Mr. Bing didn't speak about his business to me, you understand. He wouldn't consider that proper, but I've heard him complaining to Will in person and on the telephone about how much he had invested and how little he had to show for it."

Frank glanced at Sarah and saw she'd also identified another possible suspect. Disgruntled business associates sometimes took drastic steps to rid themselves of troublesome partners.

"And where were you and your daughters that night, Mrs. Bing?" Frank asked.

Mrs. Bing's eyes widened, but she quickly

schooled her expression to blankness again. "Home. We were all at home that evening. We retired by ten o'clock, I'm sure, which is what we usually do."

Frank didn't bother to glance at Sarah. Mrs. Bing was lying, and they both knew it. "I know Carrie was at the show on Saturday. Did Pearl attend it at any time?"

Mrs. Bing frowned. "How do you know about Pearl?" She turned to Sarah. "I don't believe I mentioned her to you at all."

"Pearl came to see me yesterday," Frank said. "She found my card on your desk, or so she said."

"She actually went to see you?" Mrs. Bing cried in alarm. "You didn't tell her why I was there, did you?"

"I didn't tell her anything at all. I let her believe that I had given my card to Mr. Bing when we met at the show."

Mrs. Bing's gratitude was plain. "Oh, thank you, Mr. Malloy. That was so kind of you."

"I protect my clients, Mrs. Bing, even the ones who don't hire me," he said with a smile. "Now tell me, since you and your daughters were all at home in bed when Mr. Bing met his untimely end, who do you think might have wanted to do Mr. Bing harm?"

"Oh dear, I have no idea. I mean, he rarely spoke to me about his business concerns, and I never met many of his associates. Actually, Will is the only one I know at all. I don't think I met any of his friends. He . . . We didn't entertain and we didn't receive any invitations either."

"That seems a little odd," Sarah said. "Wouldn't Mr. Bing have a lot of friends in the city?"

"Oh no. He's only lived here since . . . Well, a little less than a year, I believe."

"Really?" Frank said. This was news. "He's not from New York, then?"

"No, he . . . I'm actually not sure where he came from originally, but most recently, he moved here from Colorado, I believe."

How interesting. "What did he do in Colorado?"

"He was in mining. He was quite successful, from what I understand, so he and Pearl moved to New York. He thought he could be even more successful here."

"By investing in motorcars," Frank guessed.

Mrs. Bing smiled weakly and nodded.

"Are you sure you don't know of anyone who might wish Mr. Bing ill?" Sarah said gently. "Someone from his past, perhaps? Someone he might have mentioned, even in passing?"

Mrs. Bing looked up in surprise. "I'd forgotten but yes, there was someone. It was the strangest thing . . ."

"Who was it?" Sarah pressed when she hesitated.

"It was a woman. She came to the door one day demanding to see Mr. Bing."

III

This was promising. Sarah leaned forward to encourage Mrs. Bing's confidence. "Who was this woman?"

"I . . . I'm not sure. She looked like someone who should have gone to the back door. The way she was dressed, I mean. She was a bit threadbare, and she looked like she'd seen hard times." Mrs. Bing smiled a little sadly. "Of course, I was a bit threadbare myself when I married Mr. Bing."

Sarah tucked that admission away for later. "And she asked to see Mr. Bing?"

"Yes, she was quite insistent, and our maid was a bit distressed. The woman didn't look like someone Mr. Bing would want to see, but he agreed when the maid told him her name."

"Do you remember what it was?"

Mrs. Bing concentrated for a moment. "I don't actually think I heard it. Perhaps our maid will remember."

Sarah also tucked that away for future reference and said, "So Mr. Bing met with her?"

"Yes, but not for very long. I expected him to tell me who she was, but he didn't, and he ignored me when I asked him about her."

"And she didn't come back?"

"No, she didn't come back, but Mr. Bing

was . . . I guess you could say he was disturbed by her visit. He brooded for several days afterward."

"When did this happen?" Frank asked.

She had to think for a moment. "Last Friday, I think. Oh, and Pearl seemed upset about her, too."

"Did Pearl also see her?"

"No, she was out, but Mr. Bing must have mentioned the woman to her. She asked me what I knew about her, but I couldn't tell her anything."

Sarah had many more questions for Mrs. Bing, and she figured Malloy did as well, but the parlor door opened, and a young woman wearing full mourning came bustling in, an expression of challenge on her lovely face. She was dressed for the street, still wearing her hat and gloves, so she had obviously just arrived. She had already opened her mouth to speak, but when Malloy stood up, she stopped dead in her tracks and the words died in her throat.

For a long moment no one spoke while the young woman stared at Malloy, but Mrs. Bing finally said, "This is my stepdaughter, Pearl. Pearl, these are my friends, Mr. and Mrs. Malloy."

"Your *friends?*" Pearl said doubtfully.

"Yes," Sarah said cheerfully. "I met Mrs. Bing at the automobile show last Saturday. We had a lovely visit while my husband spoke with Mr.

Bing and inspected all the autos on display. We were so saddened to read about Mr. Bing's accident, and we thought we'd pay a condolence call to see if there is anything we can do to support the family."

"Mrs. Malloy is very kind," Mrs. Bing said, but Pearl wasn't paying her any attention. She was still staring at Malloy, now with a very satisfied expression.

"Yes, she is," Pearl said without the slightest hint that she cared one way or the other. She continued to stare at Malloy, who was meeting her gaze unflinchingly. Whatever silent communication passed between them pleased Pearl, although her smile made Sarah slightly uneasy.

Someone made a discreet coughing sound, and only then did Sarah notice that Pearl had not arrived alone. A gentleman stood in the doorway. He had obviously accompanied Pearl, as he was still carrying his hat in his hand.

"Oh, Will, I didn't see you," Mrs. Bing said. "Please come in and meet my friends. Mr. and Mrs. Malloy, this is Willard Warren, Mr. Bing's business partner."

Mr. Warren stepped forward then. He was younger than Sarah had expected, probably not yet thirty, and rather unprepossessing. Tall and lanky, he looked uncomfortable in his suit with the stiff collar and tie, and his hair was trying to rebel against the pomade he had applied and was curling at the ends. He wasn't handsome, although his shy smile of acknowledgment touched Sarah's heart. He wore a black armband to signify his mourning for Mr. Bing.

Pearl had apparently finished silently communicating with Malloy, and she said, "Whatever have you been discussing?"

Mrs. Bing glanced helplessly at Sarah, obviously not sure what she should reveal to Pearl.

"We were asking about the circumstances of your father's accident," Sarah lied. "The newspapers made it sound so mysterious."

"Yes," Malloy said. "I couldn't imagine how a man could be run over by his own motorcar."

"We really have no idea what happened," Pearl said, taking the empty chair beside her stepmother. Then she seemed to remember Mr. Warren. "Do pull up a chair, Will. You make me nervous staring down at me like that."

Will did so, and Malloy resumed his seat as well.

"Is it true the police think someone else was driving the motor and ran over Mr. Bing?" Sarah asked, realizing how grisly that sounded but wanting to see Pearl's and Mrs. Bing's reactions.

Mrs. Bing winced, but Pearl simply glared at her impatiently. "The electric automobiles are so easy to drive, anyone might have jumped into the seat and accidentally set it in motion."

"Is that what you think happened?" Malloy said.

"We can't know for certain, but it does seem the most logical explanation," Pearl said.

Sarah noticed that neither Mrs. Bing nor Mr. Warren offered an opinion.

"But why would Mr. Bing have been out of the vehicle?" Malloy asked.

With an expectant glare, Pearl turned to Mr. Warren.

"Oh, uh, any number of reasons," he said quickly. "To . . . to check something in the engine, maybe. Or a loose wheel. Or . . ."

His large hands were working the brim of the hat he still held, and Sarah noticed that his nails were stained with something dark. Mrs. Bing had said he did most of the work building the automobiles himself.

"So, you think that while he was checking whatever he was checking, some stranger jumped into the motorcar and sent it lurching forward to hit Mr. Bing," Malloy said as if contemplating this unlikely scenario.

"What else could have happened?" Pearl asked with what she probably thought was an innocent expression. She was a poor actress, though. Maeve would not have been impressed.

"Someone could have run over Mr. Bing on purpose," Malloy said, "if someone had a reason to do so."

"But who would have a reason to do so?" Pearl

said, lifting her chin in defiance. "Everyone loved my father."

Once again, neither Mrs. Bing nor Mr. Warren offered an opinion, which Sarah found very telling indeed.

"Well," Sarah said, apropos of nothing, "I suppose the police will sort it all out."

Pearl huffed in disgust. "The police are morons."

Sarah glanced at Malloy, who could have agreed with her, but he said, "They will get a lot smarter if you offer a reward for finding the person responsible."

"A reward?" Pearl echoed, as if she had never heard the word before.

"Yes. The police don't exactly overpay their detectives. They are always happy to earn a reward for solving a case."

"But that's . . . awful," Pearl said.

No one disagreed.

"I just thought you should know, if you are anxious to find out what happened to Mr. Bing," Malloy said almost apologetically.

Pearl was plainly furious at his suggestion, and her angry gaze darted back and forth between Malloy and her stepmother. Sarah couldn't help remembering that Pearl wanted Malloy to prove Mrs. Bing had killed her father, whether she had or not. Then Pearl said, "I think our money would be better spent by hiring our own private detective."

"Yes," Mrs. Bing said, "which is why I have hired Mr. Malloy."

"What?" Pearl said with a most unladylike show of emotion.

"I hired Mr. Malloy," Mrs. Bing repeated with remarkable calmness. "When I found his card on Mr. Bing's desk, I immediately went to see Mrs. Malloy, whom I had met at the automobile show, and she advised me to hire her husband." Mrs. Bing was a much better actress than Pearl.

"Of course she did," Pearl said, even more furious now to learn her stepmother had beaten her to Malloy. "How do we know he's even a good detective?"

Malloy seemed unfazed by the implied insult, but Mrs. Bing sprang instantly to his defense. "He used to be a police detective himself. I thought he would be the best one to investigate Mr. Bing's death."

Pearl glared at her stepmother. "Didn't you hear what I said before? The police are morons."

"Not all of them," Malloy said. "As I said, when they're being paid, they can be very good indeed."

"And I'm sure we will all help you as much as we can," Mrs. Bing said. "I was just telling Mr. and Mrs. Malloy about the strange woman who came to see your father last Friday. Do you know who she was?"

Pearl's anger instantly changed to alarm.

Really, Maeve should offer to give her lessons. "I . . . I don't know who you mean. What woman?"

"The one who came to see your father," Mrs. Bing repeated patiently. "Remember, you asked me what I knew about her."

"Oh yes. I . . . I'd forgotten all about her." She was actually embarrassing herself.

"Do you know her name?"

Pearl started at this. "Of course not. How could I?"

"I thought perhaps your father had mentioned it."

"Obviously, he didn't." Pearl began to remove her gloves with quick, jerky motions.

Without another word, Mrs. Bing got up and pulled the bell cord.

"I don't know why you're so interested in that woman," Pearl said when she'd finished removing her gloves and slapped them down in her lap.

The maid came in. "Yes, ma'am."

"Mary, do you remember the woman who came to call on Mr. Bing last Friday?"

Pearl stiffened, but Mrs. Bing apparently didn't notice.

"Yes, ma'am."

"Did she leave a calling card, by chance?"

"Oh no, ma'am. She didn't have no calling card. She just told me her name. She said if I told Mr. Bing her name, he'd see her."

67

Pearl gasped, but Mrs. Bing never even blinked. "And do you remember what her name was?"

"Oh yes, ma'am. Nora Rumsfeld, she said it was."

Although Mrs. Bing had proven herself a good actress, even she could not hide her shock, although Pearl made not a sound. Maybe she wasn't surprised by the news at all.

"Thank you, Mary," Mrs. Bing said, and they all waited until she was gone because people didn't discuss private business in front of the servants.

Even then, no one spoke for a long moment, and then Mr. Warren said, "Pearl, wasn't your mother's name Nora?"

Pearl was furious again, and Mr. Warren actually flinched at the way she glared at him.

"Yes, it was," Mrs. Bing answered for her. "I don't know much about Mr. Bing's life before I met him, but I do know that. How many times did he compare me to Nora? I could never quite measure up." Then she turned to Pearl. "But I thought your mother was dead."

Pearl's cheeks burned with her combined fury and whatever other emotions she was feeling. "So did I."

Another awkward silence fell, and when it became apparent no one else knew what to say, Sarah said, "Are we to assume this woman is your mother?"

Pearl drew a deep breath and let it out in a gusty sigh. "Yes."

"But . . ." Mrs. Bing began but couldn't seem to go any further. She had gone white. The implications were too enormous. Bigamy was only the beginning.

"Have you seen her?" Sarah asked Pearl.

"I . . . Yes." All Pearl's anger had evaporated, and she almost seemed to sag. "Father told me where I could find her."

"What did she have to say?" Mrs. Bing prodded.

Pearl's lips tightened as if she would refuse to speak, but after a moment, she said, "She had a sad tale. She said Father had abandoned her in some mining town. He was supposed to send for her, but he never did. It took her all this time to find him. More than five years."

No one said the obvious, that only a few days after she appeared, Bing was dead under mysterious circumstances. Then Sarah thought of something else. "He abandoned her, but he took you with him."

Pearl's head jerked up. "What does that have to do with anything?"

"It just seems odd. When a man abandons his family, he is usually trying to escape the responsibility, so why take a child with him but not his wife? That would leave all the care of the child—all the responsibility—to him."

"My father loved me," Pearl said a bit defensively. "He loved me more than anyone else in the world."

Which also seemed an odd thing to say, but Sarah didn't point that out. "And I'm sure you loved him, too."

"But not everyone loved him," Pearl said, looking pointedly at Mrs. Bing and contradicting what she herself had claimed only a few minutes ago.

"Not loving someone and wanting them dead are two very different things," Mrs. Bing said, still calm in spite of the implications of this amazing conversation.

"That's very true," Malloy said with a small smile. "Miss Bing, if you will tell me where I can find your mother, I'll be glad to speak to her and see if I can clear her name."

Sarah was impressed. Pearl could hardly refuse such a generous request.

But would Pearl want her mother's name cleared? "She may not want to speak with you," Pearl hedged.

"I certainly can't force her to speak with me, but if the police learn that she is here, they might well decide she killed your father out of revenge, just to close the case."

Plainly, Pearl knew she was being manipulated, but Malloy was doing it so well, she couldn't object. She gave him the name of a rather seedy hotel. Mr. Bing had obviously not shared any of his fortune with his first wife.

"I'd like to speak with you, too, Mr. Warren," Malloy said.

"Now?" he asked in surprise.

Malloy smiled innocently, forcing Sarah to cover her mouth and cough to hide a snort of laughter. "I can call on you later at your factory."

"I'm afraid I won't be able to help you," Warren said anxiously. "I don't know anything about how Bing died."

"Don't cheat me out of a chance to visit your factory. I'd love to see how your automobiles are made," Malloy said, still smiling.

"Oh well, yes, of course," he stammered.

"When is the funeral?" Sarah asked, deciding they had accomplished all they could today. Malloy would no doubt advise questioning each of these people separately, which would be impossible at this time.

"When is the funeral?" Mrs. Bing asked Pearl, which surprised Sarah. Wasn't Mrs. Bing involved in the arrangements?

"I . . . We decided on Saturday." Pearl glanced at Warren as if he had been part of the decision, although he just stared blankly back at her. "The police are releasing the . . ." She stopped and swallowed as if discussing her father's dead body distressed her, which it probably did.

71

". . . releasing *him* today. We'll have the funeral here. I don't expect many people will attend," she added sadly.

"Everyone from the factory will be there," Warren said. "I'll give them the time off."

"Yes, they do turn out for funerals, don't they?" Pearl said with a touch of bitterness and a glance at her stepmother.

Mrs. Bing's cheeks flooded with color, but Sarah couldn't tell exactly what emotion she was experiencing. Sarah now had far more questions to ask Mrs. Bing than when they'd first arrived, but they'd best be asked in private.

Frank handed Sarah up into the motorcar, and they slipped into their dusters and goggles for the drive home. Sarah also wrapped several yards of tulle around her head to keep her hat from blowing off. When they were suitably garbed, Frank turned to her.

"That was interesting."

"This Nora woman certainly had a good reason for killing Bing, if the story she told Pearl about Bing abandoning her is true."

"But would Nora have known how to operate a motorcar?"

"Ah, that's important to know, unless Pearl is right and it's so easy to operate an electric motor that anyone could do it."

Frank nodded. "I guess I'll have to ask Mr.

Warren to let me try one out so I can see for myself."

Sarah laughed at him. "You aren't fooling me. I see your nefarious plan."

"There's nothing nefarious about it," he said, pretending to be affronted. "It's information we will need."

"You're right, of course, because everyone else close to Mr. Bing does know how to operate an electric motorcar," she said with mock solemnity.

"Except me," he said, and hurried on before she could laugh again. "But Nora has the best motive so far for wanting Bing dead."

"But only *so far.* Mrs. Bing hasn't told us everything, I'm sure."

"No, and if she's got a better reason for wanting Bing dead than she's already revealed, she won't want anyone else to know it."

"Then I'll have to work a bit harder to find out what it is," Sarah said, giving him a look of challenge.

"Don't worry, I'll leave that entirely up to you. I'm not nearly as good as you are at getting women to reveal their secrets."

"And there's something odd about the way Bing left his wife but took Pearl with him. In my experience, men try to avoid dealing with young girls if they possibly can. And men who abandon their wives usually leave the children as well, since they're too much trouble. To take Pearl and leave her mother behind seems very strange."

"Maybe he was angry with his first wife," Frank suggested. "He could get double revenge by leaving her and taking her beloved child with him."

Sarah considered this. "You may be right. I'd certainly be devastated to lose my child."

"But not your husband?" he teased.

"Of course I'd be devastated to lose you, but I love you. We don't know how Nora felt about Bing."

Frank took a moment to savor the admission of love. He never got used to it, no matter how often Sarah said it. But only a moment. "No, we don't know how Nora felt about Bing, but she must have been furious at being left behind in a mining town. How would she even support herself?"

Sarah frowned. "The possibilities are very limited and not very appealing. She must have been shattered."

"And extremely angry."

"She hasn't forgiven him either, if she spent five years trying to find him."

"I think you're right."

"And have you realized how this will affect Mrs. Bing?" Sarah said with another frown. "This means she isn't even Mrs. Bing."

"No, she isn't. She probably won't inherit anything from Bing either, if she's not his legal wife, so she's in exactly the same situation as this Nora was when Bing deserted her."

"It's too bad she can't prove she didn't know about Nora, although I don't think she did. Knowing about her would give her another good reason to kill Bing."

"Unless it's all the same reason. Maybe she realized her marriage was bigamous and that's why she wanted a divorce."

Sarah shook her tulle-wrapped head. "But that doesn't make any sense. Why go through a divorce when your marriage wasn't legal in the first place? All she'd have to do is inform Bing she knew the truth and leave him."

"You're right, so wanting a divorce actually proves she didn't know about Nora being alive. Still, she did want a divorce and whatever her reason, it might give her a motive."

"And I will do my best to find out what her reason was."

Malloy smiled. "So shall we try to find the first Mrs. Bing before Pearl has a chance to warn her off?"

"Do you think she would?"

Frank shrugged. "Why take a chance?" He climbed out of his seat and grabbed the crank, sighing dramatically for Sarah's benefit. "Right about now, I'm wishing I had an electric motor that would start with no effort at all."

"Then isn't it lucky you know exactly where to get one?"

• • •

The hotel wasn't the worst Sarah had ever seen, but few hotels would accept a female staying alone. Such women were always assumed to be prostitutes and even the most humble establishments didn't want to become known as houses of assignation. Nora Rumsfeld Bing probably had little choice in accommodations.

The desk clerk was a young man with a pocked face, wearing a wrinkled suit with a stained collar. He eyed them slyly as they approached the desk. "We don't take people without luggage," he said with a smirk.

Malloy didn't even blink. "We're here to see Mrs. Rumsfeld."

His less-than-respectful gaze took in Sarah. "Both of you?"

"She's my wife's sister," Malloy lied with ease. "Is she in?"

The clerk frowned but he did deign to turn and look at the rack of pigeonholes that represented each of the rooms in the hotel. "Her key is gone, so she must be in."

"And what number would that be?" Malloy asked, this time with a slight edge to his voice to indicate he was losing patience.

The clerk looked over his shoulder again, as if he didn't already know the correct room number. "I don't know if I should . . ."

With a disgusted frown, Frank slid a quarter

across the desk, and the clerk promptly gave him the room number.

"Why is it," Sarah asked as they climbed the stairs to the second floor, "that the cheaper the hotel is, the ruder the desk clerks are?"

"I don't know if that's true. Desk clerks in expensive hotels can be rude, too."

When they reached the appropriate room, Malloy rapped on the door and then stepped back so Sarah would be the first person Mrs. Bing saw.

The door opened a crack, just enough for one eye to peer at them. "Who are you?"

Sarah gave her what she hoped was a reassuring smile. "I'm Mrs. Frank Malloy. Pearl suggested we speak with you about your, uh, situation." Sarah could lie with the best of them.

"Pearl?" she said in alarm, opening the door wider. "Is she here?"

"She is helping her, uh, stepmother make the funeral arrangements, but she sent us to help you."

Nora Rumsfeld Bing was probably not much older than forty, but life had not been kind to her. She was, as Ethel Bing had described, a bit threadbare. Her face had a weathered look and her eyes were hard. She'd made some effort with her hair, but the style was practical and not very flattering. "How can you help me?"

"I don't know, but we'd like to try. Pearl is worried that if the police find out about you, they will accuse you of killing your husband."

She scowled at that and turned her displeasure on Malloy. "Who's he?"

"This is my husband, Frank Malloy. He's a private investigator."

"What's he investigating?"

"Mr. Bing's death," Malloy offered. "Pearl would like us to make sure you aren't blamed."

Malloy's added assurance did not placate Mrs. Bing, but she said, "You better come in, then."

The room was small and utilitarian. A bed, a chest of drawers, and a wardrobe. One stuffed chair and one straight-backed chair.

"Have a seat," Nora said, gesturing vaguely. "I got nothing to offer you."

Malloy silently told Sarah to take the stuffed chair. He sat in the straight-backed chair, and Nora plopped down on the neatly made bed.

"I didn't kill him," she said. "So you don't need to waste your time saving me. Pearl should've known that."

"Innocent people are convicted of crimes with alarming frequency, Mrs. Bing," Sarah said. "Should I call you Mrs. Bing?"

"You can if you want. It's still my name in spite of Alvin running off. He never got no divorce, so I'm still his wife, and you can tell that to the harlot he married."

"I would hardly call Mrs. Bing—the other Mrs. Bing—a harlot," Sarah said. "She is a perfectly respectable woman who was deceived. She had no idea you were still alive until today."

Nora shifted uneasily on the bed. "She's a harlot now, though, isn't she? Sleeping with a man who's not her husband."

They would get nowhere debating this with her. Sarah decided to change the subject. "Pearl told us your husband deserted you."

"That he did," she said, warming to the subject. "We was forever moving from one town to another, looking for a big strike. He was a mining engineer, so he knew what to look for, but his luck hadn't been good. We was running a boardinghouse to make ends meet. Miners need a place to sleep and get something to eat, after all. I told him we should open a store. That's who made money in those mining towns, the people who sold stuff to the miners. He wanted to be rich, though. He wanted to strike gold or silver or copper or lead. Didn't matter to him, as long as he got rich."

"Why did he leave you?"

Nora's scowl deepened. "What did Pearl tell you?"

"She didn't really say much, just that she thought you were dead."

"Yeah, that's Alvin's doing. He was always clever, and he was clever about this, too. He said he needed to move to another town. He'd heard about a new strike, and he wanted to get there before word got out."

"And he took Pearl with him."

Nora frowned. "Yeah, well, I never agreed to that, but he snuck away in the middle of the night and when I woke up, they was both gone."

"Didn't you think that was strange? How would a man alone take care of a child?"

"She wasn't a child by then. She was almost fifteen."

"Oh, I guess I didn't realize how old she was."

Nora glanced away and some emotion that might have been pain washed over her, but when she looked back at Sarah, her gaze was cold again. "He said he'd send word when he got settled, and I could sell the house and join him. That was our plan. It took me six months to figure out he was never going to send word."

"That must have been awful for you."

"At least I had the boardinghouse. Most of the women in those mining towns made a living on their backs. I did pretty well, until the mines petered out. Then I set out to find Alvin. I didn't want him anymore, but I did want Pearl. I wondered why she'd let him abandon me like that and never even sent me so much as a letter, but I should've known it wasn't her doing. If she thought I was dead, she wouldn't expect to see me again, would she?"

"No, she wouldn't," Sarah agreed, finding herself in sympathy with Nora.

"I see he did all right for himself, too," Nora

added, gesturing to a newspaper lying on the floor. It had been folded open to a story about Bing's death. The awful engraving of the motorcar resting on his chest still made Sarah wince. "They say he was a millionaire."

"He was apparently quite wealthy, yes," Sarah agreed.

"Who gets his money now?" she asked, turning to Malloy, who had shown remarkable restraint by letting Sarah ask all the questions.

"That depends on whether he had a last will and testament," he said.

"What's that?" Nora asked with interest.

"It's a document that states how he wants his property distributed after his death," Malloy said. "He can say he wants his money to go to his family or to someone else."

"You mean he can leave his money to that hussy who isn't really his wife?"

"He might have, but since they weren't legally married, you might be able to contest the will."

"I'll contest everything. She don't have any right to his money. It should go to me and Pearl."

Sarah thought Pearl would certainly agree. Had Pearl been happy to learn her mother was still alive, though? Sarah hadn't been able to tell, and Nora hadn't really said one way or the other. "What did Mr. Bing say when you went to see him?"

Nora gave a mirthless laugh. "He was surprised,

as you can imagine. I guess he never thought he'd see me again."

"How did you find him?" Malloy asked.

"I didn't have much trouble. He cuts a wide swath, that one, and people remembered Pearl, because she's so pretty. It took me a long time to catch him up, though, because I'd run out of money and have to stop and work someplace for a while until I saved up to travel to the next place, or winter would set in and I'd be stuck someplace until spring. That took years, but he was easy to find here. Somebody told me there's a city directory and there he was."

"When you saw him, did he . . . ?" Sarah began and stopped when she realized she didn't know how to phrase her question.

"Did he say he was sorry, and he'd throw his new wife out and take me back?" Nora asked sarcastically. "What do you think?"

"Did he offer you money?" Malloy asked.

Nora nodded her appreciation at his perception. "He sure did. He said he couldn't have somebody like me dragging him down. He needed a wife who was a lady, so he said he'd give me money if I'd leave town and never come back. I was willing to take his money, but I wasn't leaving, that's for sure."

"Did he say that exactly," Sarah asked in confusion, "that he needed a wife who was a lady?"

"Yeah, he said he was rich now and he had lots of society friends. They'd never accept somebody like me, and they'd laugh at him behind his back. That's why he married that harlot, he said."

Except the second Mrs. Bing wasn't exactly a society matron either.

"Mrs. Bing," Malloy said before Sarah could think of another question, "do you know how to operate a motorcar?"

IV

"A motorcar?" Nora echoed with derision. "How would the likes of me learn to drive a motorcar? Pearl knows how, though. She took me for a ride in one when she came to see me. She said she didn't want nobody to overhear us so that was the best place for us to talk."

Frank tried to imagine holding that kind of a conversation in his noisy, gasoline-powered motor and nearly laughed out loud. "I guess Pearl is a good driver."

Nora scowled at him. "Nobody got run over, if that's what you mean."

"What plans did you and Pearl make?" Sarah asked quickly to change the subject.

"What do you mean?" Nora asked suspiciously.

"You said you weren't planning to take money from Mr. Bing and disappear, so what *were* you planning to do?"

Nora straightened almost defensively. "I didn't decide yet."

Sarah nodded her understanding, and Frank marveled at the way she could appear so sympathetic. "I can understand that. But Mr. Bing owns a large house. As his wife, you're certainly entitled to live in it with your daughter."

Frank almost winced at the thought of Nora

trying to move in with the other Mrs. Bing and her daughter. Who would win that confrontation? Nora would have the law on her side, if she could prove she married Alvin first, but could she?

"Mr. Bing's funeral is on Saturday at his house," Sarah was saying. "I'm sure Pearl will invite you, but just in case she can't get in touch with you . . ."

Frank wasn't so sure Pearl would invite her, so he couldn't help approving of Sarah's attempt to get Nora there. It would be interesting to see what happened when the two women met.

"Yes, Pearl will need me there," Nora said with a confidence Frank didn't share. He couldn't wait for Saturday.

"You are an evil woman, Mrs. Malloy," Frank said as they strolled out of Nora Rumsfeld Bing's hotel and approached their motorcar.

"I just felt Mrs. Bing should know when her husband's funeral is being held, and I knew Pearl would be quite busy between now and then and it might slip her mind to invite her mother," Sarah said with an unrepentant grin.

"Now we'll have to attend the funeral, and we'll have to bring Gino and Maeve along, too, since they'll never forgive us if they missed seeing the two Mrs. Bings coming to blows."

Sarah shook her head. "I hope they don't actually come to blows. Besides, Pearl might be the one who objects the most to having her mother there. She's probably as concerned about appearances as her father was."

They'd reached the motor and Frank helped her up. They put on their gear and Malloy picked up the crank.

"Where to now?" she asked.

"It's late, so home, but tomorrow I think I'll pay a visit to Bing's automobile company."

"You poor thing," she said with a smirk. "I hope you won't be too bored."

"I'll struggle through somehow," he assured her. "And while I'm doing that, it might be a good time to see if you can catch Pearl Bing alone."

"I was thinking the same thing."

The best part of visiting a place of business was that Frank didn't have to wait for a socially acceptable time of day to call. As long as the business was open, he'd be welcomed, or at least tolerated.

The Warren Motor Company was located in a large warehouse on the east side of the city. A regular door for pedestrians and a large double door for motorcars marked the front. Both were closed against the November chill. Frank found the pedestrian door unlocked, so he let himself in. It led directly into the shop, where a dozen men in work clothes labored at various tasks. Some stood at one of the workbenches that lined the room, and two were trying to attach a headlamp to a partially assembled automobile that held pride of place in the center of the floor.

There didn't seem to be a receptionist or any sort of secretary, which Frank thought wasn't really surprising, so no one noticed his arrival for several minutes. Finally, the man at the nearest bench hollered, "Can I help you, mister?"

"Yes, I'd like to see Mr. Warren if he's in."

The fellow didn't even set down the tool he'd been using on whatever mysterious piece of equipment he'd been working on. He just lifted his chin and shouted, "Will! A fellow here to see you."

Frank glanced around to see if anyone had responded to this crude method of communication, and just when he'd decided no one had, he saw a figure emerge from the shadows at the far end of the building. Frank soon recognized him as Willard Warren. He was also dressed in work clothes and was wiping his hands on a dirty rag. Unlike yesterday, when he'd seemed ill at ease, he seemed quite comfortable in this environment.

When he was close enough, he said, "Mr. Malloy, isn't it?" He didn't look particularly pleased, but he also didn't look like he planned to throw Frank out.

Still, Frank decided to warm up his welcome a

bit. "I decided to take you up on your offer to see your setup. I hope this is a good time."

Warren sighed. "If you're worried about me being in mourning, I'm not too grief-stricken to show you around. I'm sure Mr. Bing would have approved."

"He was certainly a big supporter of electric motorcars," Frank agreed.

Warren neither agreed nor disagreed. Instead, he turned slightly so he could see the rest of the shop. "We build all our automobiles right here. We have to make everything by hand, which is why the automobiles are so expensive. If they ever figure out how to make them more cheaply, everyone will own one."

"How much do the electric vehicles cost?" Frank asked with genuine interest.

"You can get a basic model for a thousand dollars, but most people want them fancy, so add another thousand or more if you really want luxury."

Frank let out a low whistle. His luxurious gasoline-powered motor had cost only a little over a thousand dollars.

"But think about how much use you'll get out of one here in the city," Warren quickly replied. "And your wife will love it. Let me walk you through the process of building one of these beauties."

Frank willingly followed along as Warren took

him around the room, explaining each step in the process of constructing an electric auto.

"I notice you always call them automobiles," Frank said about halfway through his tour.

"Yes, that seems to be the preferred term ever since the *New York Times* started using it last year."

Frank made a mental note and continued to follow Warren on the tour. Finally, they were finished, and Frank stood before a row of five completed electric automobiles that were parked at what Warren explained were charging stations in the rear of the building.

"Someday you'll see charging stations all over the city," Warren said with a confidence Frank didn't think he had any right to feel. The stations were about six feet tall and two feet wide. The bottom held a metal box with holes, like a box you'd carry an animal in if you didn't want it to suffocate. The top was a large metal plate with various dials and levers. A long rubber cord connected each automobile to one of the charging stations, much the way a cord connected an electric lamp to an outlet on the wall.

"I suppose I'd need one of these charging stations, too."

"If you want to be fancy, but you can plug the auto into your house's electricity, too. Really, you can get a charge at any place with electricity."

If they'd let you, Frank thought, but he said,

"Do you have an office where we can talk in private?"

"Of course." Warren seemed pleased by the question. He must think Frank wanted to discuss a purchase. Warren led Frank to the far side of the building, where a short row of offices had been roughly constructed. The interior of the one they entered consisted of a battered desk covered with papers, a filing cabinet, and a chair for visitors. The room was lit by one naked bulb hanging down from the ceiling. Warren reached up and pulled the chain to turn it on. Frank took the visitor's chair at Warren's invitation. Warren sat down behind the desk.

"I imagine you'll want a rather luxurious model for your wife," Warren said with a smile.

"Maybe eventually, but right now I need to ask you some questions about Alvin Bing."

Warren's salesman's smile faded. "I should've known."

"I did tell you I'd be stopping by."

"And Miss Bing warned me you'd be nosing around."

"Is that what she called it, *nosing around?*" Frank asked good-naturedly. "And to think she tried to hire me herself."

"Why would she want to hire you?" Warren asked in alarm.

"You'll have to ask her that yourself. I gather you're quite close to Miss Bing."

The lighting was poor, but Frank could still see Warren's face turn scarlet. "I am fortunate that Miss Bing considers me a friend."

"I'm sure she appreciates your support at this difficult time," Frank said, not bothering to sound sincere.

Warren's face tightened, but he held on to his temper. "Mr. Bing's death left his family without any male to assist them. Miss Bing naturally asked for my help."

"I guess you and Mr. Bing were close friends."

"I wouldn't call us friends," Warren hedged. "We were business associates. I was fortunate to meet Mr. Bing when he was looking for investment opportunities, and he saw the potential in automobiles right away."

"I understand the company isn't doing too well, though."

"Who told you that?" Warren asked, obviously offended.

"Mr. Bing mentioned it to his wife."

Warren drew a breath, still trying to hold his temper in check. "The automobile business is very competitive. There are over two hundred companies making them and . . . and . . ."

"And a rather limited market," Frank said helpfully.

"It will grow," Warren insisted.

"But your company wasn't doing well, so you needed an investor," Frank guessed.

"That is a very common business practice."

"I know, but even after Bing invested, the company wasn't doing well."

"It takes time to start showing a profit in any business."

"Had Bing complained to you about this?"

"Mr. Bing complained about everything. All investors want an immediate return on their money, but I explained that since we can only make one vehicle at a time, it's a slow process."

"Was Mr. Bing satisfied with your explanation?"

Warren smiled grimly. "Hardly. He was used to the quick returns he got in mining, but he was resigned, I think."

Frank nodded sagely. "And did Mr. Bing approve of your friendship with Pearl?"

Warren flushed again, but Frank wasn't sure if the emotion he was feeling was anger or embarrassment. "Why wouldn't he?"

"I don't know. Maybe because he was a millionaire and you're a . . ." Frank glanced meaningfully at Warren's clothes. ". . . a mechanic."

"I'm much more than a mechanic," he huffed. "I'm an engineer, and I design the vehicles we make here. I *own* this company."

"In partnership with Bing," Frank reminded him. "Except with Bing dead, what happens to that partnership?"

"I . . . His heirs will continue to receive his share of the profits, of course." He didn't sound certain, though.

Frank didn't challenge him. "If there *are* any profits . . . and his heirs aren't likely to interfere in the business, are they?"

Warren seemed to be alarmed. "What do you mean?"

"I mean they aren't likely to question anything you tell them, since they won't know anything at all about the business."

"Miss Bing is quite familiar with the business."

"Is she? Is that how you two became friends?"

"I don't like your tone, Mr. Malloy," Warren said, obviously having chosen to take the high ground since nothing else was working. "My relationship with Miss Bing is entirely honorable."

"I'm sure it is, but she's a very pretty young lady. No one could blame you if you had ambitions there."

"I . . . Miss Bing is indeed an attractive young lady," Warren said carefully. "A man couldn't help but notice."

"Would Mr. Bing have welcomed you as a suitor for his daughter's hand?"

His flush actually deepened. "I couldn't say."

"Ah, then your pursuit of Miss Bing only began after his death."

"What? No . . . I mean, that isn't true."

"What part isn't true? That you are pursuing Miss Bing or when you began to?"

Warren rubbed his forehead. "I don't think any of this is your business, Mr. Malloy, and it isn't at all proper for us to be discussing Miss Bing like this."

"Isn't it? I'm trying to figure out who had a reason to kill her father. I've been a detective for a long time, and I know that people usually get killed for one of two reasons: love or money. You're in an unsuccessful business partnership with Bing and you're interested in his daughter, so you qualify in both categories."

"I did not kill Alvin Bing," Warren said, furious now. "Why would I? Yes, the company isn't making money right now, but he could see that it was going to eventually. He was ready to invest even more money to make that happen."

"Was he really? I suppose you can prove that."

"He told me just the other day. We hadn't made the arrangements yet, but yes, it's true."

"And what about Miss Bing?"

"Miss Bing and I are merely friends," he insisted once again. "She sought my help in arranging her father's funeral, but I have no reason to think she has deeper feelings for me."

"And what about you, Mr. Warren? Do you have deeper feelings for her?"

"My feelings don't matter in the slightest. I will be a friend to Miss Bing as long as she needs me."

"How very noble."

Warren glared at Frank, but he had no response.

"I don't suppose you have met Pearl's mother," Frank said idly.

"I . . . No, of course not. Why would I?"

"No reason, but if Miss Bing relies on you so much, I thought she might have asked for your support."

Warren winced at that. "I do know she was very upset when she found out her mother was still alive."

"Who told you she was upset?"

"I . . . She told me when we were out yesterday. It's only natural, isn't it? She thought her mother was dead, and then to find out her father had lied to her . . ."

"Who was she upset with?"

"What do you mean?"

Frank gave him a pitying look. "You know what I mean. Was she angry at her mother for turning up or at her father for lying to her?"

"I don't . . ."

"Yes, you do. Think about it, man. Who was she angry with?"

"I . . . I guess both of them."

"What makes you say that?"

"Well, she couldn't believe her father had lied, of course, but he said he'd done it for her own good. Nora wasn't the kind of mother she needed. He was trying to protect her and give her a better life."

"That's interesting," Frank said thoughtfully, because it really was. "What did Pearl think of her mother?"

"She . . . I think she might have agreed, because she didn't have anything good to say about the woman, and she wasn't particularly happy that she was here in the city."

Even more interesting.

"But I shouldn't be talking about Miss Bing like this," Warren continued. "She's entitled to her privacy, especially considering the circumstances. I know she was devastated by her father's death. They were very close."

"Then she approved of his marriage to the second Mrs. Bing?"

"I . . . I didn't say that."

Just as Frank suspected. "So, she didn't approve?"

"She just didn't like Mrs. Bing very much, and I'm sure the feeling was mutual."

"Why do you suppose they didn't get along?"

"I don't know. I don't know much about women. I only had brothers, and my mother was a simple creature."

"The Bing women are far from simple," Frank said.

"Yes," Warren agreed sadly. Frank had to purse his lips to keep from smiling.

"What do you think of the second Mrs. Bing?"

"Me? I hardly know her."

"But you must have an opinion."

"She has always seemed like a nice lady. Simple, like my mother. When she was married to Lane, she was—"

"When she was married to who?" Frank said, cutting him off.

"Ken Lane. He was my chief mechanic."

"Was? What happened to him?"

"He . . . It was a terrible accident. Here in the shop. A vehicle rolled over him and crushed his chest."

Frank frowned. "Just like Bing."

"Not like Bing at all," Warren hastily assured him. "What happened to Lane was just carelessness on his part. He'd neglected to set the brake and . . . and it was an accident."

Frank would investigate that later, but for now . . . "How long ago did this happen?"

"I . . . Not quite a year, I guess it is now. It happened in early December last year."

Frank counted the months in his head. Ethel Bing had been married to Bing for almost nine months, and her husband had died only two months prior. "Did Bing know Lane's wife before he died?"

Warren shifted uneasily in his chair, probably guessing where Frank was going with his questions. "I don't think so. I mean, no, I'm sure he didn't. I introduced them at Lane's funeral."

So that explained Pearl's sarcastic remark about

Warren's employees showing up for funerals. "They had a very quick courtship," Frank remarked.

Warren stiffened but he had not one word to say. If Bing had known Ethel before, maybe Lane's death wasn't really an accident. But if Ethel and Bing had been lovers, why was she so anxious to divorce him so soon after their wedding? And if Bing had somehow killed Lane, that wouldn't help Frank at all in figuring out who had killed Bing. How could having so much information only have confused him more?

Maybe Sarah would have better luck with Pearl Bing.

Sarah had spent her morning trying to figure out how she could arrange to meet privately with Pearl Bing, but she hadn't come up with a plan. Even Maeve, who could usually be counted on, had failed to think of anything before leaving to take Catherine to school on her way to the office. Consequently, Sarah had decided just to visit the Bing home this afternoon and take her chances, when her maid told her Mrs. Bing had come to call.

Sarah met her in the parlor. Ethel Bing was dressed in full mourning, and she looked distraught. Was she just beginning to mourn her husband after seeming to take his death in stride up until now?

"Oh, Mrs. Malloy, I'm so sorry to come to you like this, but I didn't know what else to do," she said before Sarah could even greet her.

Sarah asked her maid to bring them some tea and invited Mrs. Bing to sit down with her on the love seat. "Has something happened?"

"Yes, something terrible, or at least I think so. Alvin's first wife has moved into our house."

Sarah needed a moment to absorb this information and couldn't help realizing her own words had probably prompted this move. What had she been thinking? Well, in her own defense, she hadn't thought Nora Bing would actually do it. That would be little comfort to this Mrs. Bing, however.

"Did she arrive this morning?"

"No, last night. She said she was Alvin's true widow, so she should be the one living in the house."

"I'm assuming she allowed you and Carrie to stay there last night," Sarah said.

"Yes, she *allowed* us," Mrs. Bing said, not bothering to hide her sarcasm. "She said we'd have to find someplace else to live, though, since the house would now belong to her and Pearl."

"What did Pearl have to say about all this?"

Mrs. Bing sighed. "Not much, but I could see she wasn't happy. I don't think she was best pleased to find out her mother was still alive, at least not after she visited Nora. Pearl would certainly be glad to be rid of me and Carrie, but I don't think she wants her mother to replace us."

"Have you decided what you'll do?"

"I don't have any idea what I *should* do," she said, her voice thick with unshed tears. "That's why I'm here. I hoped you could give me some advice."

"I can offer some, and you are free to accept it or not, but my advice would be to stay exactly where you are for the time being and to contact Mr. Bing's attorney. You need to find out if he left a will and what it says."

"A will?"

Sarah recalled the way Malloy had explained it to Nora, and she repeated it for Ethel. "Mr. Bing may have left you the house, whether or not your marriage was legal, and if so, you have every right to continue to live there, at least until the legal affairs are settled."

"And what if he didn't?"

"The attorney will be able to help you figure that out, too."

Mrs. Bing rubbed her temples and blinked back her tears. "I don't know what to think. I had no idea that Alvin's first wife was still alive. You must believe I never would have married him if I did."

"Of course you wouldn't have. No woman would knowingly enter a bigamous marriage. Did he ever mention the circumstances of his previous marriage to you?"

"Just to say that Pearl's mother had died out west. Pearl believed it, so why shouldn't I?"

"No reason. It seems highly unlikely a man would claim his wife was dead if she wasn't, and yet that appears to be the case."

"I still don't understand how it happened, though. Wouldn't Pearl have known her mother wasn't dead?"

"We, uh, visited Nora Rumsfeld yesterday after we left you. She told us the whole story." Sarah retold it as briefly as she could.

"How awful," Mrs. Bing said when she'd finished. "I never thought I'd feel sorry for Pearl, but that was a horrible lie to tell her."

"Yes, it was, and it was a horrible thing to do to Nora."

"Mr. Bing was very cruel to both his wives," Mrs. Bing said. "If he wanted to leave Nora, why didn't he just divorce her? It's easier out west, isn't it?"

"I don't know what state he was in, but some of the western states have much more lenient divorce laws than New York does. But perhaps he never imagined he'd want to remarry, so he saw no need to legally end the marriage."

For some reason that suggestion disturbed Mrs. Bing. She turned away from Sarah and stared off into space for a long moment. Before Sarah could think what to say to draw her back, her maid, Hattie, brought in the tea tray. Sarah poured them both a cup and Mrs. Bing accepted hers gratefully. By the time the little ritual was accomplished, Sarah had decided what to say next.

"Mr. Bing must have been quite taken with you to risk a charge of bigamy," she said as gently as she could.

"Oh no, it wasn't like that at all," Mrs. Bing hastily assured her. "It wasn't a love match by any means."

Sarah had a thousand questions, but she was afraid Mrs. Bing wouldn't answer any of them, since they were all rather intrusive, so she tried a technique Malloy had taught her and said nothing at all. Few people could abide more than a moment of silence and would hasten to fill it, even if that meant talking about something they shouldn't.

Mrs. Bing turned back to Sarah, her eyes guarded but her chin quivering. Sarah simply smiled encouragingly.

"I . . . You see, I'd just lost my husband. My first husband, Kenneth," she said. "He worked at Mr. Warren's factory, building automobiles. He loved his work. He said it was the future and someday everyone would drive an auto and horses would be banished from the streets."

Sarah nodded and remained silent.

"There was a terrible accident at the factory. Nobody really saw what happened, but Ken was killed. It was awful. I couldn't believe it at first, but then I saw him, laid out in the casket, and I had to believe it. We weren't rich, Mrs. Malloy, but we had a good life. Ken's job at the factory paid well, and he spoiled Carrie a bit, I'm afraid. But with him gone, I didn't know what we were going to do."

Which was why women would remarry if they could. A woman could earn only a fraction of the salary a man could earn, and Mrs. Bing was unlikely to have any skills at all. She would also be concerned about her lovely young daughter's future. The city wasn't a safe place for pretty girls with no man to look after them. "And then you met Mr. Bing," Sarah said. "Or did you already know him since your first husband worked for Mr. Warren?"

"I met him at Ken's funeral. He came to pay his respects to a great mechanic, he said. He was so kind, and he was especially nice to Carrie, who was devastated by her father's death. When I thanked him later, he said he knew what she was going through because his daughter had gone through it when her mother died. Or I guess I should say when he *told* her that her mother had died," she added bitterly.

"I'm sure you were very grateful at the time, though."

"Oh yes," she agreed with a mirthless smile. "Especially when he called on us later and brought us both flowers. I actually asked his advice about what I should do. I was terrified. We had some savings, but only enough to keep us for a few months. I would have to find some work and Carrie, too, but I had no idea how to go about it. Ken had always taken care of everything."

"And what did Mr. Bing advise?" Sarah asked, although she thought she knew the answer.

As she had expected, Mrs. Bing's smile twisted. "He suggested I marry him. He said he could take care of Carrie and me. He said Carrie would be a companion for Pearl, who had been so lonely. He said he was lonely, too, and would appreciate a good wife. It was, he said, a practical arrangement for everyone."

"Practical," Sarah echoed.

Mrs. Bing smiled sadly. "I certainly wasn't looking for romance. I had just buried my husband. I thanked him but told him no the first time he asked me, but he didn't stop asking me. He kept calling on us and bringing gifts. Before long, Carrie was begging me to marry him. He was rich, she said, and we'd never want for anything. That's all she cared about, you see. I'd already warned her our lives would be very different now that her father was gone, and she didn't want things to change. If I married Mr. Bing, they not only wouldn't change, they would get much better."

"I can see why she would think that was a good bargain."

"Yes, she's still a child and doesn't understand what being married means, but he wore me down after a while. I guess the prospect of being practically penniless was too much. Ken had hardly been dead for two months when I married Mr. Bing."

"And nine months later, you were asking my husband about getting a divorce," Sarah said.

She refused to meet Sarah's eye again. "Marrying him was a mistake. I never should have done it."

"I guess he wasn't as nice after you were married as he was before," Sarah said.

Mrs. Bing could have agreed, giving Sarah a perfectly good reason for wanting a divorce, but she said, "He wasn't the man I thought he was. I couldn't . . . We had to get away from him."

"I don't suppose you mentioned the divorce to your daughter."

"Oh no, she wouldn't have wanted to leave." Mrs. Bing still wouldn't quite meet Sarah's eye. "She . . . As I said, he was very good to her, spoiling her like her father did except that he had more money to do it with."

Sarah remembered seeing Carrie with Mr. Bing at the automobile show. She'd obviously adored him. Sarah could easily imagine the tantrum a girl like Carrie could throw if her mother wanted to take her away from such luxury. She probably would have told Bing about her mother's plans, too. "But now you don't have to worry about Carrie objecting."

Mrs. Bing's startled gaze darted back to Sarah, and she didn't answer for a long moment. "I suppose that gives me a very good reason for wanting Mr. Bing dead."

Sarah smiled reassuringly. "Only if you actually used it to justify killing him, but Malloy and I are satisfied that you didn't, since you hired us to find the real killer."

She seemed relieved and she nodded eagerly. "Yes, and Carrie wouldn't have done it either. Why would she want to kill the man who was making her life so pleasant?"

"That *would* be strange," Sarah said non-committally. "You told me that all three of you were in bed by ten the night Mr. Bing died. Are you quite sure? The automobile show was still going on and it was open until ten thirty."

"I . . . I'm sure we were. I retired early, but the girls wouldn't have gone out alone at that time of night."

"So you don't know for sure that Pearl and Carrie were at home?"

"I . . . Well, Carrie wouldn't have left the house, but I can't speak for Pearl. She does what she wants, that one, and she can go anywhere in that auto her father gave her."

That statement teased at Sarah's memory. For some reason, she hadn't realized that Pearl would have had an automobile that was strictly her own. She'd just assumed Bing owned several vehicles and the women in his family could drive whichever one they wished. "Does Pearl have her very own auto?"

Mrs. Bing shuddered slightly at the memory. "Yes, she does, and Carrie does, too. You see how he spoiled them and why Carrie would have been furious at the thought of giving all that up."

Yes, Sarah could see it clearly, but this raised a whole new set of questions. "And I suppose you have your own automobile as well?"

"Oh no, Mr. Bing didn't feel that was necessary. I could use Carrie's or one of his if I needed to go someplace," she said with just a trace of bitterness.

"So Mr. Bing had more than one auto that he drove?"

"He had two, although he made it clear to me that neither was for my particular use."

Sarah realized they had completely missed something important. "Do you know if Mr. Bing had driven himself to the show the night he died?"

For some reason, Mrs. Bing had to think about this. "I don't know. He never shared his plans with me, you see. He'd mentioned that he would be attending the show because he didn't trust Will to say the right things to potential customers, but . . . Well, I'm sure he must have driven his own auto to the show. He usually drove himself wherever he wanted to go."

"And did any of the rest of you attend the show that day?"

Once again she hesitated before saying, "Carrie went with him in the morning, but she came home later. She said it was boring."

And how had Carrie gotten home? Did she use the auto she and Mr. Bing had driven to the show? And if so, how did the auto that ran over him get there?

"Do you know what happened to the auto that was, uh, involved in the accident?"

"No, I don't. I never even thought about it."

"Then the police didn't return it to you?"

"I have no idea, but if they did, no one told me."

"Could you check? Or better yet, I'll ask Malloy to check for you."

"I can't imagine what difference it would make which auto it was," Mrs. Bing said, although she plainly knew it would or Sarah wouldn't be so interested.

Sarah smiled reassuringly. "It probably doesn't," she lied. It might actually make a great deal of difference.

V

"I've been wanting to speak with Pearl, but I'm not sure how to find her alone," Sarah said.

"Why would you need to speak to her alone?" Mrs. Bing asked. She seemed a little suspicious now.

"Because she might not be as forthcoming if you were there," Sarah said with an apologetic smile.

"As forthcoming about what?" Mrs. Bing asked, still not convinced.

"About where she was the night her father died, and what she knows about her mother's sudden return from the dead, and what else she might know about her father's death. I don't think she'd talk about any of that in front of you."

"Yes, you're probably right, but . . . I don't think she will see you before the funeral tomorrow. She's making all the arrangements herself, and she's made it very clear she doesn't want my interference, and now with Nora in the house . . ." She shrugged helplessly.

"You're probably right. I'll wait until afterward, then." Although with Nora Bing in the house, Sarah knew seeing Pearl alone would be extremely difficult.

"Do you really need us at the funeral?" Maeve asked. She and Gino were obviously not thrilled at the prospect of spending their Saturday mourning a man they hardly knew, even if it meant seeing the Bing women at odds. Gino had come to the Malloy house early Saturday as instructed so they could discuss their strategy before the event. They were gathered in the parlor, and Frank and Sarah had just finished telling them what they had learned from their visits with Nora Bing and Will Warren yesterday.

Frank tried to placate Maeve the way Sarah would, although he knew he wasn't as good at it as his wife. "We really need your help, Maeve. You met Carrie at the automobile show, so she might talk to you."

"You're closer to her age, too," Sarah pointed out helpfully. "She might not realize you work for Malloy."

Maeve seemed to be at least considering the truth of this, but Gino was still skeptical. "And who am I supposed to charm?"

Maeve's skeptical expression twisted into a smirk. "Maybe you're supposed to charm Pearl Bing. She's quite a looker."

Gino pretended to take her seriously. "Thank you for reminding me. I'll be happy to use my skills on the lovely Miss Bing."

Maeve's smirk transformed into a pout, and Frank came to her rescue. "I thought you'd enjoy chatting with Will Warren and any of the men who work for him who show up. He seemed to think they would all be there, so see if you can at least eavesdrop on them and find out what they thought of Bing and if anyone is especially happy at his demise."

"Do we really think somebody at the factory killed him?" Gino asked.

"It doesn't seem like anybody there had a reason to," Frank admitted, "but we only have Will Warren's word for that."

"We do know the company wasn't doing well," Sarah said. "That's why Mr. Warren needed an investor in the first place."

"And Bing wasn't happy with the way things were going," Frank added.

"Which might give Bing a reason to kill Warren, but not the other way around," Gino pointed out.

Maeve's smirk was back. "Which is probably why Mr. Malloy wants you to talk to Warren and the other men."

"Couldn't I just go to the factory and pretend I want to buy one of their autos?" Gino wasn't exactly whining, but Maeve apparently thought he was, since he would obviously much rather visit the factory than attend a funeral.

"There's no way I can do something I enjoy

while I talk to Carrie, so you have to come to the funeral, too."

Gino smiled in a way that he probably used to get out of trouble with his mother. "How can I refuse the opportunity to spend time with you, Miss Smith, even if it is at a funeral?"

Maeve gave an unladylike snort, but she had been successfully placated.

Frank decided to press his luck. "And, Maeve, if you can also manage a chat with Pearl, no one would complain."

"I'll try, but she knows I work for you, and she's probably still angry that you're working for Mrs. Bing instead of her, so I doubt she'll be interested in talking to me."

"Maeve is probably right. Pearl isn't going to be happy about seeing any of us, I'm afraid," Sarah said. "But we should all probably at least try. Meanwhile, Malloy and I will pay our respects to both Ethel and Nora and see what we can find out."

"I wonder which widow will be sitting in the family pew?" Maeve said a little too gleefully.

"The funeral is at their house, so no one will be sitting in any pews," Sarah said. "I advised Ethel to carry on as if she really was Mr. Bing's widow, so I'm guessing the front row will be filled."

"What an awkward situation," Maeve said. "I don't know how Ethel can hold her head up."

"She's done nothing wrong," Sarah said, and

Frank nodded his agreement. "It's not her fault that Mr. Bing was a scoundrel."

"So we're sure she and Mr. Bing weren't having an affair or something before her first husband died?" Maeve asked.

Frank exchanged a glance with Sarah. "I think we are. Ethel told Sarah she never even met Bing until Lane's funeral, so it seems unlikely they planned Lane's death so they could marry."

"It does seem unlikely," Maeve said, "but how unfair. She married him for security and now she's not even his widow."

"I hope she'll take my advice and consult his attorney. It's possible she's named in his will."

"But Nora said she'd challenge the will," Frank reminded her. "From what I know of attorneys, they'll drag it out as long as they can, too."

"And Pearl won't want Ethel and Carrie to get a cent of her father's money," Maeve said. "So this should be interesting to watch, at least."

"Imagine all four of those women living under the same roof," Gino said with a grin. "I wouldn't be surprised if the house just exploded."

Frank wouldn't be either.

Sarah hadn't known exactly what to expect except that she'd been sure this funeral would be a bit different from most of the others she had attended in her life. Death was such a constant in this world that she had attended many, many funerals. Recently, she and Malloy had witnessed a funeral where the dead man's mistress had made an appearance, but that remarkable occurrence faded into insignificance when compared to this one with the dead man's two wives as hostesses.

Sarah realized she had underestimated Pearl Bing, however. Instead of the dead man's two wives fighting for pride of place in the parlor to greet the guests, Pearl was there alone. She looked magnificent in her black gown, accented with jet beads and satin piping.

She apparently didn't care about observing the usual funeral formalities, however.

"What are you doing here?" she asked in a furious whisper when Sarah tried to take her hand.

"We came to support your stepmother," Sarah said with a polite smile.

"Ethel is not my stepmother or anything else to me, and she is doing quite well without your help, thank you."

Malloy, bless him, said, "We're also trying to find out who killed your father." He didn't add a reminder that she should be grateful for such efforts, but she plainly knew that's what they were both thinking. She obviously didn't agree.

"This is hardly the time or place for that," Pearl said, her formerly pale face now scarlet.

"Then we won't interrogate the mourners," Maeve said, stepping up to make Pearl even angrier. "I'm so sorry for your loss," she added. "Please let us know if there's anything we can do for you. Oh, and do you know Mr. Malloy's partner, Gino Donatelli?"

Frank and Sarah politely stepped aside, allowing Pearl to give Maeve and Gino the full force of her glare.

"I'm so sorry we have to meet again under such sad circumstances," Gino said as solemnly as if he really meant it.

"Is everything all right, Miss Bing?" Will Warren asked, having miraculously appeared at her side.

Sarah couldn't help but notice how his hand came up as if he had intended to place it on her back in a comforting gesture but remembered just in time how inappropriate it would be for him to touch her like that. His hand closed into a fist, and he quickly lowered it to his side.

"Everything is just fine," Gino assured him.

But Warren wasn't going to take Gino's word for it. "Who are these people?"

"They work for Mr. Malloy," Pearl said through gritted teeth.

"I'm his partner," Gino said helpfully, and introduced himself, sticking out this hand for Warren to shake.

For a moment, Warren looked as if he would refuse to shake, but he finally lifted his hand and accepted Gino's friendly gesture with little grace.

"This is a very difficult day for Miss Bing," he said to all of them in what was plainly a warning.

"We have no intention of making it any more difficult for her," Malloy said pleasantly. "We're just here to pay our respects."

Sarah bit back a smile as Malloy steered her over to the coffin to view the body. "Well done, Mr. Malloy," she whispered.

"I do try, Mrs. Malloy," he replied.

They stopped before the coffin, where Mr. Bing was laid out. He showed no visible ill effects from his encounter with the automobile. Of course, any marks would be under his clothes, but Sarah chose not to think about that. "He looks just like I remember him."

"Don't pretend you remember him," Malloy said.

"I looked at him once or twice at the automobile show," she defended herself.

"He was a nice-looking man," Maeve decreed when she and Gino had taken a look.

Gino made a choking sound.

"Well, he was," Maeve insisted. "At least that explains why two women married him."

Sarah led them away from the coffin before they caused a scene. "Let's see if we can find the rest of the family."

Maeve and Gino wandered out into the hallway, where they could see the other guests arriving. The dining room doors were closed, probably to discourage people from partaking of the refreshments until after the service. Frank and Sarah found the rear parlor—the room the family would normally use—and there, to their surprise, the two Mrs. Bings were sitting in tense silence.

Apparently, no one else had thought to seek them out, because they were quite alone.

Since Ethel was sitting closest to the door, Sarah greeted her first. "Mrs. Bing, I'm so sorry."

"She's not Mrs. Bing," Nora protested, jumping to her feet. "I am." She wore an ill-fitting black dress that someone must have lent her. Sarah couldn't imagine Ethel being so generous, but perhaps she was.

"Of course you are," Sarah said, not bothering to argue about whether Ethel deserved the title or not. "And I'm very sorry for your loss as well. I'm sure this is difficult for both of you."

"Difficult?" Nora scoffed. "That ain't the half of it."

Sarah once again decided not to rise to Nora's bait. "Pearl is doing a lovely job of greeting the mourners. You must be very proud of her."

Nora was rendered momentarily speechless by the compliment, but Ethel said, "It was her idea that neither of us do it. She didn't think it proper for me, since, as it turns out, I wasn't really Alvin's wife, and everyone would want to know who Nora was if she was there. Pearl didn't want to air our dirty linen, especially at her father's funeral."

"I don't know why not," Nora said. "It's *his* dirty linen, after all."

She was right, but Sarah didn't say so. "I didn't see Carrie, though."

Ethel frowned. "Carrie has taken Alvin's death very hard."

"She's taken to her bed," Nora reported with a hint of disgust. "I can't think why, though. Even his real daughter didn't do that."

"She was quite horrified by the way Alvin died," Ethel explained stiffly. "She's been having nightmares, so she hasn't been able to sleep. She'll be down for the service, though."

"You may not realize it," Sarah said, seeing an opportunity, "but I'm a trained nurse. I would be happy to check on her, to make sure she's well."

To Sarah's surprise, the look Ethel gave her appeared to be alarm. She recovered quickly, but there had been no mistaking that expression. "She isn't ill," Ethel insisted. "Just grief-stricken."

"She's probably worried about who's going to buy her new dresses now that Alvin is dead," Nora said slyly.

"I'm sure we're all concerned about our futures," Ethel snapped, then turned back to Sarah and Malloy. "I did telephone Mr. Bing's attorney as you suggested. He's going to meet with me on Monday."

"Meet with *you?*" Nora cried. "I'm Alvin's legal wife. He should be meeting with me."

"I'm sure you'd be welcome to join us. I was going to ask him if Alvin had made a will and what allowances it made for me and Carrie."

"Huh, then you can bet Pearl and I will be there, too."

A maid appeared in the doorway. "Miss Bing asked me to tell you to come to the parlor for the service."

"I'll go get Carrie," Ethel said, hurrying from the room.

"I guess we better get along, then," Nora said, shooing Sarah and Malloy toward the door.

Sarah exchanged a look with him. So far they hadn't had much success.

Maeve was surprised at the small turnout for Mr. Bing's funeral. Usually, rich people had a lot of friends who would at least come to be seen if not to truly mourn. But few of the guests seemed to even be affluent enough to qualify as Bing's social equals. Alvin Bing's crowd of mourners mostly consisted of mechanics uncomfortably wearing their Sunday best and a couple of their wives in dresses Maeve was certain Pearl and Carrie Bing wouldn't deign to tear into rags for cleaning cloths. One well-dressed couple looked out of place and didn't seem to know anyone else there, so Maeve naturally made a beeline for

119

them with Gino in her wake. She quickly learned they lived next door, and while they hardly knew the Bings, they had felt they should pay their respects. They were obviously sorry for their generous impulse.

Before she had a chance to send Gino off to talk to the other men and find someone else to chat with, Will Warren announced that the service was about to begin, and the guests who were still in the hallway filed into the parlor to find a place on one of the folding chairs set up there. Gino and Maeve knew to sit in the back row so they could watch everyone, but they weren't fast enough. The back two rows were already filled with the mechanics and their wives, so the two of them slipped into the next free row, saving seats on the end for the Malloys.

A woman Maeve didn't know and who looked like she might be one of the mechanics' wives accompanied the Malloys into the room. "Who's that?" Gino asked Maeve in a whisper.

"Judging by her full mourning—although that dress is a fright—she must be the other Mrs. Bing," Maeve whispered back.

The fact that she left the Malloys to their own devices and went straight to where Pearl was standing near the coffin confirmed Maeve's theory. The woman slipped a comforting arm around Pearl, but Pearl did not appear to be comforted. After shooting her mother an impatient glance, she sidestepped out of the embrace and turned to speak to the minister, who had appeared at the front of the room.

The Malloys joined Gino and Maeve, but no one spoke. Any conversation would be easily overheard in such close quarters now that everyone had found a seat and settled down. An uneasy silence hovered in the room, and then Mrs. Ethel Bing and Carrie came in.

Maeve had found Carrie to be an amusing girl when they'd met at the automobile show. She genuinely loved driving a motorcar and was eager to show off her knowledge. She had fairly sparkled with enthusiasm then, but all trace of that sparkle was gone now. The girl was pale and wan, and her eyes were red and swollen from weeping. She balked slightly when Ethel urged her to enter the parlor and she saw everyone looking at them, but then she lowered her head and let her mother direct her to the front of the room.

The minister saw them and turned from his conversation with Pearl to greet Ethel, taking her hand and saying something comforting, if his expression was any indication. Apparently, no one had explained the situation to him, and he still believed Ethel was the true widow. Nora looked as if she might make an objection, but Pearl quelled her with a glare and then said something to the minister that signaled him to begin the service. Pearl and Nora sat down at one end of the front row, and Ethel and Carrie sat on the other end.

Renewed whispers rustled through the audience, which probably meant people were wondering who that rough-looking female was and why she was sitting with the family and probably also wondering why Pearl and the strange woman were sitting as far apart as possible from Mrs. Bing and Carrie. All whispers ceased when the minister asked them to bow their heads for prayer, and then he went through a very brief, very dry, very anonymous funeral service. He read all the Scripture verses about life after death and the promises of heaven but said very little about Alvin Bing. Maeve would've bet money the two had never met.

Then it was over, without even a eulogy. The minister invited everyone to partake in the repast and informed them the body would be taken to the cemetery after the meal. With that, the mourners quietly left their seats to file by the coffin for a final farewell.

Pearl stopped by the bier and gazed down at her father for a long moment. Her face was turned away, but from the set of her shoulders, she wasn't feeling the usual emotions people exhibited at funerals. She looked more angry than anything. Nora barely spared the dead man a glance and she looked as if she'd like to spit on the corpse. Fortunately, she refrained and hurried off after Pearl.

Carrie had apparently begun to weep during the service and when she reached the coffin, she broke into sobs. Her mother wrapped an arm around her and was supporting her with her other hand, but she still looked as if she might collapse.

"Oh, Papa!" she cried, and leaned over to noisily kiss the corpse.

Kissing the corpse of a loved one wasn't unusual, but Ethel Bing actually gasped in what might have been horror and quickly pulled Carrie away. Carrie protested weakly, but Ethel ushered her out of the room before she could do anything else to cause comment. The Malloys made no move to rise until the last of the other mourners had filed out, so Maeve and Gino waited as well.

When they were alone, Maeve said, "Do you still want me to talk to Carrie?"

Sarah sighed. "If you can."

Ethel Bing had gotten as far as the dining room, but the other mourners had stopped her there to express their condolences. As far as they knew, she was the legitimate widow. Sarah could see she was trying to be gracious, but she must also be conscious of her new status as bigamous wife and couldn't help feeling awkward.

Sarah glanced around and saw Carrie had moved away from her mother and stood alone at the far end of the room, near the door to the kitchen. Perhaps she was considering making her escape. Sarah caught Maeve's eye and nodded to where the girl stood. Maeve understood immediately and strolled over to the girl.

Gino headed for the buffet table and easily struck up a conversation with one of the men from the factory.

"I don't see Pearl or Nora," Malloy said.

"Or Will Warren," Sarah noted. "They are probably in the family parlor having a conference."

"About what?"

"Who knows? We won't get close to Ethel anytime soon, so let's wander back to see if we can find the others."

They stepped back out into the hallway and encountered Nora Bing, who was apparently heading for the dining room. She stopped when she saw them and looked them up and down with apparent disapproval. "Are you still here?"

"So it would seem," Malloy said, which obviously infuriated Nora.

"Why can't you just leave us alone?"

"Because Ethel Bing hired us to find your husband's killer," Malloy said.

"Her name isn't Bing, and she's a fool to hire you."

"Why would you say that?" Sarah asked, fully expecting Nora to claim Malloy wasn't a good detective.

But Nora smirked. "Because she might not want to know who killed Alvin."

"Are you saying you know who did?" Malloy asked, somehow managing not to sound too interested.

"Let's say I have my suspicions, and Ethel wouldn't be pleased if I'm right."

Sarah could sense Malloy's annoyance, but he kept his voice calm. "If you have any proof—"

"If I had any proof, I'd tell the police, but you mark my words, Ethel is going to be sorry she hired you."

Sarah managed a friendly smile. "Perhaps you'd share your suspicions with us."

"Not a chance," Nora said with satisfaction. "You'll have to earn your fee the hard way. Now get out of my way. I want to get something to eat."

They stepped aside and Nora sailed past them, a satisfied grin on her face.

Sarah turned to Malloy. "She thinks Carrie did it."

"Yes, Carrie is the only one who would upset Ethel," he agreed.

"Do you think she knows something?"

"Maybe, but it could just be wishful thinking."

"Which would explain why she doesn't have any proof."

"Exactly. Let's see if we can find Pearl and Will."

Since the guests were all busy sampling the

delights of the funeral repast, no one else had wandered down to the rear parlor. Sarah knew they had guessed correctly when they heard Pearl Bing's outraged voice saying, "She's a conniving little witch. How dare she make a scene? He's not even her father!"

Sarah realized too late that she should have stopped sooner so she could have heard more, but she was already in the doorway and had been seen. Malloy realized it, too, and squeezed her arm before saying, "Excuse us, Miss Bing, Mr. Warren. We didn't mean to intrude."

Mr. Warren had jumped to his feet the moment they had noticed the Malloys in the doorway, but not before they'd seen him holding Pearl's hands in a way that seemed to indicate he was more to her than her father's business partner.

Pearl's cheeks were flushed, but perhaps she was just still angry at Carrie for her unseemly display of emotion.

"You, uh, you aren't intruding," Mr. Warren was saying. His color was high, too, but he was obviously embarrassed.

"Shouldn't you be out somewhere finding my father's killer?" Pearl asked.

"We still haven't spoken to all the family members yet," Malloy said.

Pearl really had mastered the condescending glare. "So, you thought you'd question us at my father's funeral?"

"Certainly not," Malloy said, not the least bit chastened. "We are just paying our respects."

"And listening at doors," Pearl said.

"Not intentionally," Sarah said, conveniently forgetting her regret over not having eavesdropped on purpose. "We made our presence known immediately, and while you may not want anyone to know how angry you are at your stepsister—"

"She's not my stepsister or any other thing to me," Pearl snapped.

"—how angry you are at *Carrie,*" Sarah corrected herself, "you have no reason to be embarrassed. Your feelings are perfectly natural. No one wants to see unseemly behavior at a funeral."

Pearl seemed surprised to find her feelings confirmed, and Sarah took the opportunity to move into the room.

"I know you probably don't feel much like eating," Sarah continued, "but perhaps Mr. Warren would fetch you a cup of tea. You still have the visit to the cemetery ahead of you, and you need to keep up your strength."

Mr. Warren looked torn. Plainly, he was willing to do anything to serve Pearl, but he also wasn't sure he should leave her alone with the Malloys. Then Pearl looked up and said, "Please, Will."

"I'll go with you," Malloy said, and that left poor Mr. Warren with no other choice.

When the men were gone, Sarah moved to where Warren had been sitting next to Pearl on a sofa. "May I join you?" She didn't wait for a reply and pretended not to notice Pearl's frown. "I really am very sorry about your father, Miss Bing."

Pearl apparently wasn't quite sure whether to believe her or not, so Sarah just went on.

"I know this has been a trying week for you. First your mother appears after you'd thought her dead for years and tells you that your beloved father has been lying to you—"

"He said he really thought she was dead," Pearl said without much conviction.

Sarah considered that for a moment. "I suppose it's possible."

"Those mining towns were very primitive. Mail service was unreliable and sometimes there wasn't even a telegraph."

Which would have meant that news of Nora's death might not have reached him, which hardly supported his claim that he'd heard she was dead. "He took very good care of you, though."

Pearl brightened a little at that. "He adored me. He called me his Pearl of Great Price, after the Bible verse."

"How sweet," Sarah said. All her training as a society girl was really paying off. She could feign sympathy with the best of them.

"For all those years, it was just the two of us. We didn't need anyone else."

It seemed important to her that Sarah understand, so she nodded. "You were young to be left without your mother, though."

"I was practically a woman," she corrected Sarah. "I was everything to him, wife and daughter and partner. And then *they* came along."

"They" were obviously Ethel and Carrie. "I know you were very close to your father, but it must have been lonely for him. A daughter isn't the same as a wife and—"

"I told you, I was *everything* to him. He didn't need a *wife*. He didn't need *her*. And he certainly didn't need that *girl*."

"But you'll want to get married yourself someday," Sarah said, relentlessly kind. "Aren't you and Mr. Warren . . . ?"

Pearl was angry again. "Aren't we what?"

Sarah smiled. "Forgive me for assuming, but I couldn't help noticing Mr. Warren seems rather, uh, devoted to you."

Pearl waved away Mr. Warren's devotion with a flick of her hand. "I'm certainly not going to marry Will Warren."

"He would probably be disappointed to hear that."

"If he is, it's his own fault for *assuming*," Pearl said, echoing Sarah's word choice. "I wasn't

planning to marry at all. Father . . . needed me."
Her voice trailed off in the first genuine show of
emotion she had betrayed today.

"I'm sure he relied on you a lot when it
was just the two of you," Sarah tried. "But
he must have had his reasons for marrying
Ethel."

Pearl's grief evaporated and she stiffened.
"What do you mean by that?"

Sarah hesitated. What had she said that Pearl
found so offensive? "I just meant what I said
before. A wife can provide companionship that
a daughter can't." Would Pearl know what she
meant? Quite possibly not, but Sarah wasn't
about to explain the facts of life to her.

"He didn't need a wife," Pearl insisted. "He
had me."

Sarah decided not to argue.

"Are you all right, Miss Bing?" Maeve asked
Carrie, who stood at the far end of the dining
room, her swollen eyes staring at nothing.

She turned to Maeve and frowned. "I'm not
Miss Bing."

"I'm sorry. I saw you sitting with Mrs. Bing
and Pearl, so I thought—"

"I'm Miss Lane," she said flatly.

"I'm pleased to meet you. I'm very sorry about
Mr. Bing's death."

"Did you know him?" Carrie asked, still

frowning. Maeve couldn't tell if she was suspicious of Maeve or just trying to figure out who Maeve was.

"Just slightly. We met at the automobile show, remember? You showed me how easy the electric auto is to operate."

"Oh yes, I remember you now," Carrie said, although she didn't look as if she really did.

"Can I get you something? You look like you could use a cup of tea at least."

"No, I . . . My stomach hurts."

From the state of her eyes, she'd been crying for a long time, so no wonder. Maeve glanced over her shoulder at the crowd of mourners helping themselves to the food. "Would you like to go someplace quieter?"

Carrie winced. "Yes, but . . ." She glanced over at where some of the guests were still expressing condolences to her mother.

"No one will miss you, I'm sure, and you really look like you need to lie down."

"I could go to my room," Carrie said softly. "No one will bother me there."

"I'll take you," Maeve said. "Quick, before someone sees us."

Luckily, Carrie didn't question why she needed Maeve's help getting to her own bedroom. She probably simply appreciated the encouragement. Only a few of the mourners were in the hallway and they were more interested in finding a place to sit down so they could eat than in wondering what the two girls were doing.

"Upstairs?" Maeve asked.

Carrie nodded and led the way up the staircase and down the hallway. She opened one of the doors and went straight for the unmade bed, flopping onto it and burrowing in like a woodland creature. Or at least the way Maeve imagined woodland creatures would burrow.

How strange that the bed would be unmade. Surely, the servants had readied the entire house for the funeral, which meant Carrie was probably in the bed until very recently.

Maeve closed the door behind her and frantically tried to think what Mrs. Malloy would do in this situation. She would probably show Carrie compassion and get her to confess her deepest fears. Maeve didn't feel much compassion for Carrie, but she could pretend.

"Are you sure you don't want anything to eat?" Maeve said, moving over to the bed.

Carrie had turned her face into the pillow and Maeve now realized she was using it to smother her sobs.

"There, now," Maeve said. "You'll make yourself sick if you keep that up."

"I'm already sick," Carrie cried into the pillow.

"Sicker, then. I'm sure Mr. Bing wouldn't want that," she tried.

It worked. Carrie lifted her head from the

pillow. "How do you know what he would want? You didn't even know him."

"If he cared for you as much as you must have cared for him, he wouldn't want to see you like this." Good, that sounded exactly like something Mrs. Malloy would say.

"He loved me," Carrie said, pushing herself up to a sitting position. "He loved me even more than he loved Pearl."

More than he loved his own daughter? Maeve somehow managed not to show her surprise. "That's . . . nice."

But Carrie wasn't listening. "And now what's going to become of us? Pearl hates me. She hates me because she knows Father liked me best. She'll never let us stay here. She'll throw us out and we won't have any money and we'll starve to death."

"I'm sure your mother won't let that happen," Maeve said lamely, not certain how to reassure her on this point.

Carrie still wasn't listening. "He should have married me. Then none of this would've happened."

VI

Gino had chosen a young man about his own age to question. The poor fellow was watching Maeve escort Carrie out of the dining room with an expression of longing that Gino understood only too well. Was it for Maeve or Carrie? Not that it mattered. He was doomed to failure either way.

Gino waited until the girls were out of sight and the fellow headed for the buffet table. Gino knew better than to betray his intentions by doing anything so obvious as actually questioning him about Bing, though. He started casually as they moved around the buffet, filling their plates.

"Do you work for Mr. Warren?" he asked the young fellow, a strapping lad of about twenty with protruding front teeth and a scattering of freckles.

He seemed surprised that Gino had guessed that. "Yeah. How did you know?"

Gino could have said he'd noticed the fellow's stained fingernails or his ill-fitting suit obviously saved for special occasions, but he said, "I just guessed. I've been thinking about buying a motorcar of my own but I'm not sure which kind to choose."

That, Gino knew, was a sure way to get an

automobile mechanic talking. The two men had filled their plates, and Gino silently led the way out into the hallway where some of the mourners were standing to shovel in their luncheon selections. Seeing no good place for them to talk, he nodded toward the open parlor door.

His companion balked at first, but when he saw that the coffin had been closed, he followed Gino and the two men pulled a couple of chairs over to the corner farthest from the bier. When they were seated, Gino introduced himself.

The fellow seemed a bit taken aback at Gino's Italian name, but he had certainly noticed his custom-made suit, which marked him as a man of means. Never mind that Mr. Malloy had paid for it. "I'm Tom Yingling."

Gino began to pepper him with questions about the various advantages of an electric motorcar over the ones powered by gasoline and steam, even though he knew all the answers Tom would give. Gino had already known a lot about all types of motorcars, and he had learned even more at the automobile show. When their plates were empty and he'd run out of questions, Gino said, "Seems like there's an awful lot of companies making automobiles."

Tom frowned. "That's true, and a lot of them are bigger than ours."

"I guess that's why Mr. Warren needed Mr. Bing to invest."

"Mr. Warren wanted to expand. He's always telling us automobiles are going to replace horses and someday you won't even see a wagon on the streets anymore."

"That's hard to believe," Gino said, although he believed it himself. "But I guess somebody will need to make a lot of them if it's going to happen."

"That's right, and why shouldn't it be our company?"

"Yes, why not? Did Mr. Bing take an interest in your work?"

"What do you mean?"

"I mean, did he visit the factory to oversee what you were doing, or did he just sit back and wait for the profits to roll in?"

Tom grinned at the image of profits rolling in. "He came sometimes, but mostly to meet with Mr. Warren or Mr. Lane."

"Who is Mr. Lane? Another partner?"

Tom's gaze drifted away, and Gino realized he was looking at the closed coffin. "No, he . . . he was our chief mechanic until he . . ."

"Don't tell me he quit for a bigger company," Gino said, managing a hint of outrage.

"Oh no, Mr. Lane wouldn't've done that. He . . . There was an accident at the factory, and he died."

"What kind of accident?"

Tom actually shuddered at the memory. "A

foolish one, but then, I guess all accidents are foolish. He was working on an engine, but he'd forgotten to set the brake. When he got it running, the auto lurched forward and knocked him over. Ran right over him. Wasn't nothing anybody could do. His chest was crushed."

"That sounds an awful lot like the way Mr. Bing died," Gino said.

But Tom was shaking his head in vehement denial. "Somebody ran over Mr. Bing on purpose. That's not what happened to Mr. Lane at all."

"You're sure of that?" Gino asked, not having to feign suspicion.

"Oh yes. We was all there, working. Anybody could see it was an accident."

Gino pretended to consider this. "It's just kind of strange that Mrs. Bing had two husbands that were run over by autos."

Tom's eyes widened but he nodded. "I know. We've all been talking about it. Not where Mr. Warren could hear," he added with a sheepish shrug, "but we all thought it was strange."

Almost like Lane's accident had given somebody the idea. Why hadn't one of them realized that yet?

"You said Mr. Bing would meet with Mr. Lane sometimes," Gino said.

"Mr. Bing thought we should be faster at making the autos. Mr. Lane tried to explain that the only way to do that was to hire more mechanics, but he didn't want to hear that. He wanted all of us to work faster, I guess."

"Would you say Bing and Lane were friends? Did they go out for a drink or anything like that?"

"Not that I ever saw. Mr. Bing never let you forget he was the boss either. I don't think he even went out with Mr. Warren."

"So I guess Bing wouldn't have met Lane's wife either."

Tom frowned again. "I wouldn't know about that, but if you think Mrs. Lane and Mr. Bing were having an affair or something . . ." Tom shook his head.

"You seem very sure."

"Mrs. Lane isn't that kind of lady."

"You know her, then?"

"She would come by the shop sometimes and bring us cookies. She . . . Well, you could tell just by looking at the Lanes that they really cared for each other. He even kept a photograph of his wife and daughter hanging up in his office. How many men do that?"

"And yet she married Mr. Bing just a couple months after Lane died."

Tom stared at his empty plate for a long moment, as if looking for an answer. "Yeah, we wondered about that, but, well, sometimes people get married for other reasons. Mr. Lane wasn't a rich man and Mr. Bing was and she had her daughter to think of."

Gino nodded. "I can see you've given this a lot of thought."

He looked up in surprise and what might have been alarm, although surely that couldn't be right. "Not me. I'm just saying what the other fellows decided. We all liked Mrs. Lane and nobody wanted to think badly of her."

Gino wondered what they'd think when word got out about Bing's bigamy. At least no one could blame Ethel for that.

While Frank and Warren walked toward the dining room to fetch Pearl her tea, Warren kept glancing back over his shoulder, as if considering abandoning his mission and returning to Pearl's side.

"She'll be fine," Frank said. "My wife will look after her."

From Warren's scowl, that was exactly what he was afraid of.

"I thought you said you and Miss Bing were just friends," Frank said. They had reached the dining room and found the table with beverages. Warren poured a cup of tea and then hesitated at Frank's question.

"We are."

"It looked like more than that when we came in just now."

Warren glared at Frank and then proceeded to stir a spoonful of sugar into the tea.

"With Bing dead, there's nobody to object to you courting her," Frank observed.

"What makes you think he would have objected?"

"Nothing at all, but even if he would have, he can't now."

Warren was still stirring the tea and he must have realized he'd been stirring it for far too long. He stopped abruptly, almost upsetting the cup, then picked it up with the saucer and started back without even glancing at Frank.

"Where were you the night Bing was killed, Mr. Warren?" Frank asked when they had reached the hallway.

Warren almost stumbled and had to catch the cup before it overturned. This time his glare was murderous. "What do you care?"

"I don't, but I need to know if you were at the automobile show that night with Mr. Bing."

Warren drew a calming breath. "I wasn't. He . . . he said I was *ineffectual* when it came to talking to customers."

"Ineffectual?" Frank echoed in amazement.

"His exact word. He thought himself quite the salesman, so I didn't bother arguing with him. If he wanted to stand around talking to idiots all day, he was welcome to do it."

"So, you weren't at Madison Square Garden that night?"

"No."

He started to walk away, but Frank said, "Then where were you?"

He stopped again, but less abruptly and turned to Frank with an exasperated sigh. "I was at my house."

Frank heard a note of pride in the word *house* and wondered at it. "Alone?" Frank raised his eyebrows provocatively.

"Of course I was alone," Warren snapped, but Frank didn't miss the color blooming in his cheeks. "I . . . I haven't owned the house long, and I don't have any live-in servants," he added for no reason Frank could see. "Now, if you're done, this tea is getting cold."

He stomped off, and Frank followed.

Sarah looked up when Will Warren entered the room bearing the obligatory cup of tea. From his expression, Malloy had been asking him questions he didn't want to answer. He went straight to Pearl and placed the cup and saucer in her hands. She didn't thank him or even spare him more than a glance. She didn't even sip the tea.

"I think we should get some luncheon," Pearl said, setting the untouched tea on a nearby table and rising imperiously. She didn't wait for a reply but strode out of the room.

Will Warren needed a moment to react, and then he followed like a puppy at her heels.

Sarah gave Malloy a questioning look.

141

"Warren says he was home alone the night Bing died. Bing thought he was ineffectual at talking to customers, so he didn't want him at the show."

"Ineffectual?" Sarah echoed with amusement.

"His exact word, according to Warren. And Warren still expects me to believe there's nothing between him and Pearl."

"He may be right about that," Sarah said. "Pearl says she isn't interested in getting married at all."

"Why wouldn't a young woman be interested in getting married?"

"That does seem strange, since marriage is the only real form of security a woman can hope for, as uncertain as even that may be."

"Yes, just ask Ethel Bing or whatever her name really is. But for all his protests, Warren seems extremely fond of Miss Bing."

"Which was obvious from the way he was clutching her hands when we caught them. And the way he looks at her, of course," Sarah added sadly. "I didn't have a chance to ask Pearl where she was the night her father died. She was too busy telling me why her father had no need to marry Ethel when he had her to look after him."

"Is that why she didn't want to get married? Was she planning to take care of her father for the rest of her life?"

"I don't know about the rest of her life, but apparently that was her intention for the time being. Until he married Ethel, that is."

"So, she was angry with her father and jealous of Ethel."

"And jealous of Carrie, too, I imagine. Ethel said Bing was very kind to Carrie, which probably meant he bought her things and paid attention to her."

Malloy frowned. "Was she jealous enough to kill her father, though? Isn't that cutting off her nose to spite her face?"

"I'd think so, but as we both know only too well, people sometimes don't consider the ramifications when they act in anger."

"And if we're going to be logical, Warren really doesn't have a logical reason to kill Bing either. He was going to need Bing to invest more money in his factory, which Bing couldn't do if he was dead."

"This is getting too complicated. Let's go get something to eat and see if there's someone else we can talk to."

Maeve had somehow managed not to gape when Carrie suggested that Alvin Bing should have married her instead of her mother. "Aren't you a bit young for marriage?"

"Papa told me girls younger than me get married out west," Carrie informed her.

Probably not to men as old as Alvin Bing, but Maeve didn't bother to point that out. "Even if you had married him, it wouldn't have been legal, just as your mother's marriage isn't legal, since he was already married to Nora," Maeve pointed out.

"He would've divorced that woman for me."

Maeve had to shake her head. How had she gotten into such a strange conversation? Surely, Carrie didn't believe Alvin Bing would have married a child. She decided to change the subject. "Your mother said you went to the automobile show with Mr. Bing the day he died."

Carrie blinked at the sudden change of topic. "I went with him every day. He liked to tell people the electric autos were so easy to drive that he'd taught me."

Just as he had told them when they'd been at the show. "Did you stay the whole time?"

"What? No, I . . . I got tired, so I came home in the afternoon."

"Did you drive your auto home?"

"Yes, I . . . I mean . . . I don't remember."

That seemed strange. How could she not remember? "How did you get home?"

"I walked."

Maeve nodded, as if this were the most natural thing in the world. Certainly, it wasn't unusual for people to walk in the city, but not spoiled rich girls. "So Mr. Bing drove the auto home."

"I . . . Well, yes."

"Do you remember which one it was?"

"Which one?"

"Yes, was it your auto or one of his?"

She didn't even wonder how Maeve knew she had her own auto. "I . . . I don't remember."

She really was a terrible liar. So many people were that sometimes Maeve thought she should offer lessons. "And what did you do that evening?"

"What evening?"

She was so very annoying. "The night Mr. Bing died. If you didn't go to the show, what did you do?"

"I . . . Nothing."

At least she hadn't claimed she didn't remember. "And where did you do this nothing?"

"What do you mean?"

"Were you at home or—"

"At home. Here. With Mother."

"And Pearl?"

"Pearl spent as little time with us as she could manage. We never saw her after supper."

"Could she have gone out?"

"She could have done anything. I'm tired of answering your questions. I don't see what business it is of yours anyway. Go away and leave me alone."

Since Maeve had gotten the information she'd come for, she did just that.

Sarah and Malloy found Ethel in the dining room. There was no sign of Pearl or Mr. Warren, and apparently, everyone else in attendance had expressed their condolences and gotten food and then gone off to eat it. Ethel was staring blindly at the buffet table as if uncertain of its purpose.

Sarah laid a comforting hand on Ethel's arm and said, "Let me fix you a plate. You should eat something."

"I'm not really hungry," Ethel said, but Sarah had already picked up a plate. She chose a few light items, a roll and a slice of ham and a bit of this and that. The servants had placed the dining room chairs along the wall, and they were mostly empty now that people had finished eating and wandered out.

Sarah took Ethel's arm and led her to one of the chairs, then sat down beside her. She was vaguely aware that Malloy was fixing himself a plate, or at least she thought that's what he was doing, but while she was encouraging Ethel to eat, he brought the plate over and handed it to Sarah.

She smiled her gratitude and turned back to Ethel. "I'm glad you made an appointment with Mr. Bing's attorney."

"He said he'd been expecting my call. I hadn't planned to take Nora and Pearl along, but perhaps that's best."

"Yes, it's better if they hear everything directly from the attorney. They might not believe you, in any case."

Sarah was happy to see Ethel absently take a bite

of the roll and proceeded to set a good example by starting on her own lunch. After a few minutes of companionable silence, Sarah said, "Mr. Warren seems very interested in Pearl."

Ethel smiled sadly. "Yes, but he's wasting his time. She has no interest in him."

"And yet she asked him to go with her to plan her father's funeral." Sarah decided not to mention having seen them virtually holding hands just now.

"Mr. Warren has been quite helpful since Mr. Bing died, but I'm afraid Pearl is simply taking advantage of his affection for her."

"Why do you think Pearl doesn't take him seriously as a suitor?"

Ethel shook her head. "She calls him a yokel behind his back. She and Mr. Bing would often make fun of him when he wasn't around, too."

Sarah wanted to be sure, though. "But perhaps Pearl was agreeing with her father just to keep the peace. Could she have secretly cared for him, and now that Mr. Bing is dead, she is free to show her real feelings?"

Ethel had taken another bite of her roll, and she considered the question as she chewed. "I don't know. It's possible, I guess. Pearl is a very secretive girl, at least around me. I'm not sure I know what she really thinks about anything or anyone."

"Except maybe you and Carrie," Sarah said with a sympathetic smile.

"Yes," Ethel said sadly. "She has made that very clear."

Gino's new friend Tom was only too happy to take him out to the Bings' garage, which was the converted stables behind the house. "Mr. Bing always said the best advertisement for an automobile was seeing one in person," Tom explained as he led Gino inside. The garage was wired for electricity for charging the autos, so it also had electric lights that enabled Gino to clearly see the four autos parked there. "That's why he had so many himself. He wanted them seen all over the city."

"That sounds like a good strategy, but he'd need more than four driving around the city if he really wanted to be successful."

Tom smiled knowingly. "I think you're probably right."

They paused for a moment to admire the autos. Two of them were small and open like a buggy, with just one seat to hold two people and a fold-up top in case of inclement weather. The only difference was that instead of traces for the horses, there was a small compartment in front to hold the battery. The others were larger and enclosed, like a carriage, with one outside seat for the driver. "I wonder which one he was driving the night he died," Gino mused.

"I, uh, I wouldn't know," Tom said. "I usually

saw him driving one of the two larger autos, though."

"Then I guess the two smaller ones belong to his daughters."

Tom did not express an opinion, so Gino started strolling around each of the vehicles, ostensibly admiring them but really looking for any signs of damage that would indicate that one of them had recently collided with its owner and crushed him to death. He wasn't sure what that might look like, but anything out of the ordinary could be a clue.

Gino had a difficult time picturing a female easily climbing up to the driver's seat of the two large vehicles. If Bing had been driving and gotten out for some reason, she would have had to manage her skirts and scramble up in a hurry. Unless, of course, she had been driving in the first place. Would Bing have allowed a female to drive him?

The two smaller vehicles were almost identical, although Gino felt certain their respective owners could tell them apart. Closer inspection, however, showed one had been more roughly used than the other. "Whoever drives this one isn't very careful," Gino said, gesturing to the nicks and small dents along the vehicle's front panel that protected the batteries. Some looked fresh and others showed a bit of rust, indicating they'd been there awhile.

Tom studied the dents, shifting uneasily from one foot to the other. "You're right. That's what comes from letting girls drive automobiles."

Gino managed not to wince and wondered if he should warn Tom not to express such sentiments around Maeve, whose driving had once helped save Gino's life. "Which girl drives this one?"

"I, uh, Carrie, I think," Tom said uneasily. Gino remember the longing look Tom had given Carrie. He probably didn't want to say anything bad about her.

And yes, it made sense that Carrie's auto was dinged up, since Carrie was probably the more careless of the two. "Hey," Gino said, "could some of these dents have come from hitting Mr. Bing?"

Tom looked up and he was definitely alarmed this time. "I . . . I don't know. How could you tell?"

Gino had been wondering the same thing, but he was no expert. In fact, he wondered if there could even be an expert in such things. In spite of the number of pedestrians in New York and the abandon with which many people drove automobiles, very few people had been run over or even hit by one. "There might be a way to know," Gino said. "I guess if somebody remembers which one of these he was driving that night, at least."

Tom continued to stare at the many dents, but Gino had wandered over to the last vehicle.

This one was pristine, inside and out. Or *almost* pristine. Right in the middle of the front panel was a rather large dent just about where a man's legs would be if he was standing in front of it.

Frank had felt a bit conspicuous in the funeral procession out to the cemetery. His was the only gasoline-powered vehicle in the line and therefore the noisiest by far. He pretended not to notice the pitying glances sent him by the various employees of Warren's factory, although he did manage to feel superior to the mourners still driving wagons. He supposed the factory jobs didn't pay enough for the workers to afford to buy an automobile.

The procession itself was rather unique. The hearse carrying the coffin was horse-drawn and splendid, with the horses prancing and the long black plumes affixed to their halters waving in the breeze. Behind the hearse was one of Bing's autos, a large one with an enclosed passenger compartment and a high seat in front for the driver. Will Warren drove while Pearl and Nora rode inside in silent dignity.

Behind them came Ethel and Carrie, although Frank wondered why Pearl had allowed them in the procession at all, much less in such a place of honor. Maybe she was worried about what people would think, though, since everyone believed Ethel was the real widow. They rode in a small, open vehicle that held just the two of them, with Carrie driving. She seemed to have recovered from her onslaught of grief, although her young face was set grimly. Ethel had chosen to wear a veil, so whatever emotions she was feeling were hidden.

The graveside service was mercifully brief, and the mourners who had made the trip politely expressed their final regrets to Pearl and Ethel, which wasn't as convenient as it should have been because they were standing as far apart as they could while still being in the vicinity of the grave. Thank heaven Sarah was with him, because Frank would have merely slunk away under the force of Pearl's glare, but Sarah always knew what to say in social situations, even those as awkward as this one. She actually pretended not to notice Pearl's irritation and simply said how sorry they were and moved on. Maeve and Gino, he noticed, didn't approach Pearl at all.

When they turned to go back to their motorcar, Gino sidled up to Frank and said, "Take a look at Carrie's auto."

This wasn't difficult because they had to pass it to reach their own.

When they arrived at their own motor, they paused to wait for the ladies, who would need their assistance getting in. "Carrie isn't a very careful driver, is she?" Frank said.

"No, she isn't."

"Do you think those marks prove she's the one who ran over Bing?"

"I would except that Pearl's auto has a big dent in the front, too."

"That's unfortunate, but it really doesn't matter. We just need to find out which one was involved in Bing's death. The police will probably know."

"Which I guess means one of us will have to go and ask them," Gino said.

"Are you volunteering?"

Gino winced. "I guess I am."

"It appears no one really has an alibi," Maeve surmised after everyone had shared what they had learned that day at the funeral. The children had been with Mrs. Malloy all day and demanded attention the moment they all had returned home, so they hadn't had an opportunity to talk privately until Brian and Catherine were tucked in bed. Now the four of them were gathered in the parlor with Mrs. Malloy sitting off in the corner with her knitting. Sarah loved the way her mother-in-law pretended not to be interested in the discussions of their cases, but every now and then would add a bit of wisdom or insight.

"We aren't sure about Pearl," Sarah reminded them. "I don't think we've asked her outright where she was."

"But Ethel insisted at first that they were all

at home and in bed by ten o'clock that night," Maeve reminded her.

"I think she must have just been thinking about Carrie and herself and included Pearl out of . . . I don't know, a sense of obligation or something."

"An obligation to protect her from being charged with murder?" Malloy asked with some amusement.

Sarah shrugged. "Women are expected to protect their children. Perhaps it was instinctive to protect Pearl as well."

"Regardless of why she lied about Pearl," Maeve said impatiently, "we now know from Carrie that Pearl didn't ever sit with them after supper and that she could have left the house without them knowing."

"And if women protect their children," Gino added, "Ethel might be lying about Carrie as well."

"Carrie also couldn't remember very much about that day, or so she claimed," Maeve confirmed.

"Let's think about this logically," Malloy suggested. "We know that Bing spent the day at the show, and Carrie admits she went with him in the morning."

"So how did they get there?" Sarah said. "Knowing Mr. Bing, he drove one of his automobiles."

"Because he thought driving his auto around the city was good advertising," Gino said.

"But which one?" Malloy asked.

No one answered.

"We don't know the answer to that yet, and Gino is going to find out, so let's move on," he finally said.

"Carrie said she got bored or tired and came home in the afternoon," Maeve said.

"And she either drove the auto or walked or took a cab or something," Sarah said.

"Except if she took a cab, why didn't she just say so?" Maeve said. "Instead, she claimed she walked."

"It was a pleasant day, so she might have," Sarah said.

"But would she?" Maeve challenged. "A young girl all alone?"

"And would Bing have allowed that?" Malloy asked. "Everyone says he was fond of Carrie, so presumably, he'd look after her safety, too."

"But it wasn't late at night, remember," Sarah said. "She went home in the afternoon, in broad daylight. Maeve, would you have been afraid to walk alone in the city at that time of day?"

"Probably not, but why should she if she has an auto she can drive?"

"Because Bing needs it himself," Gino said. "He'll need it to drive home that night."

"But he could take a cab home," Malloy argued.

"Or someone could come back to get him at the end of the evening," Mrs. Malloy said from her corner.

They all turned to look at her in surprise, but she didn't even glance up.

"Who do you think would've gone to get him, Ma?" Malloy asked with genuine interest.

"How should I know? You're the detectives."

"She has us there," Sarah said, earning a nod from Mother Malloy.

"Then who do we think went to get him?" Malloy asked.

"Carrie or Pearl," Maeve said. "They each had their own autos, and they were both fond of him."

"But Pearl was angry with him for lying to her about her mother being dead," Malloy reminded her.

"All the more reason to go," Maeve argued right back. "She'd have an opportunity to berate him in private."

"And run over him if he made her too mad," Gino added.

"Oh my, he's right," Maeve said in dismay. Gino gave her a beaming smile.

"But why would Carrie run over him?" Maeve asked. "I can see her being willing to drive to Madison Square Garden to fetch him, but why would she want to kill him?"

"Maybe it was an accident," Sarah said.

"Then why run away and leave him to die?" Malloy asked.

"She's young," Gino said. "Maybe she panicked."

No one was convinced.

"If she adored him, like everyone says, she'd try to get help," Maeve said.

"What about Ethel?" Malloy asked. "Would she have gone to get him?"

"Probably," Sarah said, "but she's the one who hired us to find the killer. Why would she do that if she killed him?"

"That does seem to put her in the clear," Gino said with a grin.

"And Nora can't drive, so that puts her in the clear," Malloy said.

"Even though she has the best reason we know of for wanting to murder him," Maeve said. "Besides, even if she could drive, why would she be the one to fetch Bing?"

"To get him alone so she could kill him," Mrs. Malloy said.

They all turned to her again.

"But if she can't drive, she couldn't have killed him," Sarah pointed out.

Mrs. Malloy finally ceased her knitting and looked up. "How do you know she can't drive?"

They all looked at one another in amazement.

"How *do* we know?" Maeve asked with a frown.

"Because she told us she couldn't," Sarah admitted.

"Actually, she didn't even say she couldn't. She said, 'How would the likes of me learn to drive?'" Malloy said.

"And we just assumed the rest," Sarah said, annoyed with herself.

"It's also not hard to learn to drive an electric motor," Maeve added. "You don't even have to change gears."

"And Pearl took Nora for a drive in her auto," Gino said. "She might've explained the finer points to her, at least."

"And whoever killed Bing didn't really have to *drive* the auto," Malloy pointed out. "They just had to somehow get him to stand in front of it and put it in motion."

"So Nora might have done it," Sarah said.

"And she has no alibi because she was alone at the hotel that night. Nobody would know if she was in her room or not," Malloy said. "I think we need to pay the first Mrs. Bing a visit."

VII

The next day, Gino arrived at the house in time for the noon meal, which was a big one on Sunday. Maeve teased him about missing Sunday dinner with his family, but he reminded her that he was there to help her entertain the children while Frank and Sarah paid a call on Nora Bing. It was the least they could do after Mrs. Malloy had watched them the previous day during the funeral. Since the weather was turning colder, they would be limited to a brisk walk outside followed by an afternoon of play in the nursery. Maeve apparently decided to be grateful so Gino wouldn't regret his decision to help.

Malloy decided to drive the motorcar, so Sarah donned her duster and goggles and wrapped the length of tulle around her head to hold her hat on. She waited patiently while he cranked the motor to life and then they were on their way. For once she was glad he insisted on obeying the five-mile-per-hour speed limit since the weather was cold enough to be uncomfortable even at that speed.

The black wreath still adorned the Bings' front door, and the maid who answered their knock seemed surprised to see visitors. "I don't know if Mrs. Bing is at home," she said. People who weren't accepting visits would simply instruct their servants to say they weren't at home.

Sarah handed the girl her card and said, "We would like to see Nora Bing, if she's receiving."

From the look of surprise on the girl's face, Nora did not usually receive visitors at all. "Yes, ma'am." She flitted away without even offering them a seat on the bench in the entryway.

"Do you think she'll see us?" Malloy asked with a frown.

"I'm sure she'll be dying of curiosity to find out why we've come," Sarah replied confidently.

Sure enough, the maid returned shortly and conducted them to the formal parlor, which had been returned to its original state after the funeral. Nora was waiting for them. She no longer wore the ill-fitting mourning gown from yesterday nor any other sign of mourning, not even a black armband. She did, however, wear a haughty expression, probably the kind she imagined the mistress of such a fine house would assume.

"What brings you here on this fine day?" Nora asked.

"Thank you for seeing us," Sarah said, always aware of what was required on visits like this. "I'm sure you must still be recovering from your ordeal yesterday."

"You think it was an ordeal to put that scoundrel in the ground?" she scoffed.

Malloy muttered something about it being an

ordeal for the gravediggers, but Sarah simply smiled sympathetically. "I was just being polite. To answer your question about why we've come, we were wondering if you could clarify a few things for us."

"I already told you, I don't know anything about Alvin's death. I hardly know anything about Alvin's *life* after he abandoned me in that stinking mining town."

"Then it will be a short visit," Sarah replied, relentlessly smiling lest Nora think to take offense.

"Well, I suppose I can spare you a few minutes," Nora allowed. She gestured to the grouping of chairs in front of the fireplace, and they gladly sat down in the circle of its warmth.

"How is everyone coping today?" Sarah asked politely.

"If you want to know if we're still crying over Alvin, you don't need to worry about us. Carrie is the only one who seems to care that he's gone."

But not Pearl? That was curious. "I'm sure it was difficult for Carrie to lose two fathers in less than a year," Sarah said.

Nora snorted. "Alvin wasn't her father, and she was old enough to know that. She's just making a fuss to get attention."

Nora might be right about that, although Sarah thought Carrie's grief seemed real enough.

"Have the four of you made any decisions about the future?" Malloy asked, reminding them both of his presence.

Nora glared at him. "I don't guess we can until we see that lawyer tomorrow. Ethel says it depends on what the will says, and she seems to think it will say something in her favor."

"What will you do if Mr. Bing left everything to Ethel?" Sarah asked.

"I'll get a lawyer of my own, I guess. I think they're all crooks, but you've got to hire one if you want the law to help you."

Neither Sarah nor Malloy had anything to say to that, so an awkward silence fell.

"It must have been a shock to you to see Pearl all grown up," Malloy offered after a few moments.

The question seemed to stir some tender emotions in Nora, and her expression softened slightly. "She wasn't exactly a baby when Alvin took her, but yeah, she's growed into a fine lady. I . . . It was a surprise."

"I remember you said she took you for a ride in her automobile, too," Sarah said. "It's a bit shocking to see a girl driving one, isn't it?"

"It was that," Nora agreed.

"Mr. Bing tried to convince my husband to buy an electric auto for me to drive, but after watching my husband drive our gasoline-powered auto, I don't think I could manage one."

"Pearl did just fine with hers," Nora bragged. "She kept saying how easy it is."

"I suppose she tried to convince you to learn to drive as well," Sarah said with some amusement.

Nora's tentative amiability evaporated. "I see what you're doing. You're trying to make it sound like I could drive so you can accuse me of running over Alvin."

"Not at all," Sarah lied. "You couldn't possibly learn to drive just by watching Pearl do it one time, even if she did try to show you how the auto works."

"You're right about that. I could hardly make sense of half of what she was telling me, and even if I could learn, I wouldn't want to drive in this town. I never seen so many people and wagons in one place. A person can hardly find room to walk on the sidewalk, much less fit an automobile onto the street."

"I can understand why you might be afraid," Malloy said as pleasantly as he ever said anything. "I'm not fond of driving in the city myself."

This amused Nora. "I didn't think men ever admitted to being afraid of anything."

"We don't like to, that's true," Malloy allowed. "But a person can get killed around automobiles if he isn't careful. Just ask Ethel."

"Ask her what?" Nora said with a frown.

"Oh, perhaps you didn't know that her first

husband was killed by a motorcar, too," Sarah said.

This was obviously news to Nora, and good news at that, if her expression was any indication. "Then that proves it. Ethel is the one killed Alvin. She probably did in her first husband, too."

"Her first husband was killed in an accident at Mr. Warren's factory," Malloy said. "She wasn't even there."

This stopped Nora for a moment, but she quickly came up with a new theory. "Then it must be Will Warren who done it. He didn't have no love for Alvin, at least."

"But didn't he need Mr. Bing's money to finance his business?" Sarah asked innocently. "Mr. Bing couldn't invest if he was dead."

But Nora waved away that thought. "He could get money from somebody else. This city is crawling with millionaires. What Will Warren really wants is Pearl."

Sarah managed to keep smiling. "I did notice he seems quite enamored of her."

"He's flat out in love with her," Nora said, "but Alvin wasn't going to let Pearl marry him, no matter how successful he got."

Sarah managed to look surprised. "How do you know that?"

"I . . ." Plainly, Nora didn't know it, not for a fact. "I just know Alvin, that's all."

"But why would he object?" Malloy asked,

probably not even pretending to be confused. "Warren has his own business and he's a skilled mechanic. Even if he doesn't succeed with his automobiles, he'll be able to earn a good living. Most fathers would be happy with a son-in-law like that."

"Pearl don't like him," Nora decided.

Sarah thought this might be closer to the truth. "But she sought out his advice about planning the funeral, and he had a place of honor yesterday, even driving Mr. Bing's personal automobile."

"She could do a lot better," Nora insisted. "No matter if he did buy himself a new house just for her."

Sarah frowned in confusion, but plainly, Malloy understood what she was talking about. "He did mention his new house to me. What makes you think he bought it for Pearl?"

"Because he told her he did. At least, I guess he told her. He told me about it, though. Wanted me to know he could provide for Pearl just as good as Alvin, I guess. He wants to marry her, and who can blame him?"

Sarah had to resist the urge to scratch her head, which wouldn't be very ladylike no matter how confused she might be. "So Mr. Warren wants to marry Pearl but Mr. Bing objected because . . . because Pearl didn't want to marry Mr. Warren?"

"I didn't say that," Nora insisted.

Sarah was pretty sure she had, but now Nora

must realize it didn't make a lot of sense or maybe that she had misrepresented some of the motivations. "I guess the important thing is if Pearl wants to marry Mr. Warren."

Nora didn't agree or disagree.

"If Mr. Bing objected to the marriage," Malloy mused, "that would give Warren a good reason to want him dead."

Nora brightened at this. "I told you!"

"But not if Pearl didn't want to marry him at all," Malloy added. "Killing Bing wouldn't help with that."

Nora's smile vanished again.

"Perhaps Pearl can clarify this for us," Sarah said. "Is she here?"

Nora shifted uneasily in her chair. "No, she, uh, she went for a drive with Mr. Warren."

Sarah didn't dare even glance at Malloy for fear one or both of them would burst out laughing at what amounted to a complete contradiction to what Nora had claimed. "That's nice," she said faintly.

"I just said she didn't want to marry him," Nora insisted. "She can still be friends with him."

Sarah was pretty sure Nora had claimed Pearl didn't like him, but maybe she could still be friends with someone she didn't like. That made as much sense as any of the rest of this. "Perhaps she finds it comforting to be with someone who was a good friend of her father's."

"They wasn't friends. Alvin never had a real friend in his life, just people he used to get what he wanted."

"You have every right to be bitter," Sarah said, nodding to encourage Nora.

"Bitter ain't the half of it. That skunk just up and left me when he decided I wasn't fancy enough for him, and he took the only person I cared about in this world. Then he turned her against me so even now he's gone, she don't want anything to do with me."

Sarah didn't bother to point out that Pearl had taken her into her own home. "I can't imagine how painful it must have been when you realized he was gone and had taken your child."

Nora took a moment to let Sarah's sympathy soak in, and then she sighed. "Do you have children, Mrs. Malloy?"

"Yes, two."

"Then you know. At first I was just mad. I knew he was leaving, but he didn't warn me he was taking Pearl, so I was furious about that, because he tricked me. But after a few months went by and no word from him, I knew what he'd done. I felt real stupid then for not figuring it out sooner. He always did dote on her. They had their little secrets, too. They'd whisper and laugh and if I asked them what was so funny, they wouldn't tell me. He was turning her against me even then."

"Have you spoken to Pearl about this? Maybe you misunderstood—"

"I didn't misunderstand nothing. He turned her against me. I could see it in her eyes that first time she come to my hotel room after he finally told her I was still alive. She didn't come to see me because she missed me or because I'm her beloved mother. She come to see was I as bad as she remembered so she could decide what to do about me."

"But surely she missed you," Sarah argued, compelled to offer what comfort she could. "You're her mother, after all."

But Nora gave her a pitying smile. "She got to be a fancy lady, but I was still a boardinghouse landlady from a rough mining town. If anything, she likes me even less now than she did then."

"I can see why you'd be angry with Bing," Malloy offered.

"Angry? Ha! I hated him the way I've never hated another human being. I might've forgiven him for leaving me. Lots of men desert their wives, and I would've got over that, but he tore my heart out when he took my Pearl, and now I can't even get her back."

"I guess Nora had a good reason for killing Bing," Frank said as they reached the place where they'd parked their motorcar.

Sarah sighed. "Yes, but we just didn't realize

exactly how good it was. I think I imagined a joyous reunion with her daughter, since Pearl allowed Nora to move into the house, but obviously, that is not the case."

"Stealing Pearl away once was bad enough, but finding out Pearl despises her must have been awful."

"I can't even imagine how painful that would be," Sarah agreed, but he could tell she was trying to, and it was a very unpleasant experience.

"So she had a very good reason for wanting Bing dead, which is more than we can say for most of our other suspects, but do we think she could have made the auto run over him?"

"I think you need to find out more about the electric motorcars and just how easy they really are to operate."

"And then find out if Bing had his auto at Madison Square Garden that night or if someone came to get him when the show was over."

"How will you find out?" Sarah asked with a frown as he opened the trunk that was fastened to the back of their motorcar for storage and started pulling out their driving gear.

"That, Mrs. Malloy, is a mystery."

Gino made an early start on Monday morning and reached Police Headquarters on Mulberry Street before most of the detectives. He took some ribbing from men who remembered him from his time on the police force, but it wasn't particularly good-natured. They were all jealous of Frank Malloy's good fortune and firmly believed it should have happened to them instead. Gino thought Mr. Malloy would have admitted his own unworthiness, but that would hardly have placated the men who envied him.

Gino finally discovered the detective who was investigating Bing's death. He wasn't someone Gino had worked with before, but he knew who Gino was.

"You the one works for Malloy?" he asked when Gino found him with his feet up on his battered desk, drinking a cup of coffee that smelled like it might be half whiskey.

"I'm his partner, yes." Gino had worn a cheap suit today—no use lording it over the other cops that he worked for a millionaire—but Paddy Doyle didn't seem to appreciate his efforts. Doyle was a typical black Irishman, with dark hair and eyes and a flushed face, although that might be the whiskey.

"Partner, eh? He give you half of his millions?"

"I'm just a partner in his detective agency."

Doyle made a rude noise. "If you're a detective, what are you doing here? You must know we can't do nearly as good a job as you can." Did he sound bitter or just annoyed? It was impossible to say.

"I never said that. New York City police

detectives are the best in the world," Gino said with a smile to tell Doyle he was buttering him up.

"Yeah, yeah, just tell me what you want so you can be on your way. You're giving me a headache."

"They told me you're working on the Bing case, the one where he got run over by an automobile."

"I'm not likely to forget that one. What do you want to know?"

"Which one of his autos ran over him?"

Doyle had been sipping on his coffee, but the question stopped him. "*Which one?* You mean he's got more than one?"

"Yes. Didn't anybody mention that? He's got four."

Doyle muttered an imprecation against rich men. "What the devil does he need with four automobiles?"

"One for every member of his family, I guess," Gino said with a grin. "He taught his wife and daughters to drive, too."

"He lets *girls* drive them machines?" Doyle asked sourly. "Is he crazy?"

"Since he's dead, we'll never know, but if you tell me which one of his autos he was driving that night, I might be able to tell you who killed him."

"Nothing is that easy," Doyle reminded him. "How am I supposed to tell you which one it was?"

"Just tell me what it looked like."

"It looked like those motorcars you see everywhere nowadays."

Gino managed not to sigh. "Was it one that looked like a carriage?"

"A *horseless* carriage?" Doyle said provocatively.

"Yes, a *horseless* carriage, or was it one that looked more like a buggy, open with one of those drop tops?"

Doyle pretended to consider the question carefully. "It was a buggy."

Gino refused to react, but a frisson of excitement ran up his spine. One of the girls had driven the offending auto, then. "Was it all banged up or did it look pretty good?"

"How should I know? It was dark and all them things look alike to me."

"Then how did you know it belonged to Bing at all?"

"His partner told me."

Gino hoped his eyes didn't actually bug out, because he wasn't able to completely conceal his surprise. "His *partner?* What was he doing there?"

"They was having an automobile show at Madison Square Garden. I guess he was there for that, just like Bing."

"How did he happen to be at the accident, though?"

"The show was over and I guess he come out and stopped to gawk, like everybody else, and he told us who the dead man was. I'd already found his card case, so I knew who he was, but the partner told me the auto belonged to him, too."

As shocked as he was, Gino did remember to check his facts. "And do you remember this partner's name?"

Doyle frowned and sipped his coffee again. "Can't say that I do, but I might've writ it down someplace."

"Will Warren?" Gino asked.

Doyle shrugged. "Could be. Claimed he designed automobiles, but he looked too young for that, if you ask me."

Gino thought so, too, but he didn't say so. "I guess you took the car into custody, then."

"Didn't nobody on the force know how to drive it, so we let this fellow take it back to Bing's house. We didn't need it for anything anyway."

So they still didn't know which auto had run over Alvin Bing, but at least they'd narrowed it down to either Carrie's or Pearl's vehicle.

"What about witnesses? If people were coming out of Madison Square Garden when the show ended, somebody must've seen who was driving."

Doyle gave him a pitying look. "Seems like Bing was one of the last to leave the show. Most everybody was gone by then, and if somebody did see what happened, they never stopped to talk about it."

"You said people were gawking, though."

"After it was over. You know how it is. If there's something dead in the street, they start gathering like flies, but nobody would admit to witnessing the accident."

So, who was driving the auto that night? And what was Will Warren doing there when he'd sworn he was home in bed?

"I think you just like looking at automobiles," Sarah teased when they pulled up in front of Will Warren's garage.

"I do," Malloy confessed unrepentantly, "but we need to get some important information and you're the only person in our detective agency who doesn't already know how to drive."

"I'm also the only person in our detective agency who doesn't get a salary."

Malloy gave her a look. "You get to spend all my money. How much more do you want?"

"I would never spend *all* your money. That would be stupid."

"Indeed it would. Shall we go in and convince Will Warren you want to spend *some* of my money on an automobile?"

Everyone in the shop looked up when they entered. Plainly, they weren't used to seeing a female in the place, even if she was dressed in driving gear. Sarah smiled at them, but nobody smiled back.

"Mr. and Mrs. Malloy," Will Warren said suspiciously, emerging from the depths of the shop. He must do far more work on the autos than merely designing them, if the dirt on his overalls was any indication. "What a surprise." He didn't look surprised. He looked annoyed, and Sarah couldn't blame him. They were rather relentless when working on a case.

"Hello, Mr. Warren," she said cheerfully.

"I told my wife what I learned from you about electric motorcars, and now she wants to see for herself."

Warren's expression softened a bit, although Sarah could see he didn't completely believe Malloy's excuse for being there. She would have to convince him, or at least get his full cooperation if they were going to learn what they came here to find out.

"My husband thinks I'll change my mind about learning to drive if I have an electric vehicle. Could you show me how it works?"

"I can do that and much more, Mrs. Malloy." Mr. Warren might not believe them, but he was determined to pretend he did. "Come with me and I'll show you some different styles. I think you might prefer a vehicle like Miss Bing's."

"I'm not sure what type she uses," Sarah said, following him through the shop. Several vehicles in various stages of construction were receiving attention from the men she had seen at the funeral. She nodded to each of them, receiving tentative smiles and nods in return. They plainly weren't sure if they should be happy to see the Malloys, but if Will was willing to welcome them, they would reserve judgment.

At the back of the shop they found a row of vehicles that were attached to what Sarah determined must be charging stations by long black cords, similar to the cords on her electric lamps. Two of the vehicles were completely open, with just a fold-up top, but the rest were enclosed, like a carriage, except all four sides were constructed of panes of glass instead of the smaller windows usually found in horse-drawn carriages. The enclosed vehicles were of various sizes, though. One was as large as the one Will Warren had driven in the funeral procession, but the others were smaller and made so the driver could sit inside.

"This is the kind Miss Bing drives," Warren said, leading her to one of the open vehicles.

"I'm not interested in freezing to death, Mr. Warren," she informed him wryly. "Winter is coming, and I've already endured one of them with an open vehicle."

Mr. Warren nodded his understanding. "Then you might prefer something like this." He took her to the smallest of the enclosed vehicles.

Inside was a bench seat that would hold two people, with the controls for the driver on the left side.

"My husband says you don't have to crank an electric motorcar," she said with a worried frown.

"No indeed. They are so easy, a child can use it. If you want, I can demonstrate."

"Yes, I'd like that."

Mr. Warren opened the door and offered his hand to help her inside.

"You know I can't drive," she said uneasily.

"Then I'll drive and explain everything to you as we go. There's an alley out back where we can try it out, and if you feel comfortable, you can try it for yourself."

Sarah knew a small thrill at the thought, but that would, of course, defeat the purpose of their visit. "I think I'll just be satisfied with your instruction today, Mr. Warren." She took his hand and climbed in.

The interior was upholstered like a fine carriage, which surprised her. It shouldn't have, of course. Their motorcar was quite fine, too. What really surprised her, though, was how few controls there seemed to be compared to their gasoline-powered motorcar.

Mr. Warren unhooked the auto from the charging station, climbed in, and took the driver's seat. There was a lever on the left side of the seat, a tiller that had been flipped up to be out of the way, which he folded down now so it was in front of him, and two pedals on the floor.

"This lever"—he clutched the one on the left of the seat with his left hand—"is the accelerator lever and it controls how fast the vehicle goes. This is the steering lever," he continued, moving the tiller bar that stretched across in front of him with his right hand. "It turns the front wheels."

"Oh yes, we have a tiller like that in our motorcar."

Mr. Warren nodded. "The pedals on the floor control the brakes. This one stops the rear wheels and this one stops the drive shaft."

"What's that?" Sarah nodded to an odd-looking thing mounted on the front panel.

"That's a meter that tells you how much battery power you have left."

"Oh, so you don't get stuck in the middle of Fifth Avenue because you ran out of power."

Mr. Warren smiled his approval. "Exactly. Are you ready to take a little tour of our alley?"

"As long as you drive," Sarah said.

Mr. Warren shouted to one of the men to open the rear doors of the garage. Then he turned to where Malloy was standing nearby, observing. "I'll have your wife back in a few minutes."

Malloy nodded and stepped out of the way. Mr. Warren pushed the accelerator lever and the auto moved forward.

"Is the motor running?" Sarah asked in surprise.

"We wouldn't be moving if it wasn't."

"I didn't even see you start the engine and why isn't it making any noise?"

"That is the beauty of an electric, Mrs. Malloy," he said with some satisfaction. He pushed the steering lever forward, and the motor turned left, circling around and then exiting through the now-open doors.

"It's so quiet," Sarah marveled, not even having to feign her delight.

"Ladies especially like the privacy. They can chat with their friends and not worry about being overheard by the chauffeur."

It did seem very private, enclosed as it was, even with all the windows. "I wouldn't be worried about being overheard. It's the opportunity to be heard at all in a motorcar without shouting that I find fascinating."

Mr. Warren smiled. The alley was only a block long, so he turned the vehicle around when they reached the end and went the other way. He even showed her how to reverse.

"How do you stop? I noticed you didn't use the brake pedals that time."

"If you aren't going too fast, the vehicle will stop if you just pull back on the accelerator lever. You only need the brakes if you're going fast and need to stop quickly."

Sarah nodded, wondering how much of this Pearl was likely to have explained to her mother.

"You could take a turn driving down the alley if you like," Mr. Warren said.

Sarah laughed at the thought. "I'm afraid I'd be too frightened of hitting something and damaging your vehicle."

"Then your husband would have to buy it for you," he teased. He was boyishly appealing when he smiled. Had Pearl Bing noticed that? Did she find him appealing in any way? So far, they had only Ethel's and Nora's word that Pearl had no tender feelings for him. Of course, Sarah hadn't seen anything in Pearl's manner toward him to indicate she did, either, and she had insisted she wasn't interested in marrying him. But who knew? Perhaps she just liked keeping her feelings to herself.

"I'm not sure my husband wants to own as many motorcars as Mr. Bing did," Sarah said.

"When he sees how convenient it is for you to have an automobile, I'm sure he'll be glad he got one for you."

Yes, Sarah could take Brian and Catherine to their schools and pick them up. Or Maeve could. Somehow Sarah couldn't imagine Mother Malloy riding anywhere with Maeve, though. Or going in a motorcar at all, come to think of it. The thought almost made her laugh out loud, but poor Mr. Warren would think she was crazy if she did.

"Mrs. Bing mentioned that you'd taken Pearl

out for a drive yesterday," Sarah said. "That's another benefit of having a motorcar."

Mr. Warren's pleasant expression grew instantly defensive. "I . . . Yes, a . . . a very pleasant benefit."

"I'm sure Pearl appreciates your support. Losing her father so suddenly must have been a terrible shock."

"It was a shock to all of us, but you're right, Pearl is devastated."

"I suppose it's a blessing that her mother returned. At least she's not alone."

"Yes, a . . . a blessing," Mr. Warren said, although plainly, he didn't think so.

"And how sad that Mrs. Bing's return caused a rift between Miss Bing and her father just before he died. But I don't suppose anyone could blame Miss Bing for being angry."

They had reached the opposite end of the alley, and Mr. Warren used the activity of turning around to avoid replying to Sarah's provocative statement.

When they were heading back to the factory doors, Sarah said, "Mrs. Bing seemed to think that Pearl was angrier that she had returned than that Mr. Bing had lied to her."

"I'm sure Miss Bing was happy to learn her mother was alive," Mr. Warren insisted, although he didn't sound like he was really sure at all.

"Perhaps Mrs. Bing misunderstood Pearl's distress. I gathered that she was a bit jealous because Pearl and her father had always been so close, and that may have influenced her interpretation of Pearl's reaction to her return."

Mr. Warren frowned. "Pearl did allow her mother to move in with her, so she couldn't have been too unhappy about seeing her again."

"Yes, that does seem to prove she still loves her mother."

Mr. Warren's head jerked as he turned to check Sarah's expression, but he saw only complete sincerity. Mollified, he returned his attention to maneuvering the vehicle back into the garage.

"Thank you so much for demonstrating the automobile to me, Mr. Warren," Sarah said when he had pulled to a stop in front of one of the charging stations. "I will have a long discussion with my husband about it."

"I'm sure you will prevail, Mrs. Malloy. You strike me as a very determined woman."

Sarah decided to take that as a compliment, in spite of Mr. Warren's grim expression.

When Malloy approached them, he was no longer alone. Gino had joined him while she had been receiving her driving instructions. Neither man returned her smile.

Mr. Warren didn't seem to notice, though. He had assumed his phony salesman demeanor. "Your wife seems quite impressed with our electric automobile, Mr. Malloy. I'm afraid you will have to get her one for her very own."

"I'm sure I will," Malloy said. "You remember my partner, Gino Donatelli, don't you?"

Mr. Warren's expression tightened. "Yes. We met at Mr. Bing's funeral, I believe."

"This morning Gino visited the police detective who is investigating Mr. Bing's murder, and he learned something very interesting."

"From the police?" Mr. Warren said with undisguised contempt. "I wasn't aware that they even knew anything interesting. If they do, they haven't shared it with Mr. Bing's family."

"This was something interesting about you, Mr. Warren," Gino said. "I asked them how they found out the auto that killed Mr. Bing belonged to him, and they said his partner told them."

"His *partner?*" Mr. Warren echoed, as if he had never heard the word before.

"Yes, his partner, so we are wondering why you told us you were at home in bed when Mr. Bing was killed when you were at Madison Square speaking to the police that night?"

VIII

Frank watched Will Warren's expression very carefully, and he could have sworn the man was truly shocked by Gino's accusation.

"But I wasn't there that night. I told you . . ."

"I know what you told me, but why would the police lie about that?" Gino asked.

"You have to admit it sounds suspicious," Frank added.

Warren was frowning, as if trying to solve this mystery, and then he seemed to remember his manners and climbed out of the auto so he could assist Sarah. "I swear to you, I wasn't there," he said as he helped Sarah down.

"Well, someone who claimed to be you told the police the auto that ran over Bing belonged to him, so it must have been someone who knew him well enough to know that," Frank said.

"Lots of people would recognize his vehicles," Warren claimed.

"Who, for example?" Frank asked.

"I don't know. Everybody who works here, for a start. We built them, after all."

"And how many of them just happened to be on Madison Square the night he was killed?" Gino challenged.

"I don't know. I told you, I wasn't there, but

184

people who are interested in autos would also be attending the auto show," Warren argued. "Some of them would recognize Bing's vehicles."

"Too bad you didn't have company at your house that night," Frank said mildly.

To his surprise, Warren stiffened, and the color bloomed in his face. "What do you mean by that?"

"I just meant it's too bad no one saw you at home and could give you an alibi."

"Yes, it's too bad, but I was alone. All alone."

But he sounded so defensive that Frank was sure he was lying, and if he *was* lying, why would he lie about something that could prove his innocence?

"Then maybe you can at least tell us which of Mr. Bing's autos was the one that killed him," Gino said.

"What?" Warren asked, startled. "No, I can't. I have no idea."

"The police said this fellow who claimed to be you drove the vehicle off and presumably returned it to the Bings," Gino said.

But Warren was already shaking his head. "I never . . . I just . . . I just know all the autos were in the garage when I checked the next day."

"Why did you think to check?" Frank asked.

Warren frowned again. "I . . . The police had been there, asking questions. They told the ladies the auto had been returned, and Miss Bing asked me to make sure."

"Did the police ask you whose auto was involved in the accident?" Gino asked.

"I didn't talk to them, so I don't know."

Gino exchanged a glance with Frank. "I doubt they asked about it. Detective Sergeant Doyle didn't even know Bing owned more than one auto."

"And it would never occur to them that girls like Pearl and Carrie would have their own autos," Sarah added with a sly grin.

She was right, of course. Hardly any men in New York City would expect a young girl to have her own auto.

"And you don't remember which one was in the accident," Frank said.

"I told you I wasn't there," Warren snapped. "How many times do I have to say it?"

Frank sighed dramatically. "Too bad no one can vouch for you, isn't it?"

"Do you believe him?" Gino asked when they had made their way out of Warren's garage to the sidewalk.

"I don't know," Frank said. "He seems like he's telling the truth, but Doyle told you he was at Madison Square Garden that night."

Gino frowned. "He couldn't remember the man's name, but the man told Doyle he was Bing's partner. Who else could it have been?"

"Did Mr. Bing have other partners?" Sarah asked.

"Not that we know of. I guess you can ask

186

Ethel, although she might not know, either," Frank said, not happy with this at all. "You need to go see her and find out what the attorney said about Bing's will, in any case, so you can add that to your list of questions."

"Even if Warren wasn't at Madison Square that night, he's still hiding something," Gino said.

"Yes, he is," Sarah said. "He's definitely lying about being home alone and snug in his bed when Mr. Bing was killed."

They hadn't quite reached the spot where Frank had left his motorcar, but both he and Gino stopped dead in their tracks and turned to gaze at her in amazement. So Frank wasn't the only one who thought Warren had been lying. "What makes you so sure?" Frank said.

"Didn't you notice how he blushed when you said it was too bad he didn't have company that night?"

"I thought he was just mad," Gino said.

Sarah gave him a pitying look. "No. He might have been at home and even snug in his bed, but he wasn't alone."

"Then why . . . ?" Gino muttered.

"Because he's embarrassed to tell us who he was with," Frank said, feeling like an idiot for not figuring it out himself.

"Or he doesn't want to embarrass someone else," Sarah said. "We just have to figure out who that is."

"Pearl Bing," Gino suggested. They started walking toward the motorcar again. "He's been mooning after her like a lovesick cow."

"He'd certainly want to protect her, too," Sarah agreed, "but no one who knows her thinks she cares a fig for Will Warren."

"Which makes it unlikely she was alone with him that night, in his home or anywhere else," Frank said. They had reached the motorcar and he opened the trunk so they could pull out their dusters and goggles.

"Who else could it have been, then?" Gino asked.

"I can think of a lot of possibilities, but we need to find out more about Will Warren before we can know for sure," Frank said. "Do you think your new friend from the factory would join you for a drink at the end of the day, Gino?"

"We got so excited about Gino's news that we completely forgot to ask you about your driving lesson," Malloy said when they had settled in the parlor after arriving at home. Gino had joined them since it was almost time for lunch and the Malloys had an excellent cook. Maeve would miss it since she was holding down the fort at the office.

"Ah yes, if we only had an electric auto, we could have discussed it on the drive home," Sarah couldn't resist saying.

Malloy rolled his eyes, and Gino smirked.

"You're going to have to buy an electric auto," Gino informed him.

Malloy gave him a mock scowl. "Maeve wants one, too."

"Then you are doubly doomed."

"I was hoping Maeve's *husband* might buy her one," Malloy said.

Gino never even blinked. "Is Maeve getting married?" he asked innocently.

"Apparently not," Sarah said, ending their little squabble. "And to answer your question, I learned a lot from Mr. Warren."

"Enough to really operate the auto?" Gino asked, eagerly leaning forward.

"Enough to set it in motion, at least. It's amazingly simple. There aren't any gears to worry about. All you can do is drive forward or backward, and there's a lever on the driver's left side that controls how fast you go and in which direction. The steering is the same as our motorcar, and you don't really need to use the brakes if you aren't driving fast. Just pulling the accelerator lever to its upright position stops the vehicle, although the engine keeps running. It's apparently always running or at least able to propel the vehicle forward without needing to be started in any way."

The two men considered this information for a few moments.

"So if someone was in the vehicle . . ." Malloy said.

"And the person knew all you had to do was push the lever to make the vehicle move . . ." Gino added.

". . . then all they'd have to do was wait until Bing was in front of the auto and then push the accelerator lever to make it hit him."

"And pull it back to make the auto stop," Sarah said.

"How exactly did it kill him, though?" Gino asked. "The pictures in the newspapers showed the wheel resting on his chest, but is that what really happened?"

"That is a very good question, Gino," Malloy said. "While you're enjoying a pleasant drink with Tom Yingling this afternoon, I'll be going to the morgue to see if I can find out exactly how Mr. Bing died."

The police didn't always use Doc Haynes to do their autopsies, but Frank took a chance that a prominent citizen like Alvin Bing would have been taken to the morgue at Bellevue Hospital. Luckily, he had guessed correctly.

"Oh yes," Doc said after he and Frank had exchanged pleasantries in the doctor's cluttered office, where the smell of death wafted faintly off Doc's clothes and had permeated everything else. "I remember him. Don't see many people getting killed by those newfangled contraptions."

"Do you have any idea how it happened?"

Doc started shuffling through a stack of files piled precariously on his desk until he found the one he wanted. "Let's see now." He opened the folder and scanned the notes he'd made. "Like I said, I don't usually see folks who get hit by motorcars. They might end up in the hospital, but they don't often die. Those things are dangerous but not particularly fast, so people can usually get out of the way."

Frank thought they went plenty fast, but he didn't bother to say so. "How did one kill Bing, then?"

"Ran right over him. Twice, if my opinion counts for anything."

"Twice?" Frank marveled.

"Yes. It was easy to see because of the dirt marks on his suit."

Frank was trying not to imagine what it would be like to have a motorcar run over him even once. "How could it have run over him twice?"

"That's up to the police to figure out, but he had a badly injured leg where the motorcar hit him to knock him over, I presume. Then there was a wheel mark across his abdomen." Doc made a slashing motion with his hand across his own to illustrate. "And another one across his chest." He made another slashing motion, this time higher up. "They told me the wheel of the motorcar was resting on his chest when they found him."

Frank winced. "I guess that would kill him."

"Easily. His ribs and sternum were crushed and his lungs and heart—"

"That's fine. I get the idea," Frank said.

"The wheel left a clear mark when it passed over his belly and his chest," Doc mused. "What are those wheels made of anyway?"

"Wood, just like a wagon wheel."

"I thought it might be metal, but wood is unforgiving enough, I suppose."

"And you think the motor went over him twice?"

"The internal damage lower down was just as bad, so yes, twice."

"But how could that happen?"

Doc shrugged. "Don't those machines go backward?"

"They do, yes."

"Then I'd say whoever hit him knocked him down and proceeded to run completely over him, then went backward over him again or at least halfway, stopping when the wheel was on his chest."

Which told Frank a lot more about the killer than he had realized before. Hitting Bing and even running over him once might have been an accident, but doing it again showed a definite desire to do Bing as much harm as possible.

Who among Bing's circle hated him that much? Frank could think of only one person.

Sarah knew she was probably on a fool's errand, but she resolutely climbed the steps to rap on the Bings' front door. The reluctant maid took her card and eventually escorted her to the parlor, where Ethel waited to receive her.

"Have you learned anything?" Ethel asked by way of greeting.

"I'm sorry to get your hopes up, but no, we're still investigating."

Ethel sighed and then apparently remembered her manners. "Please sit down. Can I offer you some tea?"

"That would be lovely. It's rather brisk outside." The cab ride over had been chilly and Sarah couldn't help thinking longingly about that neat little electric auto she'd ridden in this morning.

Ethel rang for the maid and ordered a tea tray. When they were alone again, Ethel said, "I went to see the attorney this morning."

"I hope the news was good."

Ethel smiled a little wanly. "Oddly, it was, at least for Carrie and me."

"I'm so glad for you." Sarah knew better than to ask outright about the terms of Mr. Bing's will. Ladies didn't normally discuss money, and they certainly didn't *inquire*.

Her silence had the desired effect, however. "He left me almost everything. Well, between me and Carrie, at least. He left her a trust, a rather large one. The attorney said a trust was best for someone who isn't of age yet."

Sarah nodded encouragingly. "I'm sure it is."

"And I got the house and a trust of my own."

"And you can still receive it, even though your marriage wasn't legal?"

Ethel nodded. "Nora was with me, of course, and she made sure the attorney knew she was Alvin's legal wife, but Alvin must have known Nora was alive, because he worded the will in a specific way so I would be the heir, regardless. The attorney explained it all very thoroughly."

What a cad. Sarah wanted to tell Alvin Bing exactly what she thought of a man who would deceive a woman as vulnerable as Ethel Lane, but she said, "That's a relief, I know. I hope he left Pearl something, too." Because if he hadn't, the girl would be rightfully furious and would certainly contest the will.

"He left her a dowry, for when she marries," Ethel reported with a frown. "I think he expected her husband would take care of her so he didn't need to."

"And if she doesn't marry?" Sarah asked, getting a bad feeling.

"She can live here as long as she wishes. That's one of the terms of the will. I get to keep the house but only if I give Pearl a home as long as she chooses to live here. But she only gets the dowry if she marries."

Now Sarah really wanted to give Mr. Bing a piece of her mind, but she bit her tongue. How awful of him to provide so generously for his bigamous wife and stepdaughter and neglect his own child. "And I suppose Nora wasn't mentioned at all."

"No, she wasn't, but believe me, she had a lot of questions for the attorney. She wants to contest the will. I think that's the right term."

"Yes, I think it is. Did the attorney give her any encouragement?"

"He indicated that while he himself didn't know that my marriage to Mr. Bing was bigamous, Mr. Bing certainly did and wrote his will as if he were leaving a bequest to an unrelated individual. Something about not saying that I was his wife but merely listing my name. The attorney said Nora was certainly free to sue, but that a judge might well rule in my favor anyway. They could even accuse Nora of deserting Alvin, in which case she'd certainly lose."

"Poor Nora," Sarah said.

From Ethel's expression, she felt little sympathy for her rival. "If she was as disagreeable with Alvin as she has been with me, I can see why he left her."

"I'm sorry you've had to endure that, but I'm

sure she's just taking out her frustrations with Mr. Bing on you."

"She's made that pretty clear, but it doesn't make my life any more pleasant."

"I don't suppose you have to let her continue to live here."

"Not by the terms of the will, no, but . . ." Ethel looked away, her gaze fixing on the fireplace.

"But?" Sarah prodded.

"But Pearl seems to have reconciled with Nora since Mr. Bing's funeral. Pearl was so angry at first, after Nora's sudden appearance, but perhaps I misjudged her true feelings. I thought she was angry with Nora, but now I think she was only angry with Alvin."

"I'm sure Nora explained what happened and that she never wanted to lose Pearl."

"I suppose. She hasn't reconciled with *me,* though, and she's been very rude to both me and Carrie. I may have to keep Pearl, but I don't have to share a house with Nora. I just haven't figured out how to tell Nora she must leave."

"I can understand why you'd be reluctant to do so. If she's rude now, she could become quite unpleasant if you evict her."

Ethel sighed. "You do understand. And Pearl will be offended as well. If only Mr. Bing had left Pearl some money of her own. Then she and Nora could find a place together."

The maid knocked then and brought in the tea

tray. Sarah fortified herself with a nice hot brew and a few tea cakes. When the maid had gone, she asked the other question she'd come to ask. "Did Mr. Bing have any partners besides Mr. Warren?"

"Business partners, you mean? Not that I know of."

"I don't suppose he'd invested in any other automobile companies."

Ethel smiled and shook her head. "One was more than enough, from all the complaining he did."

"What about from his earlier days? Maybe a partner in one of his mining ventures."

But Ethel shook her head again. "Not that I know of. He'd cut his ties with all of that, or so he said. Sold everything and was investing the money in other things."

The parlor door opened abruptly, and Carrie Lane stepped in. She wore a frilly dress more suited to a much younger girl and which didn't pay the slightest heed to her mourning status. Her pretty face was twisted into a suspicious frown. "What are you talking about?"

"Don't be rude, Carrie. We have a guest," her mother chastened her.

"I can see that, but she's not really a guest. She works for us, doesn't she? You're going to figure out who killed Papa, aren't you?"

"I hope so," Sarah said, intrigued by Carrie's belligerent attitude.

"Have you found out anything yet?"

"Carrie," her mother tried again, more sharply this time.

Carrie ignored her. "Have you?"

"A bit," Sarah said.

"Nobody has asked me anything. Don't you want to ask me something?" She plopped down on an unoccupied chair and snatched a tea cake from the tray.

Maeve had, of course, questioned her, but Carrie probably didn't know Maeve worked with them, too. Maybe Carrie would give her different answers than she'd given Maeve. "How did you and Mr. Bing travel to the automobile show the day he died?"

Ethel drew in her breath with a hiss, as if she wanted to stop this, but she apparently thought better of it and remained silent.

"We drove, of course." She took a bite of the tea cake and chewed it leisurely.

"Which vehicle did you use?"

"I don't remember. We drove to the show every day, and Papa liked to use different vehicles. How can I remember which one we used on a certain day?" She crammed the rest of the tea cake into her mouth.

"What time did you leave the show that day?"

Carrie shrugged and when she'd swallowed, she said, "I didn't pay attention. In the afternoon sometime."

"And how did you get home?"

"I walked. It was a beautiful day."

This was what she'd told Maeve, but she seemed to have grown more confident in her story now. She picked up her mother's teacup and drained it.

Sarah watched her carefully, but she saw no signs of dishonesty. "What did you do that evening?"

"I sat with Mother until I went to bed around ten o'clock, like I do every night." She glanced at her mother as if confirming her statement, but Ethel just stared woodenly back at her.

"And you were home all evening?"

"Of course. Mother and I both were." She didn't even glance at her mother this time. She was either telling the truth, or she'd practiced lying until she was good at it.

"What about Pearl? Was she home that night?"

"Of course she was," Nora snapped from the still-opened doorway. She strode in, glaring at Carrie, who simply glared back.

"How would you know?" Carrie challenged. "You weren't even here."

"You can't believe a word this girl says," Nora informed Sarah.

"Now who's being rude?" Carrie asked her mother sweetly.

"Nora, this is a private conversation," Ethel tried.

"I thought it was Mrs. Malloy trying to find out who killed Alvin. What's private about that?"

"Nothing," Carrie said firmly. "And she was asking me if Pearl was home that night." Carrie turned to Sarah. "Do you still want to know?"

Nora made a rude sound, but Sarah said, "Yes."

Carrie smiled with satisfaction. "She was out. She goes out all the time at night."

Nora looked like she wanted to claw Carrie's eyes out, and she strode close enough to the girl to make Ethel rise to her feet in case she had to protect her child. "Liar!"

Ethel was angry, too, although in a much more ladylike manner. "Carrie, that isn't true, and you know it."

"She does!" Carrie insisted. "Why do you think she wouldn't ever sit with us? She didn't want us to know when she was home and when she wasn't."

"Then how would you know she was out?" Nora challenged.

"I'd go to her room to check. Sometimes she was out for hours," Carrie announced smugly. "You can ask the servants if you don't believe me."

"Servants," Nora hissed, as if she couldn't imagine a less trustworthy lot.

"But where would she go so late at night?" Ethel asked. Her troubled gaze darted between Carrie and Nora, who still stood as if ready to attack Carrie for maligning Pearl's good name.

"I'm sure I don't know," Carrie said innocently. "Maybe you should ask her. Or Will Warren."

"Mr. Warren would never . . ." Ethel began but stopped when she apparently had second thoughts.

"I don't know what Will Warren might do, but Pearl would never sell herself so cheap," Nora said. "I raised her better than that."

Carrie actually laughed, earning a dark look from both the Mrs. Bings.

"Did she really go out the night Mr. Bing died?" Sarah asked.

All three of the others turned shocked gazes at her. Carrie was the first to recover. "Yes, she did. Lately, she's been going out most nights, too."

"That ain't true," Nora said. "Not since I been here, at least."

Carrie gave her a pitying look. "Do you really think Pearl goes to bed at eight o'clock?"

"We aren't interested in what she did any other night," Sarah said. "Just the night when Mr. Bing died."

"How many times do I have to say it? She was out that night for sure," Carrie said. "She took her auto and didn't get home until almost one o'clock."

"How do you know?" Nora demanded.

Carrie smiled sweetly. "I saw her out the window."

"And you waited by the window until one o'clock when she got home?" Nora scoffed.

"I heard her come in. My room is next to hers."

"How do we know you were home yourself?" Nora asked, furious now. "You've got your own auto, too. You could've been anywhere."

"Because my mother knows I was home, don't you, Mama?"

Sarah thought her tone sounded taunting, but Ethel didn't seem to notice. She took her seat again with elaborate care, arranging her skirt carefully before saying, "We were both here all evening. Besides, we didn't have any reason to want Alvin dead." She raised her guileless gaze to Nora, although Sarah knew Ethel had wanted a divorce she couldn't get, which could have been a very good reason indeed.

Nora sniffed. "And you're saying I did have a reason. Well, it's true enough. I wouldn't've spit on Alvin Bing if he was on fire."

"He'd deserted you and turned your own daughter against you," Sarah said. "You told me that yourself."

"Yes, and I hated him for it, but I don't have no idea how to work one of them motorcars, so I couldn't've killed him," she added with a satisfied smile.

"Pearl could have, though," Carrie said, earning a scowl from Nora.

"Don't you go blaming my Pearl. She loved her father even if he was a rat."

In Sarah's experience, loving someone didn't always stop a person from killing them. In fact, it often gave the killer an added reason to do so. "And why do you think she would have wanted to kill him?"

"Because she was jealous," Carrie said confidently.

"Jealous of who?" Sarah asked.

"Me, of course. Papa loved me more than he loved her. He told me so."

"Carrie, please," Ethel tried, but no one paid her any attention.

"That's crazy," Nora said. "He'd never say no such thing."

"He did, too. He loved me more than he loved Mama or anybody else, and he didn't love you at all," she finished triumphantly to Nora.

Nora's face twisted into a bitter smile. "He might've said that, but he loved me once and he loved Pearl, so if he stopped loving us, he would've stopped loving you someday, too, and then you'd be penniless and abandoned just like we are. Is that what happened? He said he stopped loving you and was going to throw you out, so you killed him?"

Sarah had expected Carrie to laugh at this as she'd laughed before, but her face flooded with color and she surged to her feet. "You're an evil witch and you don't know what you're talking about," she screamed.

Ethel was up in an instant and caught Carrie when she would have lunged for Nora. "Stop it, Carrie. Stop it this instant!"

With her mother's arms wrapped around her, she had no choice, but the look she gave Nora could have drawn blood. Sarah realized she was on her feet as well, and she decided she could help defuse the situation.

"Perhaps you'll see me out, Mrs. Bing," she said to Nora, who registered first surprise but then comprehension.

"Sure. Come on." Nora led the way. "That girl is trouble," she said when she had closed the parlor door behind them.

"She's been through a lot in the past year," Sarah said diplomatically.

"I been through a lot the past twenty years, and you don't see me accusing *her* of murder."

But Sarah was pretty sure she had.

Tom Yingling looked up in surprise when Gino called his name as he made his way down the sidewalk after leaving work. They'd exchanged a greeting that morning, when Gino had arrived at Will Warren's garage, and Tom would no doubt be wondering why Gino was back again.

"Can I buy you a drink?" Gino asked with a friendly smile.

"How can I say no to that?" Tom replied. "There's a bar just around the corner."

This was something you could claim for most streets in New York. Gino fell in beside Tom as they worked their way through the growing crowds of pedestrians trudging home—or some-place else—after a day of labor.

"What brings you back here?" Tom asked, plainly suspicious.

"I found out something interesting today about Mr. Bing's death, and I wanted to ask you about it."

For some reason, Tom looked alarmed at this. "Ask *me?* I don't know nothing about his death."

"Not about his death exactly," Gino hastily explained. "In fact, I just need to know more about Mr. Warren."

Tom was really alarmed now. They'd reached the saloon, but he stopped in front and made no move to go inside. "Why do you need to know anything about Mr. Warren—or Mr. Bing's death, come to that?"

Gino tried his friendly smile again. "Because I'm a private detective and I'm investigating Mr. Bing's death for his wife."

Plainly, this was not good news to Tom. "I should've known. I saw you talking to that other detective in the shop this morning. He was in before, asking questions and getting Mr. Warren all mad."

"We're just trying to find out who killed Mr. Bing," Gino said. "I can't imagine why Mr. Warren would be angry about that."

Tom obviously could and shared his feelings, but he must also understand that refusing to cooperate would look bad for him. "I don't know what I can tell you."

"Then let me buy you a drink, and if you can't answer my questions, it's my loss."

Tom just grunted, but apparently it was in agreement because he continued on into the saloon. The place was rapidly filling up with men seeking refreshment after a hard day's work, so it took a while at the bar before they got served.

Gino suggested they find a place to sit, so they carried their tall beer glasses to a scarred table and scavenged two empty chairs.

"How long have you worked for Mr. Warren?" Gino asked when he'd given Tom time to take a few gulps from his glass.

"A little over a year. He hired me right after he set up the shop."

"Did you already know something about building automobiles?"

"No. Who does? I was good with my hands, though. Didn't take any time at all for me to learn. Mr. Lane was a good teacher."

"Were Mr. Lane and Mr. Warren good friends?"

"Not friends. Mr. Warren is the boss, and he makes sure we remember it."

"That must've been hard for Mr. Lane. He would have been a lot older than Warren."

"He couldn't design autos like Mr. Warren, though, so he respected Mr. Warren. And Mr. Warren respected him right back. He'd ask Mr. Lane what he thought about things. They got along good, I'd say."

"I guess it was a shock when Mr. Lane got killed."

Tom frowned and took another long draw on his beer, not quite meeting Gino's eye. "It was hard on all of us."

"How well do you know Mr. Warren?"

Tom blinked at the sudden change of subject. "I . . . Not real well, I guess."

"Does he have a girl?"

"A girl?"

"Yes, is he keeping company with a young lady? Is there gossip that he might be getting married? I heard he just bought himself a house."

"Yeah, the fellows was talking about that. It's a real nice place, they said. We kind of wondered why he'd spend so much money on a house when the business wasn't doing good."

"Was he losing money, do you think?"

"We did all right, but he wasn't getting rich, and we thought . . ." He looked away, embarrassed.

"What?"

"We thought he should've give us a raise instead of buying a house."

His workers would naturally think that, but there was also some logic to it. If the business was doing so poorly that Warren needed an investor like Bing, where did the money for the house come from?

"But you hadn't heard about Warren having a girl he wanted to marry?"

Tom considered the question for a moment, and then said, "He liked Miss Bing, but everybody does."

"You mean everybody at the shop?"

"Sure. We all thought Miss Bing was fine, but we didn't think she was going to look at any man who has grease on his hands."

Will Warren was more than a mechanic, though. He owned the company, so maybe he had higher hopes than Tom or the other men. Had he bought the house to impress Pearl Bing? And where had the money come from?

IX

Although Frank and Sarah had shared their news with each other, they didn't hear from Gino until he came to the house that night after dinner. With the children tucked in bed, they were able to discuss murder motives freely, and Frank suspected Gino also enjoyed having Maeve's attention without worrying about the children distracting her.

They brought Maeve up to date on what Doyle had told Gino about Bing's "partner" identifying the vehicle and how Will Warren had denied even being at Madison Square that night. Gino also told them about his visit with Tom Yingling and the little information he'd gleaned about Will Warren from him.

Frank then gave Gino and Maeve a summary of his visit to the morgue.

"So whoever killed Bing ran over him and then reversed and ran over him again?" Maeve asked with a wince when Frank had shared what Doc Haynes had told him.

"Well, not all the way over him, apparently," Frank clarified. "It seems the picture in the newspapers was right and the auto's wheel was resting on his chest."

"Ouch. So we can forget the theory that it

might've just been an accident and the driver panicked and ran away," Gino said.

"It does seem that the driver was rather determined to do Mr. Bing some serious harm," Sarah said.

"And do you think Nora could have managed that kind of a maneuver even though she doesn't know how to drive a motorcar?" Maeve asked Sarah.

"After Mr. Warren's instructions this morning, I'm sure I could, so I guess it depends on how much instruction Pearl gave her mother."

"Or Nora could have just observed what Pearl did," Gino said. "Driving one of those electrics is so simple, a child could do it."

"This child would love to do it," Maeve said wistfully.

"Don't look at me," Gino said, raising his hands as if to defend himself. "But you might try cozying up to Will Warren. From what Tom told me, his attempts to impress Pearl Bing have been disappointing."

"Disappointing to who?" Maeve asked with interest.

Gino shrugged. "To Pearl, I guess, which is why Will is also disappointed. The men at the shop think he bought a house to impress her. That's what Tom said, at least."

The two women stared at him in amazement, but Frank said, "He told me he'd recently bought a house, but I didn't have a chance to ask him why."

"How did he happen to tell you that?" Sarah asked.

"He claims he was home the night Bing was killed, and I asked if anyone could confirm that. He said no, he doesn't even have live-in servants yet because he had purchased his house so recently."

"I wonder if he could have another reason for not hiring live-in servants," Sarah mused.

Now everyone stared at *her*. "What do you mean?" Maeve asked.

"I mean Carrie insists that Pearl frequently leaves the house in the evenings, not coming home again until late."

"Would a girl like her really do something so reckless?" Maeve asked with a frown.

"Who knows? Ordinarily, it wouldn't be safe for her go out alone at night, but most girls like her don't have their own motorcars," Sarah said.

"That's true," Maeve marveled. "She might feel perfectly safe in her auto."

"But where would she go?" Gino asked, obviously having missed the implications.

Frank bit back a smile at the contemptuous glares Sarah and Maeve shot him.

"To meet her lover, of course," Maeve said as if explaining something to a child.

"I could've guessed that," Gino said impatiently, "but she doesn't have a lover."

"That you know of," Mother Malloy said from where she sat in her corner. The glow of the electric light cast her face in shadow, making her look even more formidable than usual.

"Mother Malloy is absolutely right," Sarah said, confirming her position as his mother's favorite daughter-in-law. Frank managed not to chuckle at the thought. "If Pearl really is sneaking out at night—and Carrie seemed very sure of that and wasn't just trying to malign Pearl's good name— then she must have a lover we didn't know about."

"Or a lover we know a lot about but didn't know was her lover," Maeve added.

"Do you mean Will Warren?" Gino asked, still obviously confused.

"I think they do," Frank said. "Remember we thought Will was lying about his alibi, but we couldn't figure out why."

"Yes, if he was with Pearl, he wouldn't want to ruin her good name," Sarah said.

"And she's hardly likely to give him as her alibi for the very same reason," Maeve said.

"But everybody thinks Pearl doesn't like him," Gino argued.

"Which means no one would ever suspect they were lovers," Maeve said.

Everyone took a few moments to consider the possibilities.

"Why would they need to keep it a secret, though?" Sarah finally asked.

"Obviously because they thought someone wouldn't approve," Maeve said.

"And Mr. Bing seems the logical choice," Gino added.

"Nora certainly wasn't in any position to approve or disapprove," Sarah said, "and I doubt Pearl would have cared what Nora thought in any case."

"You're probably right," Frank said, considering the other, very limited possibilities. "That leaves Bing and maybe Ethel, although I can't imagine Ethel's opinion would have mattered to anyone."

"But if they just wanted to keep their affair a secret from Mr. Bing," Maeve mused, "why are they still keeping it a secret now that he's dead?"

"Maybe because it gives both of them a good reason to kill her father, so they don't want you to know," Mrs. Malloy suggested from her corner.

"I'm going to put you on the payroll, Ma," Frank said.

"About time, too," she muttered, not even looking up from her knitting.

Frank had to cough to cover a laugh, and he noticed everyone else appreciated his mother's comment as well, although they dared not show it.

"And what if they not only had a reason to kill Mr. Bing but they actually did?" Maeve said, her voice rising with her excitement as she formulated her theory. "What if they decided to drive down to Madison Square that night and confront him?"

"Yes," Sarah said, warming to the topic herself. "Maybe they didn't intend to kill him at all. Maybe they were just going to tell him they were in love and wanted to marry."

"But for whatever reason," Maeve continued, "he still refused to give his consent, so who-ever was driving Pearl's auto ran him over in revenge."

"They would both have had to flee, though," Gino said. "No one would believe his daughter and his partner ran over him by mistake."

"So Pearl headed home, but Will stayed to see what happened," Maeve suggested.

"And that's why Doyle said Bing's *partner* identified the auto," Gino said. "Because Will Warren really was there, no matter what he claims."

"And if he and Pearl ran over Bing, of course he'd deny that he was there," Maeve said.

"And Carrie was telling the truth when she said Pearl goes out at night," Sarah said.

"And Tom thought it was strange that Warren bought himself a house when the business wasn't doing well, but obviously he needed a place to meet Pearl where they wouldn't be seen," Gino said.

"Wait a minute," Frank said. "Did Tom say he didn't think Warren could afford to buy a house?"

"Yes. We already knew the business wasn't doing well," Gino reminded him. "That's why Warren needed Bing to invest, and his employees thought he should have spent the money on the business instead of buying himself a big house he didn't need since he's a bachelor."

"I wonder where the money for the house came from," Sarah said.

"If it came from Mr. Bing's investment and Bing found out, then Warren had another reason for killing him," Maeve remarked.

"We need to speak to Pearl and Warren," Frank said.

"Together or separately?" Gino asked.

"It might be difficult to get them together," Sarah said. "I've found it impossible to even find Pearl at all."

"Then we'll talk to them separately," Frank said. "Gino and I will track down Warren tomorrow."

"He'll probably be in his shop," Gino said.

"You could call on Ethel in the morning," Maeve told Sarah. "Maybe she can tell you a good time to catch Pearl."

Sarah nodded. "Or I can be there before Pearl has time to leave the house."

"Do we really expect them to confess?" Maeve asked with a smirk.

Frank shrugged. "I'd settle for a reasonable explanation. Maybe we're completely wrong about them."

Mother Malloy made a noise that might have been a laugh. "It's happened before."

Sarah had wrestled with the decision of how early was too early, and finally decided that nine o'clock would be a good compromise. Pearl Bing was hardly likely to be out before then, but the residents of the house would most likely be awake and dressed. Maybe not Carrie, but Sarah didn't need to speak to her.

The maid who answered the door seemed a bit distressed, much more distressed than an early caller would explain, and she tried to convince Sarah to leave her card and return later. From the way she kept glancing over her shoulder, however, Sarah didn't think her reluctance to announce Sarah had anything to do with the time of day.

"Is something wrong?" she asked.

The girl actually winced. "I'm sure I don't know, ma'am."

"Something *is* wrong, I can tell, but perhaps I can help."

"I don't know, ma'am." She glanced anxiously over her shoulder again.

"Just tell me what's going on," Sarah said, using the "lady of the manor" voice as she had before. It always worked on reluctant servants.

"Mrs. Bing is sick, ma'am," the girl whispered, her eyes wide with apprehension.

"Ethel?" Sarah asked in surprise.

"No, ma'am, the other Mrs. Bing."

Sarah simply nodded. "I'm sorry to hear it, but I happen to be a nurse, so I will be happy to see what I can do for her."

She strode in without waiting for permission, and the girl stepped back to avoid being knocked down.

"Perhaps you will tell Mrs. Ethel Bing that I'm here."

"I . . . She's with the other Mrs. Bing and—"

"Then I'll just go on up. Which room is it?"

The maid scurried after her, determined to fulfill her duties, no matter how unorthodox Sarah's entrance. She managed to squeeze between Sarah and the door of the room she had indicated, so she could be the one to knock and announce the visitor.

The instant the door opened, Sarah knew Nora was seriously ill. The odor of vomit and excrement assailed her, and she found Ethel standing over Nora's bed, holding a metal bowl while Nora retched into it. Pearl hovered at Ethel's shoulder, wringing her hands helplessly. Neither woman had taken the time to dress yet.

Both Pearl and Ethel looked up impatiently when the maid announced Sarah. Ethel went immediately back to her task while Pearl shot her a venomous glare.

"What are you doing here? Can't you see you're intruding?"

"The maid told me Mrs. Bing was ill, and since I'm a trained nurse, I thought I would see if I could help." Sarah pulled off her gloves and set them and her purse on the dresser before moving to the bed. "How long has she been like this?"

"We aren't sure," Ethel said. "I heard her early this morning. It wasn't quite six yet, but she'd obviously been ill before that."

"She was perfectly fine last night," Pearl said a bit grudgingly. Plainly, she wasn't happy to see Sarah but was willing to accept her help.

Nora had finished and fallen back against the pillows in exhaustion. Sarah nudged Ethel out of the way and touched Nora's forehead. "She doesn't seem to have a fever."

"She was *fine* last night," Pearl insisted desperately.

"Perhaps she ate something bad," Sarah said.

"We all had the same thing for supper," Ethel said. "Mr. Warren ate with us, too. Such a nice young man."

"And no one else is ill?" Sarah asked.

"No one, unless Mr. Warren . . ." Ethel turned to Pearl.

"I can go to the factory and ask him," she said.

Sarah remembered that Malloy was going to see Will Warren this morning, but would he think to let her know if he heard Warren was sick?

"I can drive my auto," Pearl was saying. "It won't take long."

"Yes," Sarah said, "and then we'll know for sure if it was something she ate."

Pearl hurried out. She would have to dress, which would slow her down a bit, but perhaps in the meantime Sarah would have figured out what had made Nora so ill.

"Nora," Sarah said, hoping the woman could hear her.

Nora's eyelids fluttered and finally opened, although she didn't look directly at Sarah. "Can you tell me how you felt when you first got sick?"

Nora blinked a few times and tried to focus on Sarah's face. "I . . . tingly."

"You felt tingling? In your hands? Your feet?"

Nora nodded, and her eyes slid closed again.

"Nora, stay with me. Open your eyes," Sarah urged.

She did, although it took a tremendous effort. "Did you eat or drink anything that no one else did?"

"I . . . don't know."

Sarah turned to Ethel. "We need to call a doctor, and do you have any milk in the house?"

"I'm sure we must, or I can send someone—"

"Get me some milk, as quickly as you can."

"What's wrong with her?" Ethel asked, glancing nervously at Nora, who was lying completely still, hardly even breathing.

"I don't want to say until I'm sure but get the doctor and the milk. Please."

"Yes, of course."

Ethel hurried out even more quickly than Pearl had.

"Stay with me, Nora," Sarah begged, but Nora made a strangled sound and her body began to shake with convulsions, and Sarah knew it was already too late.

Frank's appearance at Warren's garage excited very little notice. The men working near the front nodded a greeting that Frank returned, and one silently indicated that Will Warren was in his office. Frank found him there, working on some papers that were scattered over his desk.

He looked up impatiently, probably ready to scold an employee for interrupting him, but when he saw Frank, the words died on his lips. He just sighed and slumped back in his chair and rubbed a hand over his face. "What is it now? And don't pretend you're interested in buying an electric."

Frank took a seat on one of the wooden chairs available for visitors. "I was just wondering why

Alvin Bing didn't approve of you marrying his daughter."

He watched with interest as various emotions flickered across Warren's face. He finally settled on annoyance. "I wouldn't know. I never wanted to marry his daughter."

"So you were content with having her sneak out to visit you like some doxy?"

Warren was on his feet in defense of Pearl's honor before he realized he shouldn't need to defend it. Frank had risen, too, ready to defend himself, but fortunately, Warren realized his mistake in time and sank back into his chair with a defeated sigh.

"I obviously offended you, Mr. Warren," Frank said by way of apology, "so let me ask you a different way. We know you bought yourself a house where Miss Bing could visit you without being observed by some disapproving landlady or nosy servants. We also know she did visit you, driving herself to your house in her very own auto and staying until late at night, unchaperoned."

"I don't know who told you that, but they're lying. Miss Bing would never do such a thing. Besides, what business is it of yours anyway?"

Frank leaned back in his chair and pretended to consider the question. "It's my business because I'm trying to figure out who killed Alvin Bing. It's turning into a thankless job, because I don't know of anyone except maybe his stepdaughter who seems the least bit sad that he's dead, but nevertheless, I've been hired to do a job and I'll do it. Unfortunately for you, I've found out that you had at least one very good reason for wanting Alvin Bing dead."

"If you mean because I wanted to marry Pearl, that's crazy. She will be of age in a few months, so she wouldn't need Bing's permission for anything."

"But you did need Bing's money."

Warren's eyes narrowed, but he obviously decided not to rise to Frank's bait. "I told you, he invested in my company. That was strictly a business transaction and had nothing to do with me and Pearl."

"Except that you still needed more money, didn't you? Your autos aren't selling well, and you already spent Bing's investment on your new house, didn't you?"

Frank watched in fascination as color flooded Warren's face and neck. He looked as if he might actually explode, and he was half out of his chair when the office door flew open.

"Will, are you all right?" Pearl Bing asked desperately.

Both men blinked at her in surprise. She was obviously distressed and had dressed in a hurry, if the condition of her hair was any indication. Frank rose to his feet instinctively, drawing her attention.

"What are you doing here?" She turned to Warren. "What is he doing here?"

"Asking me questions, as usual."

"And you're all right? You aren't sick?"

"No, not at all. What's wrong?" His annoyance with Frank forgotten, he came around his desk and slipped his arm around her.

"Mother is ill. Very ill." She turned accusingly to Frank. "Mrs. Malloy came for a visit. She's also a nurse, in addition to being a society matron and a detective, it seems. She thought perhaps Mother had eaten something bad, but we all had the same thing for dinner last night and no one else is ill. Mrs. Malloy suggested I make sure you weren't as well."

"Your mother seemed fine last night," Warren said, as if that helped.

"I know. It came on suddenly in the night, I guess." She sighed. "I should get back to her."

Warren glanced dismissively at Frank. "I'll go with you. I'm sure Mr. Malloy will excuse us, under the circumstances."

Under the circumstances, Mr. Malloy would go with them, but he didn't bother to say so.

Ethel had returned almost at once with the milk, but Nora's convulsions made it impossible to get her to drink any. By the time she fell still again, she was beyond help.

"She can't be dead," Ethel insisted in dismay.

223

"She was perfectly fine last night. Pearl said so."

"Try to think, Mrs. Bing," Sarah said gently. "Did Nora eat or drink anything that no one else did?"

"I . . ." Ethel wrung her hands and refused to meet Sarah's eye.

"What is it?"

Ethel glanced at where Nora lay so very still on the bed.

"Come," Sarah said, taking her arm and leading her out of the room.

"We can't just leave her," Ethel protested.

Sarah smiled reassuringly. "She won't know. Which room is yours?"

Ethel pointed and Sarah took her into the bedroom and closed the door. The room was decidedly feminine and was probably the wife's bedroom of the master suite. In spite of the unmade bed, the room was lovely. A pair of stuffed chairs sat in front of the window, and Sarah led Ethel over to them. When they were seated, she said, "You were going to tell me something about Nora. What did she eat that no one else did?"

"Not eat," Ethel said, looking away again as if ashamed.

"Drink, then. What is it?"

"Nora . . . Well, she . . . I suppose being alone all those years in rough places, she developed some unfortunate habits."

"Like drinking?" Sarah guessed.

"At first I was just confused when I thought I smelled liquor on her breath, but then I saw her . . ." She shook her head in silent denial.

"You saw her drinking something?"

"She kept a silver flask in her pocket. She . . . she'd pour a little something into her coffee or tea or whatever she was drinking. She was discreet, but I caught her a few times."

"Do you know where she kept the flask?"

"In her pocket, like I told you."

"But at night or when she wasn't using it?"

"I don't know. Her room, probably."

"What would she have filled it with?"

"Mr. Bing had quite a collection of liquor. I suppose she just took what she wanted."

"Who else would know about her . . . habits?"

"I don't know. Anyone who saw her with the flask, I suppose."

"Did anyone else ever mention it to you?"

Ethel shook her head. "Pearl wouldn't talk to me about her mother, and I doubt if Carrie would care."

"But they could have known?"

"I suppose, but a dollop of whiskey couldn't have killed her. This is so awful. How will I tell Pearl?"

"Don't worry. I'll tell her."

"I still don't know how this could happen, how someone could be well one minute and dead the next."

Sarah knew or at least suspected, but she simply nodded.

She left Ethel to get dressed and returned to the sick room. She would leave the evidence of Nora's last illness for the doctor to examine, but she needed to find Nora's flask before Pearl returned and sent her away.

It was the work of a moment. The flask lay on Nora's bedside table, empty. Sarah still picked it up and dropped it into her own pocket. There might be traces left that could be tested. In Nora's wardrobe she found a bottle of whiskey. It was a brand Sarah recognized as one of her own father's favorites. Mr. Bing had expensive tastes.

Sarah was holding the bottle up to the light to better examine the residue that had collected at the bottom when Ethel escorted the doctor into the room.

"What are you doing there?" he demanded of her.

She gave Ethel an apologetic look. "Checking for arsenic."

Frank was beginning to agree with Sarah that they needed an electric auto. By the time he had cranked his motor to life, Warren and Pearl were well on their way to the Bing house. At least they wouldn't see him following them, which he supposed was a small blessing.

He had to knock at the Bings' front door, and he wasn't at all surprised when it took a while for someone to answer. If Nora was ill, things were bound to be upset in the household. Finally, a harried maid opened the door and was ready to send him away when he pushed past her.

"Sir, you can't just come in!"

"My wife is here, Mrs. Malloy. She's . . ." He stopped when they both heard the anguished cry from upstairs. Could that be Nora?

But no, Frank recognized the tone of it. He'd heard grief like that before. "Is Mrs. Bing . . . ?" he asked, gesturing vaguely.

The maid winced. "I think so, sir. The doctor came, but it was too late."

Poor Nora, who had just discovered her beloved child. Poor Pearl, who had now lost her mother twice. And poor Sarah. She so hated to lose a patient.

The wail of grief had given way to shouting, and Frank's instinct was to find a quiet corner to wait it out, but he knew better than to show cowardice. "Maybe I can help," he told the astonished maid. Luckily, she made no move to stop him when he started up the stairs.

"You did something to her," Pearl was shouting at someone, and when he reached the top of the stairs, he saw the someone was Sarah. The two were standing in the hallway with Ethel hovering anxiously nearby.

Sarah bore the accusation stoically. "I did what I could, but it was too late," Sarah said gently. "I'm so very sorry."

"She was alive when I left! I never should have left her!" Pearl cried.

"There was nothing you could have done," Ethel said. "Right after you left, she started shaking and then . . ."

"No! She can't be dead!" Pearl screamed, covering her ears as if she could shut out the truth.

Will Warren tried to put his arm around her, but she shrugged him off, refusing to be comforted.

"Why is everyone screaming?" a new voice demanded.

They all turned to see that a sleep-tousled Carrie had emerged from her bedroom, looking disgruntled.

"It's Mrs. Bing, dear," Ethel said, hurrying to her daughter, who hadn't even bothered to pull a robe on over her nightdress. Carrie's full breasts strained against the fabric, making Frank realize she didn't look like a child, even if she still was one. "She's . . . she's quite ill, I'm afraid," Ethel added.

"She's ill?" Carrie echoed with a frown.

"Well, she *was* ill, and now . . . now I'm afraid she's passed away."

"Passed away?" Carrie repeated as if it were a challenge. "You mean she's dead?"

Pearl moaned, covering her face with her hands.

"Yes, she's dead," Ethel said as if the words hurt her.

Carrie nodded and, without another word, returned to her room, closing her door decisively.

"Miss Bing?" An officious-looking man of middle age who must be the doctor had emerged from the door nearest the gathered group. "You may come in now."

Pearl's face drained of all color and she reached out blindly for Will Warren, who took her arm and was finally allowed to assist her. The doctor led the two of them back into the bedroom while Sarah and Ethel looked on.

Only then did Sarah seem to realize Frank was there.

"Malloy, I'm so glad to see you," she said, smiling in spite of everything.

He went to her. "What happened?" he asked in a whisper.

She drew him farther down the hallway, away from Ethel, who just continued to stare helplessly at the open bedroom door. "Nora got very sick during the night. Ethel and Pearl were trying to care for her when I arrived but . . . Oh, darling, I'm afraid she was poisoned."

"Poisoned? Are you sure?"

"As sure as I can be without actual proof. According to everyone, Nora was fine last night.

The only thing she ate or drank that was different from everyone else was when she took a nip from her flask. Maybe more than a nip, in fact."

"She was a drinker?" he marveled.

"According to Ethel, and I did find the flask on her bedside table, empty. I also found a half-full bottle of whiskey with a suspicious residue in the bottom hidden in her room."

Pearl was sobbing now as Warren escorted her out of her mother's room. Ethel hurried to help, although Frank couldn't imagine Pearl would welcome her assistance.

"I suppose we'd better talk to the doctor," he said, and Sarah rolled her eyes.

"I haven't been able to convince him, but maybe he'll listen to you."

Yes, he would, Frank decided, and Frank would make sure he was sorry he hadn't listened to Sarah in the first place. She followed him into Nora's bedroom. The lingering odors nearly gagged him, but he braced himself, having learned to deal with such things as a beat cop collecting drunks on Saturday night.

The doctor looked up from where he had been returning his instruments to his medical bag. "And who are you?"

"Frank Malloy. You've met my wife, I assume."

The doctor glanced impatiently at Sarah. "Yes, she has expressed her theory that Mrs. Bing was poisoned, although I can see no evidence of it. This is clearly a case of gastritis."

"Do your patients usually die in a matter of hours from gastritis?" Frank asked.

Plainly, the doctor wasn't used to being challenged. "It varies, of course. Some succumb more quickly than others."

"But a few hours would be unusual, wouldn't it?"

"I . . . I suppose it would," he admitted reluctantly.

"What evidence would you expect to find if it was arsenic?" Frank asked.

"Well, I . . ." He glanced at Nora's body. She looked shrunken now, without the force of her personality to fill her. "Jaundice, I suppose."

Sarah stepped around Frank for a closer look. "She does look a bit jaundiced, doesn't she?"

The doctor glared at her but didn't disagree.

"I asked her how she'd felt when she first got sick," Sarah told Frank, obviously having given up trying to reason with the doctor. "She said she had tingling in her hands and feet."

"That's a symptom of arsenic poisoning, isn't it?" Frank asked the doctor.

"It can be caused by many things," the doctor hedged.

"And my wife said she found a bottle of whiskey with some kind of residue in it."

"I cannot make a determination from something

like that. What kind of a doctor would I be if I went around announcing that people had been poisoned just because they had a bottle of whiskey nearby?"

"You'd be a good doctor if you let the police know you attended a suspicious death and request the bottle be tested, along with the flask we know Mrs. Bing drank from."

"I am not in the habit of notifying the police whenever one of my patients dies," the doctor informed them.

"Are you unaware that this lady's husband was recently murdered?"

The doctor's eyes grew big. "I had no idea."

"You are probably also unaware that my wife is a trained nurse whose first husband was a physician like yourself. For my part, I am a private investigator and have been hired to find Mr. Bing's killer. We both have investigated arsenic poisonings, and I fully intend to notify the police that Mrs. Bing has died under mysterious circumstances. I will also be happy to see the incident is duly reported in all the important newspapers. May I have your name, so I can give it to the reporters? They'll want to know why you didn't report it yourself."

"You certainly may not have my name!" the doctor huffed, outraged.

"That's all right. The family will know it.

Don't bother to engage a funeral home. We'll be sending Mrs. Bing's body for an autopsy."

"You can't do that!"

"The family can," Sarah said, "and that is certainly what we will advise them to do."

The doctor glared at both of them for a long moment and finally heaved a sigh. "All right. I suppose it's possible that Mrs. Bing was poisoned, but who would do such a thing and why?"

"Answering those questions is my job, Doctor."

"It would probably be someone in this house," the doctor pointed out.

"We have thought of that already," Frank said.

"I suppose you expect me to notify the police," the doctor said, resigned now.

"Let me suggest you speak to the detective who is investigating Mr. Bing's death."

The doctor sighed again. "I guess I have no choice."

X

While Malloy finished up with the doctor, Sarah went to find Ethel and Pearl. They were in the back parlor, which was the room where the family would typically gather. Pearl and Will were sitting on the sofa. Pearl was weeping quietly, and Will Warren was patting her back the way one did to offer comfort, although Sarah had never figured out how that could help. Maybe just the physical contact was enough.

Ethel hovered nearby, obviously wanting to help but having no idea how. She seemed relieved to see Sarah. "What did the doctor say?"

"He agrees that you should request an autopsy," Sarah said, fudging the truth just a bit.

"An autopsy?" Pearl echoed, looking up from weeping into her handkerchief. "What's that?"

Sarah took a moment to select the proper phrasing. "A physician associated with the police examines the body to discover how the person died." No use explaining any more than that since the full facts would only horrify her listeners.

"But the doctor said it was gastritis," Ethel said with a worried frown.

"An autopsy would tell us what caused the gastritis, though. I know you both were surprised it came on so suddenly."

"But it could have been something she ate," Ethel said. "You said so yourself."

"We all ate the same thing," Pearl said, "and none of us is sick."

Ethel's expression hardened. "We didn't all drink from her flask."

Pearl's face flushed scarlet. "How dare you?" she asked through gritted teeth.

"Excess drinking can make a person gravely ill," Ethel insisted.

"Mother didn't drink to excess," Pearl insisted right back.

"There's no need to be unkind," Mr. Warren said. The women looked at him in surprise. Obviously, they had all forgotten he was there.

"If that is the case," Sarah said, "the autopsy will show it."

"Then by all means, we will have one," Pearl said, still glaring at Ethel. "What do I have to do?"

"The doctor will notify the police," Sarah said.

"The police?" Ethel echoed in dismay.

"I'm sorry, but yes, they will have to be involved."

Ethel was now wringing her hands. "But this is so unnecessary. You can't think . . . I mean, who would even want to harm Nora? And why? It doesn't make any sense."

It made sense to Sarah, though. They'd thought perhaps Nora had killed Alvin Bing out of revenge, but Nora may have just known something that made the real killer fear she would figure out the truth.

"Why aren't we eating breakfast?" Carrie asked from the doorway. She'd dressed since her last appearance, although her hair was still hanging loose and tangled. "I'm starving."

"You ate like a pig last night at dinner," Pearl said nastily. "I can't imagine you'd be hungry again for a week."

But Carrie simply ignored her. "It made my stomach hurt, too," she complained to her mother.

"You should have told me, dear. I would have given you something."

But Sarah wanted more information. "Did you say it made your stomach hurt?"

Carrie frowned. "Yes," she admitted reluctantly.

"Did you vomit? Or—"

"She gets heartburn," Ethel quickly explained.

"And no, I didn't vomit. How disgusting," Carrie snapped, giving Sarah the kind of glare that Pearl had perfected.

"How often does she get it?" Sarah asked, wondering if someone could possibly be trying to poison Carrie, too, but with less success.

"Mostly after supper," Ethel said reluctantly, obviously not sure if she should be answering Sarah's questions or not.

"Because she stuffs herself," Pearl sniped.

"I do not stuff myself," Carrie sniped right back. "I have a healthy appetite. Papa said so!"

Pearl jumped to her feet. "You have no right to call him *Papa*. He wasn't your father!"

"He told me to!" Carrie cried. "He said I was a better daughter to him than you ever were!"

"Liar!" Pearl screamed, and lunged for Carrie.

Only Will Warren's quick reactions saved Carrie. He grabbed Pearl and held her back.

"I'm not lying, and you know it," Carrie taunted. "He told you. I know he did. I heard you arguing about it."

"Carrie, stop," her mother pleaded as Pearl struggled against Will's restraint.

"Carrie, come with me," Sarah said, taking the girl's arm in a no-nonsense grip.

"Let me go," Carrie tried, stumbling as Sarah pulled her from the room.

"You're being cruel," Sarah informed her. "Pearl just lost her mother, and you're only adding to her pain."

"She shouldn't have made fun of me," Carrie whined as Sarah propelled her to the staircase. "Where are we going?"

"To your room, where you can't upset anyone."

Malloy and the doctor were coming down the stairs, so they had to wait.

"The doctor is going to explain to Miss Bing why he recommends an autopsy," Malloy told her smugly as they passed.

"Thank you, Doctor." Sarah had managed to say it without a trace of irony.

The doctor pretended not to hear her.

Sarah bit back a smile and nudged Carrie into motion again. This time Carrie seemed determined to prove Sarah wasn't forcing her, so she marched up the stairs and went straight to her room.

Sarah caught the door when Carrie would have slammed it behind her, and stepped inside.

"Now what do you want?" Carrie said. "And I'm still starving."

"I'll ask your mother to send you up a tray. I was wondering about your stomachache."

"I told you, I get them all the time."

"All the time? Since when?"

Carrie shrugged. "A week or two, I guess."

"And you never throw up or have loose stools?"

"Ew, no."

At least it appeared that no one was trying to poison Carrie, although Sarah could certainly understand the temptation. "You should be kinder to Pearl. You know how painful it is to lose a parent."

Carrie groaned. "But she's so mean to me."

Which reminded Sarah of something Carrie had said downstairs. "You overheard Pearl and her father arguing."

Carrie smirked and plopped herself down on her unmade bed. "Yes, I did."

"When was this?"

"The night before he died." She was still smirking.

"Do you know what they were arguing about?"

"Of course I do. Papa told her I was his favorite now and she should think about getting married and moving out of his house."

What a horrible thing to say to one's daughter, if Carrie was indeed telling the truth. It would also give Pearl a very good reason for running over Alvin Bing and leaving him to die in the street. "I gather Pearl wasn't too happy to hear this."

"She was furious. They both said some ugly things, but Papa won the argument because what could Pearl say?"

What indeed? How awful for the poor girl, and what a horrible man Alvin Bing was. No wonder Ethel wanted a divorce. "She must have been terribly hurt, and now she's lost her mother, too. Perhaps you could at least try being kinder to her. She might return the favor."

Carrie's lovely eyes narrowed. "What do you care anyway?"

Sarah sighed. Indeed, the well-being of the Bing clan was really none of her concern, since it hardly brought her any closer to figuring out who had killed Alvin and now his long-lost wife, Nora. "I can't help myself, and there's no reason for all of you to be at odds."

Carrie made a rude noise. "You don't know everything, do you?"

"What does that mean?"

"See, you don't even know what I meant!" Carrie crowed.

"Do you mean I don't know everything about your family? I'm sure that's true. What do you think I should know?"

"I don't think you should know anything at all. I think Mother and I should throw Pearl out and be done with her. Papa was already done with her, so why shouldn't we be?"

"Was Mr. Bing planning to throw Pearl out?" Sarah asked in amazement.

Carrie didn't answer immediately, letting Sarah know she was making up her answer. "He would have, if I'd asked him to."

"He would have thrown his own daughter out of his house because his stepdaughter asked him to?" Sarah asked, letting her skepticism show.

"He would've done anything for me, and he sure wouldn't've let me go hungry. I told you I want my breakfast. I'm starving."

"Yes, and you have a healthy appetite," Sarah said with a sigh. "As I promised, I'll ask your mother to send up a tray."

Glad for the opportunity to escape this annoying child, Sarah fled. What on earth had made her think she could talk sense to the girl?

Frank found the beat cop for that neighborhood and asked him to use the nearest call box to send for Detective Sergeant Doyle. Doyle must have been intrigued by the summons because he wasted no time in getting to the Bing house. The doctor had left long since, pleading a waiting room full of patients, but he had assured Frank he wouldn't try to convince Doyle not to order an autopsy.

Sarah had, in the meantime, gotten the remaining women of the house to eat some breakfast, and Carrie even brushed her hair. For his part, Will Warren hadn't even hinted that he should return to his shop. He obviously wasn't going to waste this opportunity to be of service to Pearl.

When Doyle arrived, he didn't look nearly as happy as he should have, considering Frank was handing him a murder case. "Malloy. I should've known I'd have to deal with you sooner or later after your flunky came around."

Frank grinned without humor. "I won't tell my *partner* that you called him a flunky, and you can thank me for saving your life."

Doyle snorted his dismissal of such a prospect. "Where's the dead woman?"

Frank took him upstairs to show him the body and the whiskey bottle and flask Sarah had found. Frank hadn't known what to expect, but in spite of his lukewarm attitude, Doyle was at least taking Frank's explanations seriously.

"And this woman was married to Alvin Bing?" Doyle said, scribbling in his notebook.

"She was his first wife, and as far as we know,

he never divorced her, although he married another woman about nine months ago." Frank briefly explained Nora's recent reappearance.

"And all of them were living here in the same house?" Doyle marveled.

"Only for the past week or so. Nora here"— Frank gestured to the figure on the bed—"moved in after Bing died and she realized she probably had a claim to the house, since she was still his legal wife."

"*Do* you think that's why somebody poisoned her? To get the inheritance?"

"Uh, no. Bing left a will, and she didn't inherit anything at all," Frank said.

Doyle frowned. "Then why kill her?"

"We think she may have figured out who killed Bing."

Doyle sighed. "But I don't suppose you've figured it out yet, have you?"

As frustrated as he was, Frank had to admit he didn't mind telling Doyle the truth, since it would annoy him. "Not yet, no."

"Have you at least narrowed it down?"

"We think it's one of the women or his partner, Will Warren."

"Thank God for small favors."

"You can also thank *me,* because they are all still right here in the house for you to question."

Doyle's glare held no gratitude. "I suppose you'll want to sit in, too."

"If you wouldn't mind," Frank said graciously.

Doyle looked like he minded very much, but he said, "Where are they?"

Sarah had separated Ethel and Carrie from Pearl and Will, and Doyle wanted to speak to each of them individually, so Frank suggested starting with Will, who could then be dismissed to return to his shop. Doyle agreed, so Pearl went to her room while Doyle sat down opposite Will Warren in the formal parlor. Frank took a chair off to the side so he could more easily watch Warren's reactions.

Doyle asked the usual questions about Warren's identity, his occupation, and his relationship to the family. Warren identified himself as Alvin Bing's partner, jogging Frank's memory about something Gino had told them earlier.

"Wait a minute, Doyle," Frank said, earning a scowl from both Doyle and Warren. "Don't you already know Mr. Warren?"

Doyle glanced at Warren as if just making sure and said, "I don't think so."

"But you told my *partner*," Frank said, taking a small amount of pleasure in the word, "that Alvin Bing's *partner* had identified him and his motorcar for you the night Bing was killed."

"And I told you, I wasn't there that night," Warren said.

Doyle took another considering look at Warren. "This isn't the fellow who told me about the automobile belonging to Bing."

Warren seemed to think he was exonerated. "I told you," Warren reminded Frank again.

Which only proved that Warren wasn't the one who told Doyle about the automobile belonging to Bing. He still could have been there to run over Bing.

"And I suppose Miss Bing will swear that the two of you were together somewhere else the night Bing died," Frank said.

But Warren wasn't going to be tricked into betraying Pearl. "Nobody has to swear anything because we weren't there. He just proved it," Warren insisted, gesturing to Doyle.

Doyle scratched his head, but Frank guessed he wasn't really confused. "Where were you, then, if you don't mind my asking?"

"I was at home. Mr. Bing didn't think I did a good job of talking to potential customers, so he didn't want me at the automobile show."

"Were you alone?"

Warren glanced at Frank, and while his instinct still might be to protect Pearl's good name, he couldn't help the flush that crawled up his face. "Yes, I was alone."

"That's too bad. Prosperous young fellow like you should have a loyal wife to swear you were home all night," Doyle said pleasantly. "Of course, I wouldn't believe her, but you should still have one."

Warren's flush grew darker, but he bit back whatever he might have wanted to say.

"However, the reason I'm here today is because Mrs. Bing is now dead," Doyle said when Warren remained silent. "I don't suppose you have any idea who might've wanted her dead."

"I don't know that anyone did."

"Well, we're pretty sure somebody put arsenic into her bedtime libation, so it would appear that someone did."

"Maybe she did it herself," Will said.

Doyle seemed to consider that possibility for a moment, and Frank *actually* considered it. Could they have missed something? "Why would she do that?"

"Well, she came to New York to find Pearl and get revenge on her husband," Warren said. "Pearl wasn't very glad to see her and didn't want a reunion with her mother, who turned out to be somewhat of a drudge."

"That's pretty mean, Mr. Warren," Doyle said.

"I'm just telling you what Pearl thought, at least when Mrs. Bing first got here," Warren said. "I think she was a bit embarrassed by her. Nora's daughter didn't want her, and her husband had married another woman, so she . . . she killed Bing."

"Did Mrs. Bing know how to operate a motor-car, Mr. Warren?"

"It's not difficult." He glanced at Frank again.

"I showed Mrs. Malloy how to drive one in just a few minutes."

"Did somebody show Mrs. Bing how to operate one?"

"I don't know, but Pearl might have. In any case, Nora probably ran over Mr. Bing, but then her conscience started to bother her, and she realized Bing hadn't left her anything and Pearl didn't want to acknowledge her, so she killed herself."

It could be true, Frank had to admit. They had considered Nora a good prospect to be the killer. Still, others had a good reason for killing Bing, too, and Nora didn't seem like the type to let her conscience bother her that much. "Tell Detective Sergeant Doyle how you could afford to buy yourself a house, Mr. Warren," Frank said.

This time Warren's face turned almost purple as he glared at Frank.

"Yes, Mr. Warren, do tell," Doyle said.

It took Warren a few moments to find his voice. "As Mr. Malloy knows, I used the money Mr. Bing had invested in my automobile business."

"Did Mr. Bing know that?" Doyle asked.

Warren looked like he could chew nails. "No."

Doyle nodded sagely. "I'm guessing he wouldn't have been too pleased if he found out, though."

Warren didn't bother to answer him.

"What could he have done if he did find out, Mr. Warren?" Doyle asked with interest.

Warren shifted uncomfortably in his chair. "Asked for the money back, I assume."

"Or taken the house?" Doyle guessed.

"I don't know. You'd have to ask a lawyer."

But Frank was nodding. "And your efforts to impress Miss Bing would have been for nothing."

"Is that what the house was for?" Doyle asked. "To impress Miss Bing?"

Warren could hardly control himself now. Plainly, Miss Bing was his weak spot. "I won't discuss Miss Bing with the likes of you."

"The likes of me?" Doyle echoed in feigned amusement. "In that case, I guess I need to speak with Miss Bing myself."

Before Warren could object to that, the maid tapped at the parlor door to tell them the men had arrived to take the body to the morgue. Doyle went to oversee the process, leaving Frank and Warren alone.

"Why can't you just leave Miss Bing alone?" Warren demanded. "She's suffered enough."

"I would be glad to leave her and you both alone if you'd just tell me the truth about what happened the night Bing died."

"I keep telling you, I don't have any idea what happened."

"Because you were at home," Frank remembered. "Were you at home alone with Miss Bing that night?"

"If you expect me to slander Miss Bing to save myself, you're crazy."

"What about saving Miss Bing? She had reasons to be angry with her father as well."

"You can't prove she was at Madison Square that night either."

"I can prove she wasn't at home that night," Frank lied, figuring he was probably right about Pearl being with Warren, "and if she wasn't with you, where was she?"

Warren opened his mouth to protest, but Sarah came in the still-open door and distracted him. "Mr. Warren, Detective Sergeant Doyle asked me to tell you that he's finished with you. You can return to your shop now."

"But—"

"He's going to question Miss Bing next, and you can't be with her," Sarah said as nicely as if she were apologizing to him.

"You can't expect her to be alone in a room with two men," Warren protested valiantly.

"I'll sit with her," Sarah said, exchanging a look with Frank, who nodded his approval.

"My wife will make sure no one offends her."

Plainly, offending Miss Bing had not been Warren's concern. "I'd like to speak with her before I go."

Sarah glanced over her shoulder, and they all heard the tromp of feet as the men from the morgue carried their burden down the stairs. "I'll go up for her as soon as . . ." She stepped into the room, out of the men's way while the procession passed the doorway, and they all waited for the grim task to be completed.

Detective Sergeant Doyle was apparently bringing up the rear and when he reached the parlor door, he stuck his head in and said, "You can go back to your place of business, Mr. Warren. I'll let you know if I need to question you again."

"But I need to speak with Miss Bing."

"Not before I do," Doyle said cheerfully. "Do you need a maid to show you out?"

Warren sighed in defeat. "I can find my own way."

He did, and when he was gone, Frank said, "Have you met my wife, Doyle?"

"Pleased to make your acquaintance, Mrs. Malloy," Doyle said. He knew better than to show Sarah any disrespect, but Frank could see he was actually impressed. Sarah knew how to be impressive.

"I'd like to sit in with Miss Bing when you question her, if you don't mind," she said, showing Doyle much more deference than Frank thought he deserved.

"Yes, I guess we must observe the proprieties," Doyle said, plainly amused by that thought.

Sarah smiled. "I may also know some things you don't, and I can help you get the truth out of her."

Doyle widened his eyes, but he didn't respond as most men would have, by dismissing such a claim out of hand. "I would appreciate your help."

"Thank you," Sarah said. "I'll go fetch her, shall I?"

Sarah went up to Pearl's room and knocked. Pearl came to open the door instead of just inviting her visitor in, peering out a crack before pulling the door completely open. "What do you want?"

"Detective Sergeant Doyle would like to speak with you now."

Pearl sighed in dismay. "Must I?"

"Yes, I'm afraid you must. I'll stay with you, though, so you don't have to face him alone."

"I'm not afraid of him," she protested.

"Mr. Warren was concerned about the propriety of you being alone with a policeman, I think."

She actually laughed at that. "He's a fine one to be concerned about my good name. I don't want *him* there, though."

Now, wasn't that interesting? "He's gone back to his shop, I believe."

"Thank heaven for that."

Sarah wanted to ask why Pearl was so glad to see the last of Will Warren, but she bit her tongue and followed Pearl downstairs.

Sarah was glad to see Malloy had chosen to remain in the room for Pearl's interview, although

Pearl cast him a murderous glance before taking her seat on the chair opposite Doyle.

Doyle began with the usual questions about her name and her relationship to the dead woman.

"I understand you had been estranged from your mother for a number of years," Doyle said.

"Not estranged. I thought she was dead," Pearl said.

"Why did you think that?"

Pearl's lips tightened and her hands closed into fists, but she managed to say, "My father told me she was."

"Do you know why your father would tell you your mother was dead when she wasn't?"

"I think . . . I think he wanted to get rid of her, and he left her behind when we moved on to a new town. By telling me she had died, he ensured I wouldn't ever wonder why she didn't join us or want to go back and look for her."

"You must have been pretty angry at him when you found out he'd lied to you and she was still alive."

"We had words, yes, but he . . ." She sighed with what might have been resignation. ". . . he explained that he wanted to get me away from her. She wasn't a good influence and he wanted me to become a fine lady."

"Did you agree that she wasn't a good influence?" Sarah asked, earning a frown from Doyle, which she ignored.

Pearl turned to her impatiently. "You met her. She certainly isn't a fine lady."

Sarah noticed Pearl still spoke of Nora in the present tense. "But she is still your mother."

Pearl chose not to reply to that and turned back to Doyle. "And before you ask, no, I did not want my mother to really be dead. For all her failings, she is still my mother."

"Were you surprised when she moved in here?" Doyle asked.

"Not at all. I suggested it. She was my father's lawful widow, after all, and she had every right to live in his house."

"You were reconciled, then," Doyle observed.

"As I said, we were never estranged in the first place. We were getting to know each other again, however, and I had no reason to want her dead. I'd just lost my father, and that was painful enough."

"Were you and your father arguing over Nora the night before he died?" Sarah asked.

This time Doyle didn't look annoyed, just interested, but Malloy actually gasped, although Sarah forced herself not to glance over at him. Pearl was the one who looked annoyed. "What makes you think I argued with my father?"

"Someone overheard you," Sarah said. "Was your father upset that you had gone to see your mother?"

"If someone overheard us, then you probably

already know what we argued about," Pearl said in disgust.

"But *I* don't," Doyle said, "so why don't you tell me?"

Pearl's lips and fists tightened again, but she lifted her chin as if bracing for a fight. "He was encouraging me to marry."

"He wanted you to marry Mr. Warren?" Doyle asked in apparent surprise. Indeed, Sarah had to agree Warren didn't seem like an equal match for Pearl, regardless of the indications that she was seeing him secretly.

"I don't think he particularly cared who I married. He just thought it was time some man took me off his hands now that he had a new family to think of." She didn't even try to hide her bitterness.

How horrible. Sarah couldn't help feeling sympathy for a girl whose life had revolved around her father only to have him reject her when he took a new wife.

But was it the wife who had supplanted her? Ethel herself had said her marriage to Alvin had been loveless. Carrie was the one claiming to have taken Pearl's place in his affections, and he had obviously doted on her, too.

"So, you had a good reason to be angry with your father," Doyle was saying.

Pearl stiffened, but she said nothing, meeting Doyle's gaze defiantly.

"Did you drive your automobile down to Madison Square that night and when he came over to meet you, knock him down and run him over?"

"I wasn't there that night," Pearl said.

"Where were you, then?" Doyle asked.

Pearl took a breath. "I was at home."

"No, you weren't," Sarah said. "We know that."

Pearl gave her a long, considering look. "I was with Mr. Warren."

"At the automobile show?" Doyle asked eagerly.

Pearl's gaze drifted back to him and she actually smiled. "No. I was with Mr. Warren at his home. Alone."

Sarah almost sighed with relief, but she knew better than to show a reaction.

"Mr. Warren said he was home alone," Doyle said.

Pearl shook her head at this. "What else would you expect a gentleman to say?"

"Why did you go to see Mr. Warren that night?" Sarah asked.

"Why do you think?" Pearl asked haughtily.

"Then you and Warren are lovers?" Doyle asked.

Pearl sighed in dismay at their naïveté.

"But you must have had a specific reason for going to see him that night," Sarah said. "Your mother, who you'd thought was dead, had suddenly returned and was demanding your attention. You had discovered that the father to whom you were devoted had been lying to you

254

for years. Then you'd quarreled with him because he wanted you to marry and leave his house. You must have been very upset."

"Do you think I went to Will for *comfort?*" Pearl scoffed.

"If that's what you want to call it," Doyle said snidely.

"Mr. Warren was obviously correct in worrying about Miss Bing being alone with you," Sarah said sharply, making Doyle flinch.

"My apologies, Miss Bing," Doyle said with only slight reluctance. "But let me get this straight—you were with Mr. Warren at his house the night your father was killed."

"Yes."

"Can you tell me when you arrived and when you left?"

"I usually wait until Ethel and Carrie have retired, around ten o'clock. Then I drive my auto to Will's house. That night I believe I stayed until a little after one o'clock."

"Usually? Does that mean you've been there before?" Doyle glanced at Sarah and was careful not to leer.

Pearl narrowed her eyes, but she said, "Yes. Several times."

Doyle scratched his head, as if he were puzzled. "If your father wanted you to get married and he had no objection to Mr. Warren, why would you have to sneak out to meet him?"

"I have no intention of marrying Mr. Warren."

Doyle blinked in surprise and Sarah had to admit she was probably blinking herself. She didn't dare meet Malloy's eye. She held her breath, hoping Doyle would ask the right question next. Fortunately, he did.

"If you aren't going to marry Warren, why were you, uh, meeting him?"

"To make my father . . . notice."

"Notice what? That you had a lover?" Doyle asked, not having to feign confusion now.

Pearl shook her head, obviously despairing of Doyle's insight. "Yes."

Sarah's mind was racing. Pearl was sneaking out to meet Will Warren at his house, presumably so they could do what lovers did, but she had no intention of marrying him. She had taken a lover only to make her father pay attention to her because . . . Because why? Because she was jealous of her father's attentions to Carrie? That seemed extreme and also rather childish. Surely, Pearl was beyond such pettiness, and why would she destroy her reputation for such a stupid reason? Besides, it had obviously been for nothing since her father apparently hadn't cared.

Doyle cleared his throat as if to rid himself of his confusion. "So, you and Mr. Warren were together at his house the night your father was killed."

"Yes. If you tell him that I have revealed it, he

will confirm it, I'm sure. He has only been trying to protect my reputation, which is why he hasn't admitted it before."

"And I don't suppose you had any reason to kill your mother," Doyle said with obvious resignation.

"No reason at all. I had just found her again. We were planning to find a place of our own, so we didn't have to rely on Ethel anymore."

Sarah wondered how they were planning to pay for that, but she decided not to ask.

"If that is all, I'd like to return to my room," Pearl said. "I just lost my mother, after all, and I'm quite distraught."

"Sure. I'll let you know if I have any more questions," Doyle said, standing when Pearl did and watching with narrowed eyes as she left the room.

"What do you think?" Malloy asked.

Doyle shrugged. "One will lie and the other will swear to it. There's no telling where they were the night Bing died."

"Yeah," Malloy said. "They could've been together at his house or one of them could've been off killing Bing and the other would say they were together."

"Or," Sarah said, "they could have both been at Madison Square killing Mr. Bing."

Doyle gave Malloy a dark look. "I thought you were going to *help* me with this case."

XI

Frank had thought they would finally get Pearl or Will to tell the truth, but now they were all more confused than ever. He turned to Sarah.

"How did you know Pearl and her father had argued?"

"Carrie told me."

"Carrie is a regular little busybody, isn't she?"

"Carrie is the other Mrs. Bing's daughter, right?" Doyle asked.

"Yes," Frank said wearily. "She also claimed to have seen Pearl sneaking out at night and coming back home late."

"Maybe she saw somebody poison Nora Bing," Doyle said sarcastically. "I suppose we could ask her."

"And she'd probably make up an answer for you," Sarah said. "I'm not sure Carrie always tells the truth."

"She's been pretty reliable so far," Frank pointed out.

"I don't suppose her mother will let us question her alone," Doyle said.

"I can offer to sit in as I did for Pearl," Sarah said. "She might agree to that. Maybe if you question Mrs. Bing first and she sees what a gentleman you are, she'll feel better about it."

"Of course, you'd have to *act* like a gentleman," Frank reminded Doyle, who glared at him.

Doyle didn't dignify Frank's jibe with a reply, but he turned to Sarah with a spark of annoyance. "Do you know anything else that you haven't told us?"

"Carrie *just* told me about the argument between Pearl and her father a little while ago and I didn't have an opportunity to let you know," Sarah said by way of apology. "She also claims that Mr. Bing would have thrown Pearl out of the house if Carrie asked him to."

"And she probably would have asked him to," Frank said.

"Maybe she already did and that's why Bing was trying to marry Pearl off," Doyle guessed.

"You should certainly ask Carrie," Sarah said, "but bear in mind, she may not tell you the truth."

"I guess we need to question the mother first," Doyle said, "so I can show her how nice I am."

"I don't think you'll need me for this," Sarah said. "I'll send her in."

Sarah left, and Doyle turned to Frank. "Where did you find a woman like that?"

Frank couldn't help smiling. "You wouldn't believe me if I told you."

"Just tell me, was it the money?"

Frank couldn't help laughing at that. "No. I won her long before I got the money."

Doyle didn't look like he believed that, but he didn't challenge it.

Ethel Bing wasted no time in answering their summons, but when he saw her, Frank began to regret not having Sarah to help with this interview. Ethel looked as fragile as an eggshell and as nervous as a cat.

"There's nothing to worry about, Mrs. Bing," Frank hastened to assure her, ushering her to a chair as if he were the host and she the guest. "We just need to verify a few facts with you."

Her face was white, and she had clasped her hands together tightly in her lap, probably to keep them from trembling. "I don't know anything I haven't already told you."

"Maybe you don't realize what you know," Doyle said, taking the seat opposite her. "We understand that Pearl sometimes goes out at night in her automobile."

"Oh dear, I don't think I should gossip about poor Pearl. She's been through so much . . ."

"Mrs. Bing . . ." Doyle caught himself. "Should I call you Mrs. Bing?"

She actually flinched. "I don't suppose you should. I truly thought myself married to Mr. Bing, but I was also wrong. I . . . . You may address me as Mrs. Lane. I do know I am legally entitled to that name."

To his credit, Doyle nodded and went on without making any snide comments. "Mrs. Lane, information you give to the police is not considered gossip, even if it reflects poorly on someone. We just need to know what happened. Miss Bing has already confirmed that she sometimes left the house alone at night and went to visit Mr. Warren at his home."

Poor Ethel looked stricken, but she said, "I knew she went out, but I couldn't know where she went, of course."

"And you didn't ask her?"

"I . . . I didn't feel it was my place. I was also fairly sure she wouldn't tell me."

"Would Mr. Bing have objected to his daughter seeing Mr. Warren?"

The question seemed to surprise Ethel. "I don't think so, no."

"Then why do you think Miss Bing chose to sneak out to see him?"

"I don't know. You'd have to ask Pearl."

"We did ask her, and her answer confused us," Doyle admitted. "That's why I'm asking your opinion."

Ethel seemed to be growing alarmed. "What did she say?"

"She said she wanted her father to notice."

Ethel had no reply to that. She simply stared back at Doyle with wide eyes.

"Do you think he did notice, Mrs. Lane? Did Mr. Bing know Pearl was sneaking out at night to meet a lover?"

"I don't know what he knew, but . . ." She looked away, wringing her hands in distress.

"But what, Mrs. Lane?"

"But they argued rather frequently, Pearl and her father. She was . . ." She turned back to Doyle, desperate to make him understand. "Pearl was jealous. I know, it sounds silly, but she resented the attention Mr. Bing paid to Carrie."

Doyle nodded as if he understood completely, a technique that usually encouraged people to speak more freely. Frank had to admit he'd underestimated the detective. "I guess Miss Bing was close to her father, since she thought her mother was dead and he was all she had."

"Yes, that's it. Pearl didn't understand why Mr. Bing needed to marry me. She already took good care of him, and she didn't think he needed anyone else."

"But Miss Bing is a young, attractive female," Doyle said. "Most girls like her are thinking about getting married and having their own homes."

Ethel had no answer for that. She just stared back at Doyle helplessly.

"Did Mr. Bing want Pearl to marry Mr. Warren?" Frank asked.

Ethel's brow wrinkled as if she were trying to remember. "He would tease her about Mr. Warren."

"What do you mean, tease?" Frank asked.

Ethel gave the question a moment's thought. "He would tell her Mr. Warren was sweet on her and she should catch him while she could."

"And how did Miss Bing react to that?" Doyle asked.

"She didn't like it. She was annoyed. Sometimes she was even angry."

"Miss Bing said she was the one who suggested that her mother come to live here. Is that true?"

"If she said it, then it must be. All I know is that Nora arrived here after Mr. Bing died and informed me she had more right to be here than I did. That was probably true, since she was Mr. Bing's legal wife, so I didn't object. I also thought having her mother close might be a comfort to Pearl."

"Was it?"

"I don't really know. Nora wasn't always pleasant to me, but I can understand that. Perhaps she was kinder to Pearl. They did seem to be getting along better the past few days."

"Did Pearl ever complain about her mother?" Frank asked.

Ethel gave him a pitying look. "She was hardly likely to complain to me if she did. They didn't quarrel where I could hear them, but I have no idea what they did when they were alone together."

"Did Pearl treat her mother well?" Frank tried.

But Ethel shook her head. "Pearl doesn't treat anyone well. She's an angry girl, Mr. Malloy, and a bit spoiled and used to getting her own way in everything. She has not enjoyed sharing her home and her life and most of all her father with me and Carrie. She was often rude to Nora, but as I said, I never heard them quarrel. Nora seemed to understand why Pearl was so unhappy."

"So, you don't think Pearl would have killed her mother," Doyle said.

Ethel looked alarmed again. "I don't know why anyone would have killed her. Surely, if she really was poisoned, it was a terrible accident."

"That's possible, I guess," Doyle said. "I don't suppose you had any reason to want to be rid of her."

"Me?" she asked, clearly startled by the suggestion. "I . . . I suppose if Mr. Bing were still alive and she died, he might have married me again, to make it legal, but Mr. Bing is not still alive. I would gain nothing from her death."

"But she had moved into your house," Doyle reminded her.

"Because I thought she had a right to, but after I found out what the will said, I could have sent her away if I wanted. I had no reason to want her dead."

Doyle considered her answer for a long moment. "Do you keep arsenic in the house, Mrs. Lane?"

She blinked at the sudden change of subject. "I suppose we do. Everyone keeps some for rats and mice, don't they?"

"Do you know where it's kept?"

"I . . . In the kitchen somewhere, I suppose."

Frank could tell by Doyle's expression that he had decided Ethel had given them all she had to give.

"We'd like to question Carrie, too, Mrs. Lane," Frank said. "If you think she'll feel uncomfortable talking to us, my wife has offered to sit with her while we do. She did that for Pearl, and it worked out very well."

"Carrie? Do you really need to speak to her?" she asked, newly alarmed. "She's just a child."

"She's the one who told us about Pearl going out to visit Mr. Warren," Doyle reminded her. "She may know other things that will help us figure out this case."

"I don't know. She might . . . She's easily upset," Ethel said, wringing her hands again.

Doyle smiled his understanding. "I don't like dealing with young ladies who are upset. All those tears . . ." He feigned a shudder. "So don't worry. We'll take good care of her."

"Is it absolutely necessary?"

"I'm afraid it is, Mrs. Lane."

Ethel didn't look convinced, but as Doyle had intended, she didn't feel that she could refuse to allow them to speak with Carrie either.

Frank escorted Ethel out and found Sarah waiting for her in the family parlor. "We're ready for Carrie now," he said.

• • •

Carrie actually looked pleased when Sarah told her the police would like to speak with her. She'd been sulking in her bedroom, but she perked right up at the news.

"What will they ask me? I can tell them a thing or two," she said, checking her reflection in her dressing table mirror and adjusting a few of her curls.

"I don't know what they'll ask, but you need to tell the truth," Sarah warned.

Carrie laughed at that, as if it were a joke, and Sarah sighed inwardly. This should be interesting.

She escorted Carrie down to where Doyle and Malloy waited for them. Carrie sailed into the room as if making her entrance into a ballroom full of admirers. Doyle and Malloy rose to their feet, and after giving Malloy a dismissive glance, she went to Doyle and offered him her hand.

"Are you the police?"

Doyle smiled and took her hand. "Detective Sergeant Doyle, at your service."

She didn't seem to notice the hint of sarcasm in his voice. She literally batted her eyes at him. "Oh my, should I be frightened of you?"

"If you like," he replied. "Please, sit down, Miss Bing."

"My name is Lane," Carrie said, seating her-self with much ceremony in the chair Doyle

266

indicated and taking a moment to arrange her skirts. "Mr. Bing wasn't my real father."

"I'm sorry, Miss Lane. I hope you don't mind if we ask you a few questions."

"I'm happy to help." She actually leaned forward eagerly, her eyes bright. "What would you like to know?"

"Tell me what happened the day Mr. Bing died."

Carrie instantly sat back and frowned. "I thought you were going to ask me about Nora and Pearl."

"We'll get to them, but first I want to know what you can tell me about that day."

"I already told *them*"—she gestured to where Sarah and Malloy stood nearby—"everything I know."

"You still need to tell me. As I remember, when I came to the house after Mr. Bing died, you were too upset to talk to me."

"Yes, I was very upset. I still am." She sniffed as if to prove it. "Papa had been very good to me, and I loved him very much."

"That's unusual, isn't it?"

"For a girl to love her stepfather?" she scoffed. "I hope not. Life isn't a fairy tale, Mr. Doyle. Stepparents can be good and kind."

"And I guess Mr. Bing was good and kind to you."

"He gave me everything I ever wanted," she

said smugly, as if that were the only reason to love someone.

"Your real father had recently died, hadn't he?"

"Yes," she admitted reluctantly.

"I guess that was a shock to you."

"A terrible shock."

"But Mr. Bing took his place."

Plainly, Carrie didn't like that insinuation. "No one could take my father's place, but Mr. Bing did his best to comfort me."

"And exactly how did he do that, Miss Lane?"

To Sarah's surprise, the color blossomed in Carrie's cheeks. "I told you, he gave me everything I ever wanted."

"So, he gave you gifts?"

"Not gifts exactly," she hedged.

"Then what, exactly?"

"He brought us to live in this house. He let me buy as many clothes as I wanted. He took me to the theater and to concerts and to museums."

"I'm sure you and your mother enjoyed going to all those places," Doyle said.

Carrie sniffed again, this time in derision. "Mother doesn't enjoy those things, so she didn't go along. He also gave me my own automobile and taught me to drive it."

"Ah yes, and you drove him to the automobile show that last morning, didn't you?"

She didn't like that question at all, but she said, "He asked me to drive him. He enjoyed seeing young ladies operating automobiles, he said."

"And you drove yourself home later in the day when you got tired."

"I . . . No, I . . . I walked home. It was a lovely day, and I left the auto for Papa to drive himself home later."

"Are you sure, Miss Lane?"

"Of course I'm sure."

"I just thought maybe he told you to drive yourself home and come back for him that evening."

"Why would he do that?"

"I don't know, but you did say he liked watching young ladies drive automobiles. Maybe he wanted to watch you again."

Carrie just glared at him.

"All right, what did you do when you got home?"

"Do?"

"Yes, how did you spend the rest of the day?"

"I . . . I don't remember."

"But you do remember overhearing an argument between Mr. Bing and his daughter the night before."

"Oh yes." Carrie was instantly in a good humor again. "They quarreled all the time."

"And what time was this?"

"I don't know. Late. Papa had been at the automobile show and it ended at ten thirty, so it was after we got home."

"What were they arguing about?"

She feigned outrage. "You don't think I listened at the door, do you?"

"I wouldn't think of suggesting it," Doyle lied, "but if they were angry, maybe they were shouting, and you couldn't help but overhear."

That seemed to placate her. "It was something about Pearl getting married."

"Did he object to her getting married?"

"Oh no! He wanted her to. He was tired of her always berating him about marrying Mama." Carrie smiled slyly. "She was jealous, you see."

"Of your mother?" Doyle guessed.

That delighted her. "No, silly. She was jealous of me. Because Papa loved me more than he loved her."

Even though Sarah had heard this before, she still flinched. While a man might prefer one child over another for many reasons, it was simply cruel to say so. How painful it must have been for Pearl.

"That must have made Pearl pretty angry," Doyle said.

"She was furious, and the more things Papa bought for me, the madder she got. That's why he wanted her to get married, so he didn't have to listen to her anymore."

"Do you think Pearl might have wanted to kill her father?" Doyle asked, as if he'd just thought of it.

"I'm sure she did," Carrie said eagerly. "She must've gone out that night. She took my auto and ran over Papa in the street."

"Why would she take your auto to do it?" Doyle asked.

Carrie hesitated, obviously trying to think of a reason. "So she could blame me for it," she said at last. "She hates me, remember."

"And was it your auto that ran over Mr. Bing?"

Carrie hesitated again. "How would I know? I just . . . I was guessing, that's all. I would've used her auto if I did it. To make you think it was her."

"And did you use her auto?" Doyle asked.

She stiffened at that. "Of course not. I didn't do it at all. But Pearl would want me to take the blame, you can be sure of that."

"What about Mrs. Bing?" Doyle asked.

"Mrs. Bing?" Carrie echoed, obviously confused.

"Yes, Nora Bing. You remember, the lady who died this morning. You must have been pretty angry when she showed up here."

"I didn't like it, if that's what you mean. She didn't have any right to be here."

"Whose idea was it for her to move in here?"

"I have no idea. Pearl's, probably. She would have done it just to annoy us."

"Did Pearl enjoy having her mother with her?"

Carrie wrinkled her nose in disgust. "Pearl

doesn't enjoy anything. I don't even think she liked her mother."

"What makes you say that, Carrie?" Sarah asked, earning a dark look from Doyle.

"She was embarrassed by her. You could tell."

"Do you think she wanted to get rid of her mother?"

"I'm sure she did."

Even Doyle looked taken aback by her frankness. He had to clear his throat to go on. "Did you know about Mrs. Bing's flask?"

Carrie smiled again, this time conspiratorially. "We all knew about it. She wasn't very good at sneaking."

"Carrie, where do you keep the arsenic?" Sarah asked.

But her attempt at catching Carrie unawares failed. "I don't know. In the kitchen, I suppose, although that doesn't sound right, does it? It might accidentally get into the food."

"Is that what you think happened to Mrs. Bing?" Sarah asked.

"No, I think she killed herself," Carrie said quite confidently. "She knew Pearl despised her, and Mother was going to put her out of the house. She couldn't face it, so she drank the arsenic."

"That seems a little drastic for a woman who spent years tracking down her husband and daughter," Malloy remarked. "She didn't strike me as someone who would give up so easily."

"And yet she did," Carrie said smugly. "She was old and tired and nobody loved her. What else could she do?"

No one had an answer for her. They were all a bit shocked, or at least Sarah was. She figured the men must be, too.

"Is that all? May I go now?" Carrie said. "I thought being questioned by the police would be more entertaining."

"I'm sorry I disappointed you," Doyle said with mock solemnity.

She smiled sweetly and tilted her head flirtatiously. "I'm sure you did your best, Mr. Doyle."

With that she rose and flounced from the room.

"I hope I never have daughters," Doyle said.

"Did you hear what she said?" Sarah asked when she'd shut the door behind Carrie.

"I think I heard every word," Doyle assured her, "which is why I'm never going to marry."

Sarah gave both men an impatient glare. "She said that Pearl took her auto that night and ran over Mr. Bing."

Both men frowned, trying to figure out her point.

"She only said that to make us think Pearl killed Bing, though," Malloy said.

"Yes, but she had already claimed that she left her auto at Madison Square Garden so Mr. Bing could drive himself home that night. She told us that she walked home in the afternoon."

"That's right," Malloy said, finally understanding.

"Then why did she claim Pearl took it?" Doyle asked, not understanding at all.

"She must know her auto was the one that ran over him," Sarah said. "And if Pearl was driving it, Carrie would have had to drive it home in the afternoon."

"And she thought I must know that, too," Doyle said, catching on.

"And she needed a way to explain why *she* wasn't driving it," Malloy said.

"But why would Carrie have killed Mr. Bing?" Sarah said, sinking down into the chair Carrie had vacated. "She's been devastated since his death, and he adored her and showered her with gifts and attention."

"Not *gifts*," Doyle corrected her. "He just bought her things."

"He bought her everything she wanted," Sarah recalled. "She had every reason to keep him alive."

"We're missing something," Malloy said. "I thought if we just talked to everyone, we could figure it out."

"So did I," Doyle said with a weary sigh. "I'm so grateful for all your help."

"The answer is here somewhere, I'm sure," Malloy said, ignoring his sarcasm.

"Maybe we just need to think about it some

more and put all the pieces together," Sarah said.

"You two can do that," Doyle said. "I'm going to talk to the servants and find out where they keep the arsenic. You're both officially finished with the case."

"But if we figure it out, we'll let you know," Malloy said, unfazed.

Doyle just grunted, and Sarah had to cover a smile.

"Come along, Sarah. I'll take you home," Malloy said.

When they were safely outside and walking to their motorcar, she turned to him. "Are we really finished with the case?"

"Maybe as far as Doyle is concerned, but Ethel hired us to find Bing's killer, so I think we're still doing that."

"Good. I know the answer is here. We just haven't found it yet."

"You're right, but I don't know how we're going to find it when everyone in that house is so intent on protecting everyone else."

"Or casting blame on them," Sarah said.

Malloy opened the trunk to get out their dusters. "The worst part is that we don't really know why someone wanted to kill Bing or Nora."

"No one liked Nora," Sarah reminded him.

"But people don't murder someone just because they don't like them."

Sarah nodded. "Yes, Carrie and Pearl obviously

don't like each other, because they were both vying for Mr. Bing's attentions, but neither of them is dead."

"And I think the girls genuinely loved Bing, even though Pearl was angry with him recently. Warren might've been afraid Bing would want his money back, but is that really a good reason to murder someone?"

"And don't forget Ethel wanted a divorce that she couldn't get."

"But we still don't know why she wanted to divorce him."

Sarah let Malloy help her into her duster. "Maybe that's the clue we're missing."

"Maybe, but don't forget Ethel is the one who hired us to find the killer."

"That does seem to eliminate her as a suspect," Sarah agreed.

"You may be right that we need to take some time to think about this."

Sarah sighed. "I just hope we're not missing something very obvious. We'll feel really silly."

"I hate feeling silly, so we need to find that clue."

Malloy stayed at home long enough to have a late lunch, and then he left for the office, determined to run everything new they had learned by Gino and Maeve to find if they could see something he and Sarah didn't.

Sarah was determined to use the afternoon to think, at least until the children returned home from school, but her plans were thwarted when her maid gave her a note that had just been delivered.

"Mrs. Ellsworth's maid brought this over," Hattie informed her.

How strange. Her long-time neighbor thought nothing of simply dropping in at any time of the day or night if she needed to speak to Sarah. On the other hand, Mrs. Ellsworth's daughter-in-law, Theda, was pregnant and Mrs. Ellsworth was understandably anxious about her progress. If Mrs. Ellsworth called on Sarah, Sarah couldn't examine Theda to make sure everything was going well.

Sarah tore open the envelope and smiled as she read the short note asking Sarah to drop in at any time that was convenient "just to make sure everything was as it should be with Theda and the baby." She also requested that Sarah not mention she had been summoned.

Sarah had made her living as a midwife for years before she married Malloy, and she still delivered the occasional baby at the maternity hospital she had established on the Lower East Side of the city. She was only too happy to help Theda, but she suspected that Theda had no reason for concern and her mother-in-law was just being overly cautious. Still, she could use a distraction from this very frustrating case, so she gathered her medical bag and told Hattie she'd be back soon and headed across the street to the Ellsworths' house.

The maid who answered the door greeted her warmly and smiled knowingly, since she was probably the one who had delivered Mrs. Ellsworth's note in the first place. She took Sarah into the parlor, where Mrs. Ellsworth and Theda were sewing baby clothes.

"Mrs. Malloy, what a pleasant surprise," Mrs. Ellsworth said quite convincingly.

Theda just shook her head, not fooled at all, but she rose to greet Sarah and brought her to sit next to her on the sofa.

"How are you feeling?" Sarah asked, although she didn't really need to inquire. Theda was practically glowing in the way only healthy, pregnant women did.

"I feel wonderful."

"That isn't strictly true," Mrs. Ellsworth said with a worried frown. "She's been complaining of a stomachache in the evenings."

"Just a little heartburn," Theda told Sarah. "You warned me that might happen."

Something tickled at Sarah's memory, but she ignored it. "No morning sickness?"

"No. I'm so lucky. I only had it twice, and not at all for the past month."

"But the pains are here," Mrs. Ellsworth said,

touching her breastbone. "So near her heart and—"

"Which is why it's called heartburn," Theda reminded her patiently.

"It doesn't hurt to be careful," Mrs. Ellsworth said. "I know Mrs. Malloy wouldn't mind checking you and—"

"I wouldn't mind at all. I even brought my bag with me just in case."

Theda gave her an apologetic look, but Mrs. Ellsworth was unrepentant. "That would be so good of you."

"Perhaps we should go to your bedroom," Sarah told Theda. "For privacy."

"Yes, that would be fine." Theda rose and led the way.

Mrs. Ellsworth rose to follow, but Sarah stopped her. "If she really is having any trouble, she'll be more likely to tell me if you aren't there," she whispered. "She won't want to worry you."

Mrs. Ellsworth's worried frown vanished. "Oh, Mrs. Malloy, I never thought of that. I'm so glad you came."

Sarah patted her arm and followed Theda, who was halfway up the stairs by now.

As soon as they were alone in Theda's bedroom, she said, "I'm so sorry. She sent for you, didn't she?"

"Yes, but I don't mind. I'm always happy to see

you. Now let me examine you so I can reassure her that you and the baby are fine."

Sarah listened to the baby's heart, which was beating strongly, and to Theda's heart and lungs, which were also operating just as they should. She asked all the usual questions and learned that Theda's breasts were enlarged and sore and that she often suffered from heartburn after the evening meal. Both were normal for this stage of the pregnancy.

Sarah gave her some tips for how to avoid irritating her stomach. "Other than that, is anything else bothering you?"

"Just the usual from my dear mother-in-law," Theda said with a sheepish grin.

"You mean the superstitions?" Sarah guessed. Mrs. Ellsworth was notoriously superstitious.

"You have no idea how many superstitions there are about babies. I can't even keep track of them, much less try to avoid doing all the things that can be dangerous, and that is only for when I'm expecting. After the baby is born, the list just gets longer."

"What does she have you doing?" Sarah asked, not bothering to hide her amusement.

"Mostly, she has me not doing things. I can't go to a funeral because I can't look at a dead body or step over a grave. I have to be careful around cats, too, and I can't look at the moon too long or the baby will be moonstruck."

"What does that mean?" Sarah asked, trying not to laugh.

"I'm afraid to ask. And I can't be frightened by anything because that will mark the baby, and look at this." She reached into her pocket and pulled something out.

"Is that a . . . a sock?" Sarah marveled.

"Yes, Nelson's sock. If you carry around your husband's sock, you won't go into early labor."

"It's just because she loves you so much," Sarah said. "She doesn't want anything bad to happen."

"I know, but I hate that she's so afraid all the time. I won't even be able to cut the baby's nails until he's a year old or else it will stunt his growth."

"But you have to cut his nails, or he'll scratch himself."

"Apparently, the mother is supposed to bite them off instead."

"Oh my."

"Yes, well, I already told her she'll have to do that herself."

They both laughed at the thought.

Sarah was pleased to report to Mrs. Ellsworth that Theda and the baby were doing well and the heartburn was an ordinary issue with pregnancy. After an hour spent drinking tea and listening to Mrs. Ellsworth's reports on all the gossip in the neighborhood, Sarah was able to return home.

As she crossed the cobblestone street, she reflected on how nice it was to not think about the Bing murders for an hour. Her mind felt clearer now, and maybe she would be able to figure out what she had been missing.

And that was when she put it all together.

XII

"This business about the automobiles is so confusing," Maeve said when Frank had finished bringing her and Gino up to date on what they had learned. Maeve and Gino were sitting in the client chairs in Frank's office, where they could talk privately.

"Let me see if I've got it straight," Gino said. "Carrie admits that she drove Bing to the automobile show that morning."

"That's right. And she stayed for a while but got bored or something and left in the afternoon."

"But she claimed that she walked home and left her auto for Bing to drive himself home," Maeve said.

"And now she's claiming that Pearl took her auto and drove it back to the show that night and used it to run over Bing," Gino concluded. "Didn't you challenge her on that?"

"No, because Doyle had finished with her by the time we figured it out."

"We?" Maeve asked archly.

"Well, Sarah figured it out," Frank admitted. "But we had already suspected Carrie drove herself home in the afternoon."

"But she loved the attention she got at the

show," Maeve said. "Bing always let her explain the automobile to the female customers."

"How do you know?" Gino asked with a frown.

"Because she told me that day when she was showing *me* how it works."

"She said she loved the attention?" Gino scoffed.

"She didn't have to say that," Maeve replied smugly. "It was obvious. She did say Bing always let her demonstrate for the women, though."

"All right, so for some reason, even though she *liked the attention,* Carrie left the show and came home. Did she argue with Bing? Maybe she got angry about something and decided to come back that night and run over him," Frank said, glad to see their skeptical frowns.

"That's hard to believe," Maeve said.

"Yeah, what could he have done to make her that angry?" Gino asked.

"I know it sounds unlikely, but *somebody* was mad enough to run him over."

"It would've had to be pretty bad for Carrie to go from adoring her papa to wanting him dead," Maeve said.

"If they had an argument, maybe somebody noticed it," Gino said.

"How would we find out, though?" Maeve asked. "We have no idea who might have been at the show that day."

Gino straightened in his chair. "We do know

somebody who was there when Bing was killed."

"Yes, his killer," Maeve said with a pitying look.

But Gino had figured it out. "Not only his killer, but whoever it was who told Doyle he was Bing's partner and identified the auto."

"That's right, and now we know it wasn't Warren. Doyle confirmed that for me today."

"So, who was it?" Maeve asked.

"It must be somebody who worked with Bing," Gino said. "Why else would he claim to be Bing's partner?"

"But Bing didn't really have a job or even a business," Frank reminded them.

"Except for his interest in Warren's shop," Maeve said.

"Could it be somebody else from the shop besides Warren?" Gino asked.

Maeve shook her head. "Nobody there except Warren could claim to be Bing's partner."

"That's where you're wrong, Maeve," Frank said with a grin. "Anybody could *claim* to be Bing's partner."

Now Maeve straightened in her chair. "Of course! He could claim anything with Bing lying dead and unable to contradict him."

"And he'd want the police to take him seriously," Gino mused, "so he'd try to make himself more important. Did he give Doyle a name?"

"Doyle couldn't remember it, and from what he said, he may not have even written it down. He did say the fellow seemed young to be Bing's partner, though."

"Warren could fit that description," Gino said.

"But we know it wasn't him," Frank said. "Who else at the shop is young?"

Maeve poked Gino's arm. "Your pal Tom is young."

"Yes, he is, and the other mechanics are all older," Gino said.

"Do you think he'd let you buy him another drink after work today?" Frank asked.

"He's not feeling as friendly to me as he did before he knew I'm a detective, but I'll give it a try."

"Why do men get to have all the fun?" Maeve asked with feigned annoyance.

"I'll remind you of that the next time I'm cranking the motorcar for you," Gino replied.

At the end of the workday, Gino followed Tom for a few blocks without making his presence known. The things he wanted to ask about this time were a bit more sensitive, and Tom might not want to discuss them in a public place. Sure enough, Tom eventually made his way to a house and disappeared inside. He probably planned to head out again, but he'd want to change his clothes and get cleaned up first.

Gino climbed the front porch steps and knocked on the door. After a few minutes and another rap or two, an older lady opened the door and eyed him with reluctant approval. Mr. Malloy's advice about dressing well was correct. "I don't got no rooms available just now," she said with apparent regret.

"I'm just looking for Tom Yingling. Has he come home yet?"

"Tom, eh? I think I heard him come in. Is he expecting you?"

"No, although we agreed to meet up later."

"Go on up, then. Second door on the right."

Gino made a show of wiping his feet because landladies liked that.

"He don't get many visitors," she remarked a little suspiciously.

Gino gave her his most charming smile. "He probably doesn't want to disturb you."

"Oh, I don't mind, so long as there's no shouting or fighting. And I don't allow women, of course."

"I could tell this was a respectable place," Gino said solemnly.

"Oh, the men are always trying to sneak a girl in, but I usually catch them."

"Not Tom, though," Gino said, just to see.

The landlady rolled her eyes. "Even Tom. They never learn."

"And you always catch them."

This time she just frowned. "I do try. You can go on up, but no shouting and no fighting."

Gino raised a hand as if taking an oath and then headed for the stairs. He couldn't help wondering what kind of girls would be willing to sneak into Tom Yingling's rooming house to be with him. Certainly not someone as *fine* as Pearl Bing.

Gino rapped on the door, and Tom opened it, a towel in his hand and a scowl on his face. "I told you I'd pay—" He caught himself when he saw who his visitor was. "What are you doing here?"

"I've got a few questions to ask you, and you might not want anybody else to hear the answers."

Tom glared at him, but he stuck his head out and glanced up and down the hallway. Finding it empty, he said, "I already told you everything I know."

"I think you might know something more. If you don't let me in, I might have to cause a disturbance. Your landlady told me she doesn't tolerate that."

He sighed in dismay. "You better come in, then."

The room was spartan but clean, the battered furniture dust-free, and the iron bedstead neatly made. Tom had gotten as far as washing his hands and face. He hung the towel on the washstand and indicated a threadbare, overstuffed chair, the only one in the room.

"I don't know what else I can tell you," Tom said, plopping down on the bed. "I already said I don't know who ran over Mr. Bing, and if it's about that lady he was married to, I never even saw her except that day at the funeral."

"You know about her dying, then," Gino said.

"They was talking about it in the shop. Miss Bing come to fetch Mr. Warren and he was pretty grim when he got back. Somebody said she was poisoned."

"Did they? Do you believe it?"

"I can believe just about anything about that bunch." He sounded bitter. "Is that what you came to ask me?"

"No. I was wondering why you were at the automobile show the night Mr. Bing died."

Tom opened his mouth, but he couldn't seem to make a sound. Plainly, he had no idea how to respond. After a painful silence, during which Gino knew better than to speak, he said, "Who told you I was there?"

"Detective Sergeant Doyle, who is investigating Bing's murder."

"But I didn't—" He caught himself and color flooded his freckled face.

"You didn't what?" Gino prodded. "You didn't give him your real name?"

Tom pressed his lips into a bloodless line and then said, "I didn't give him any name."

"But you told him you were Alvin Bing's

partner, so he'd believe you when you identified him."

He shrugged. "You know how it is. When you're young, people don't listen to you."

"There's no law against not giving your name or even claiming a title you don't hold," Gino said pleasantly, having no idea if he was right or not. "But if you were there, you might've seen something."

"I already told you, I didn't see him get run over."

"Why were you there at all?"

To Gino's surprise, Tom's eyes widened, and the color drained from his face. "I . . . Mr. Bing invited me."

From the way he said it, Gino thought that might actually be the truth, but there was obviously much more to the story. "I thought he liked to talk to the customers himself. He didn't even want Will Warren there."

"He, uh, he didn't want me to talk to the customers."

"Then why did he invite you?"

"I . . . He was going to, uh, introduce me to his daughter."

"Pearl?" Gino asked in surprise.

Gino would have bet Tom couldn't get any paler, but now even his freckles were fading. "No, uh, Carrie."

Gino suddenly remembered the way Tom

had watched Maeve and Carrie leaving the dining room the day of Bing's funeral. He could understand Tom wanting to meet Carrie, but why would Bing even consider introducing his daughter—or rather, his stepdaughter, of whom he was also very fond—to a mechanic from the shop? "You're lying."

Tom jumped to his feet, obviously outraged. "I am not!"

"Alvin Bing would never allow someone like you near his daughters."

Tom's outrage turned to scorn. "That's how much you know. He was going to give her to me."

This time Gino found himself nearly stunned. "Why would he do a thing like that?"

Tom opened his mouth to reply but stopped himself just in time. "None of your business."

"If you killed Alvin Bing because of it, it's everybody's business."

"How many times do I gotta say it? I didn't kill him."

"Maybe not, but you were there. Was Carrie there, too?"

"Yes. That's why I went that night. Bing had it all fixed up."

Gino could hardly believe his ears, but even if this whole story was a fairy tale, he had to hear it all. "He was going to introduce you to Carrie," he said skeptically.

"He was going to tell her."

"Tell her what?"

Tom sighed in defeat and plopped back down on the bed. "Tell her that she was going home with me that night."

None of this made any sense. "I don't believe you. Why would he pimp out his daughter to you, Tom?"

"You shouldn't talk about her like that," Tom said, pretending to be offended.

"What else would you call it?"

Tom shrugged and looked away.

"All right, why would Bing give his sweet, innocent daughter to you?"

Tom rubbed his palms against his thighs as if trying to scrub away some dirt. "He . . . he liked me."

"Even if I believed that, no man gives away his daughter's virtue just because he likes somebody."

Tom had no answer for that, which gave Gino a moment to consider the possibility that Tom was telling the truth. And if he was, what might explain it.

"You knew something about him, didn't you?" Gino guessed. It was the only explanation that made sense.

Tom looked up in surprise, but he didn't reply.

"That's it, isn't it? You knew something about him, and you were blackmailing him."

Tom rubbed his pant legs again, then closed his hands into fists. "I don't guess it matters now, with him dead and all." He swallowed audibly. "I saw him kill Mr. Lane."

For a full minute, Gino could only stare. "What do you mean, you saw him kill Mr. Lane?" he finally managed to ask.

Tom just shrugged, still not meeting Gino's eye.

"You told me it was an accident," Gino reminded him.

"That's what everybody thought, but I saw what really happened."

"What really happened?"

Tom sighed, this time in resignation. "Mr. Bing came in that afternoon. He brought a cake. Said it was his birthday and he wanted to treat the men."

"Go on," Gino prodded when he hesitated.

"We put it on Mr. Warren's desk, and all the men crowded around, eating it. Bing took Mr. Lane aside and they was talking. I didn't hear what they said, but then they walked over to where Mr. Bing had left his auto, just inside the shop doors but not really in sight of where the men were eating cake. I got the idea there was something wrong with the auto and he wanted Mr. Lane to fix it."

"What gave you that idea?"

"The way Bing was pointing at it and Mr. Lane looked concerned. Then Mr. Lane lay down in front of it so he could look at the front axle, I think."

"You said the brake wasn't set and he accidentally started the engine," Gino remembered.

Tom winced. "I know that's what I said. That's what we told the police. Mr. Warren said it wasn't a good idea to give the police too much information. They might spread the word that our autos weren't safe, and they didn't know nothing about how the autos work anyway."

Of course they didn't. "What really happened?"

"Nobody was looking except me, you see, so nobody really saw. When Mr. Lane lay down, Bing reached in and pushed the accelerator lever forward."

Gino winced. "Could it have been done accidentally?"

"Oh no. He done it on purpose."

"And you're sure of that?"

Tom gave him a pitying glare. "He pushed the lever and the auto went forward, right over Mr. Lane's chest. Then Bing stepped back and just stood there watching while Mr. Lane tried to call out, but I guess he couldn't get his breath. He just made some awful sounds and when Bing saw me looking, he started shouting for help. There wasn't nothing we could do, though. Mr. Lane wasn't dead yet, but he died before the doctor got there. Never could say a word, so nobody knew but me."

Gino's mind was racing while he put all the pieces together. Bing had killed Lane and within months had married his widow. "So, Bing knew that you had seen what he did."

"Yes," Tom said with some satisfaction. "I was still trying to decide what to do about it when Bing told me he'd give me money to forget what I saw."

"How much did he give you?" Gino asked out of curiosity.

"He give me the same amount I make in a week. He'd give it to me every week, so he doubled my salary," Tom reported with some pride at the deal he'd made.

Gino almost choked. Bing had been a millionaire, and Tom had been pleased with a pittance. But Gino wouldn't point that out, at least not until he'd gotten Tom to tell him everything. "Bing paid you and you were happy with that for . . ." He thought back. ". . . for months, so where does Carrie come into it?"

Tom frowned, his sense of grievance almost comic. "I found out he'd sent Miss Bing to Mr. Warren."

"You think Bing ordered Pearl to . . . to visit Will Warren?" Gino asked to clarify.

"Why else would she do it? She's not a whore, is she? She's a respectable girl, or at least she was."

"How did you know she was *visiting* Warren?"

"I saw her. Everybody was talking about his new house, and I hadn't seen it yet, so I went over one night. I went late so he wouldn't see me, and I'd been drinking, to give me the courage. Then who drives up in one of our autos but Pearl Bing. She parks around back of his place. I guess she thinks no one will see her. Then she just goes inside, bold as you please. There's only one reason a woman goes to a man's house late at night."

He was probably right. "So, you decided Bing was using Pearl to . . . to do what?"

"To keep Warren quiet. I figured he must've seen what Bing did, too, or maybe he just guessed."

Gino rubbed a hand over his face. He'd need something strong to drink after this, but he wasn't going to invite Tom to join him. "All right. I see how you got the idea to ask Bing for Carrie."

"I didn't *ask* him nothing," Tom boasted. "I told him I wanted her, and he said to come to the automobile show that night and he'd fix it up."

Gino decided not to challenge his version. "What happened when you got there?"

"Bing was talking to some people about the autos, so I just stood around and waited. When everybody else left, I asked Bing where she was. He said not to worry, she was coming to get him, and he'd tell her to go home with me instead." He met Gino's eye with a look of triumph.

Gino was starting to feel sick, but he couldn't leave until he'd heard it all.

"And did she?" he asked, not bothering to keep the contempt from his voice.

"She never got the chance," Tom groused. "We walked out to wait for her. The show was over for the night, and most everybody was gone by then. Bing told me to wait by the building. I guess he didn't want her to see me or something."

"But you saw her," Gino guessed.

Tom frowned. "I . . . He told me to wait under the overhang, you know where I mean?"

"Yes, I know."

"It was dark and she drove down Madison, I guess. He was going to meet her on the corner of Twenty-Sixth."

"But you saw the auto, at least."

"Oh yeah, I saw it. And I saw a woman driving, but she had on goggles and her head was all wrapped up, like they do."

"Was it Carrie?"

"I guess. Who else could it be?"

Gino almost groaned. The only female suspect who couldn't drive was now dead, so it could have been any of them.

"He had to cross the street to talk to her. He was going to tell her she was going home with me. She'd drive me in her auto, and he'd get a cab home. It seemed like it took him a long time to make her understand, though."

Gino could only imagine.

"Then he started back across the street to get me, and she rammed right into him. Knocked him down and rolled completely over him. I couldn't believe my eyes."

"I guess you didn't go to help him either."

"It happened so fast," Tom said, oblivious to Gino's sarcasm. "I only took a step or two before she reversed and ran over him again. Or I guess I should say she almost did. She left the wheel right on his chest. Then she jumped out of the auto and ran off."

"Did you ever go to help him?" Gino asked without much hope.

Tom looked affronted. " 'Course I did! But he was already dead by the time I got there, or as good as. Other people came up, too, but just like with Mr. Lane, there wasn't nothing we could do. I thought about moving the auto from off of him, but he was dead by then, and a beat cop was telling everybody to stay back."

"And you didn't get a good look at the driver?"

"It was Carrie. It had to be. It was her auto, after all."

"You're sure about that, are you?"

"About the auto? Yeah, I got a good look at it."

"You didn't tell the police it belonged to Carrie, though."

Tom scowled. "I told them it belonged to Bing, which it did."

298

"And did you tell the police you saw the driver was a woman?"

His scowl turned into a wince. "I told them I didn't see what happened. No good comes of talking to the police, you know."

Gino did know. "So, you lied to the police when you told them you didn't see what happened, and you lied to me about the same thing. How do I know any of what you said is the truth? Maybe you ran over Bing yourself."

"Why would I do that? He was paying me regular. I'd be stupid to kill him."

This was true. Gino rubbed his forehead where a headache was forming. "Did you really think you could sneak Carrie up to your room without your landlady noticing?"

Tom snorted. "We do it all the time. Once the old lady is in bed, nothing can wake her up."

Now all the pieces had fallen into place, and they made a pretty ugly picture. Gino no longer cared who had killed Bing. He deserved whatever he got. But somebody had also killed Bing's wife, Nora. "I don't suppose you have any idea who might've killed *Mrs.* Bing?"

"Pearl's mother? How would I know that?"

"No reason," Gino said, rising from the lumpy chair.

"Are you leaving?" Tom asked hopefully.

"Yes."

"Are you going to tell the police what I told you?" he asked with a frown.

"Don't worry about it. I don't think the police care much one way or the other."

Tom sighed. "I hope not."

Gino headed for the door.

"Will you tell Carrie . . . ?" Tom began, stopping Gino in his tracks. But something about the expression on Gino's face when he turned back made him add, "Never mind."

With that, Gino left. At least he'd solved one mystery.

Sarah had spent the afternoon in the nursery with Brian and Catherine after Maeve and Mrs. Malloy brought them home from school. She needed to bask in their innocence and uncomplicated affection after what she figured out about the Bing household.

Brian was signing madly, trying to make her understand something that had happened at his school, the New York Institution for the Deaf and Dumb. Sarah's skills were improving, but she still needed Catherine's help with some of the new words. Catherine seemed to learn the signs even more quickly than Brian did.

"What is he saying about Grandfather?" Sarah asked, signing her question for Brian's benefit.

He rolled his eyes at her slowness and signed it again.

"He wants to tell Grandfather about something he learned at school," Catherine interpreted.

Sarah's father had recently begun learning to sign, and Brian had been thrilled. "I'll let him know," Sarah signed.

Brian beamed.

Sarah blinked at the prickle of tears. The children would be upset if she suddenly started to weep, but the contrast between her safe and loving home and the Bings' twisted one was so great, she almost couldn't bear it.

"I think Grandmother needs to see how I rearranged my dollhouse, too," Catherine said.

"I'm sure Grandmother wouldn't let Grandfather come alone," Sarah assured her.

"I should hope not. That wouldn't be fair, would it?" Catherine asked.

Brian signed his agreement. They were both acutely aware of what was fair.

Sarah only wished the world were always fair.

She hadn't mentioned her suspicions about the Bings to Malloy or Maeve after they got home. Malloy told her that Gino had gone to question Tom Yingling about who might have attended the automobile show that night. He'd be dropping by later to tell them what he learned, so she had decided to wait until they were all together.

Sarah helped Maeve get the children tucked in, although she always thought that her help only prolonged the process, since the children had to think up delaying tactics to make her stay with them longer. When they were finally settled in, the two women found Malloy and Gino ensconced in the parlor with Mrs. Malloy knitting in her usual corner.

To Sarah's surprise, Malloy was serving Gino a whiskey.

"He just told me what he found out from Yingling," Malloy explained. "He needs it."

"Oh dear," Maeve said, sitting down beside Gino on the sofa. "Should we have a drink, too?"

"I heard him, and I'm doing just fine without one," Mother Malloy said from her corner.

Sarah and Maeve exchanged an amused glance, but they sobered immediately when they turned back to Gino. Sarah took the empty chair beside Malloy. "I suppose you'd better tell us, too."

He did, stopping periodically to sip his whiskey. Sarah saw her own dismay reflected on Maeve's young face.

"Men are horrible," Maeve said in disgust.

"Not all of us," Gino insisted. "I'm just as mad about this as you are."

"I doubt it," Maeve said. "How could a father send his daughter to a man like that, just to protect himself?"

"His *stepdaughter*," Gino corrected her.

"All right, stepdaughter," Maeve said. "But how could a man do that to a girl? To any girl?"

"I don't know," Malloy said firmly, "and

neither does Gino. We couldn't do a thing like that."

Maeve sighed. "I know you're right, not all men are horrible."

"Too many are, though," Sarah said.

They all sat in silence for a long moment, contemplating the state of the human race.

"It must have been Carrie driving the auto, don't you think?" Maeve said at last.

"If Mr. Bing did what Tom said he was going to do and told her that he wanted her to go with Tom," Sarah said, "then she would have been furious."

"And she's young and impetuous, so she might have acted without thinking," Malloy agreed.

But Gino was shaking his head. "I've been trying to figure it out ever since Tom told me what happened, and remember, Carrie was with Bing at the show that day. What if he told her that afternoon what he expected her to do? We've been wondering why she left the show early."

"Yes, she went with him to the show every day, so why did she leave early on that particular day?" Maeve said.

"But if he did tell her, that would have given her a good reason to leave," Sarah said.

"And a good reason not to return," Maeve said. "You've met Carrie. Do you think she would meekly agree to do something so awful, even for her beloved papa?"

"We don't know what kind of a hold Bing had over her," Malloy reminded them, "but it does seem likely that she would have been angry at Bing for demanding such a thing."

"Or maybe she was just hurt," Sarah said. "I can't imagine a worse betrayal. She thought he loved her."

"That's right," Maeve agreed. "She thought he loved her more than he loved Pearl. In fact . . ." She wrinkled her nose in distaste. ". . . she actually told me he should have married her instead of her mother."

"She did?" Sarah asked in surprise. The hairs on the back of her neck prickled.

"Yes, she did. I'd almost forgotten that. I pointed out that she was young for marriage, but she said Bing told her girls her age get married out west all the time. Then I reminded her that Bing was already married to Nora so the marriage wouldn't have been legal, but she thought Bing would have divorced Nora for her."

"She spent a lot of time thinking about marrying her papa," Gino said with a frown.

"That's disgusting," Maeve said.

No one disagreed.

Sarah decided she couldn't keep her suspicions a secret anymore. "I think Carrie may be pregnant."

Everyone gaped at her. Even Mother Malloy stopped her knitting to look up.

"What makes you say that?" Malloy said finally. He obviously believed her. A midwife should know, even one who wasn't practicing much anymore.

"The heartburn. She complained that her stomach was bothering her in the evenings. I thought it was odd in a girl so young, but maybe she does overeat, as Pearl seemed to think. But then I realized she might also be eating more than usual if she is expecting and . . ." She glanced at Gino in dismay.

"What?" he demanded uneasily.

"I hate to mention it in front of you, but her bosom . . ." Sarah shrugged apologetically.

"She is very well endowed," Maeve said with a sly glance at Gino, who was turning red.

"I noticed the morning Nora died," Sarah said. "Carrie came out of her bedroom in just her nightdress."

Malloy coughed uneasily and refused to meet her eye.

"You noticed, too, didn't you?" she accused.

"I, uh, I may have," he allowed, still not meeting her eye.

"It was difficult to miss," she excused him. "I went to see Theda Ellsworth this afternoon. She was complaining about heartburn, and that's what jogged my memory about Carrie. When I thought about it, I also realized she has that pregnancy glow."

"Glow?" Gino asked with a confused frown.

"It's hard to explain, but sometimes you can tell just by looking at a woman," Sarah said.

"All that sounds a little thin, though," Maeve said. "She's only fifteen."

"I know. I'll need to examine her or at least talk to her some more."

"Do you think she knows?" Malloy asked. "A girl that young might not realize."

"I have no idea, but I would guess she doesn't, at least not yet."

"And if she is," Malloy said grimly, "who is the father?"

"If he was sending her to Tom, could he have done that before, with other men?" Gino asked.

"I think it might be even worse than that," Sarah said.

"What could be worse than that?" Maeve asked.

She hated to disillusion her dear friend, but there was no help for it. "I think it might have been Bing himself."

Sarah's heart ached at Maeve's horrified expression.

"Ewww!" she cried. "How could he?"

"But that would explain everything," Gino said, equally horrified but determined to figure it out.

"What does it explain?" Maeve demanded.

"Why Bing killed Lane. He wanted to marry Mrs. Lane."

"What would that have to do with Carrie?" Maeve argued.

"Maybe so he could get close to her," Gino said grimly.

"But how would he even know Carrie existed?" Sarah asked.

"Lane kept a photograph of his family in his office," Gino said. "Tom mentioned it once. Bing would meet with Lane from time to time, so he must have seen it."

"Ewww," Maeve said again, looking a bit green.

"So, maybe Bing decided he wanted Carrie," Malloy said, "but why marry her mother?"

"Because her parents were hardly likely to allow him to marry a fifteen-year-old girl," Sarah guessed. "He doesn't care about the sanctity of marriage anyway. He was already married when he proposed to Ethel."

"I see, he just needed access to Carrie," Maeve said. She still looked a bit ill. "If he married Ethel, Carrie would be living in the same house."

"But Ethel found out," Mother Malloy said. They all stared at her again. She put her knitting down and gave them a pitying look. "She found out about Bing and her daughter. That's why she wanted to get a divorce."

XIII

"And that's why she wouldn't tell us her reasons for wanting a divorce," Frank said. He could see that everyone else understood as well.

"Of course," Sarah said. "She wouldn't want anybody to know what had happened to Carrie, except . . ."

"Except what?" Maeve asked when Sarah hesitated.

"Except she wouldn't be able to keep it a secret much longer if Carrie is with child."

"She would have at least been able to get Carrie away from him, though," Maeve said.

"Let's not get ahead of ourselves here," Frank said. "We aren't sure that Carrie is expecting, and even if she is, we don't know Bing is responsible. If he was going to give her to Tom Yingling, he might've done the same thing with some other man, too."

"Even though Bing wanting Carrie for himself explains just about everything we didn't understand before," Gino said.

"Then how do we find out for sure?" Maeve asked.

Sarah sighed. He could see that she hated everything about this, and he hated that she was even involved. "I'll have to go visit them."

"And tell Mrs.—well, whatever her name is— Carrie's mother, about the baby, if there is one?" Maeve said.

"If she doesn't already know. But if she knows Bing was interfering with Carrie, that may well be how she found out."

"And do we think that Carrie killed Bing when he told her she had to, uh, go with Tom?" Gino asked.

Frank frowned. "That would certainly give her a good reason to want him dead, but why kill Nora?"

"Maybe Nora knew Carrie killed Bing," Maeve guessed.

"How would she know that? She didn't even move into the house until after he was dead," Gino said.

Maeve glared at him, but she had no answer.

"There's still too much we don't know," Frank said. "Sarah, do you want me to go with you to see Ethel tomorrow?"

She shook her head. "She isn't likely to talk about such a sensitive topic with a man in the room. She may not even want to talk to me, but I don't intend to give her any choice."

"Are you sure it's safe to go there alone?" Maeve said. "Look what happened to Nora."

"I promise not to eat or drink anything while I'm there," Sarah said with a grim smile.

Gino smiled, too, but his was sly. "Maeve just

hates that she hasn't done much on this case, and she wants to go with you."

"As a bodyguard?" Frank asked with a grin.

Maeve refused to be embarrassed. "They aren't likely to try to kill two of us, are they?"

"They aren't likely to try to kill even one of us," Sarah said, "but if Maeve thinks she can be useful, I'm happy to let her tag along."

Frank had the feeling Maeve wanted to clap her hands in delight, but her dignity prevailed, and she merely smiled her triumph.

"You won't be sorry," she promised.

Sarah and Maeve took a cab to the Bings' house the next morning. Just as they arrived, a rather homely young man in work clothes was coming down the front stairs. He had his hands in his pockets and was whistling a cheerful tune. He glanced appreciatively at Maeve as she climbed out of the cab, dismissed Sarah as unworthy of his attention, and then sauntered on down the street.

"What a heel. Shouldn't somebody like that be using the servants' entrance?" Maeve asked in disgust.

"You'd think so," Sarah said. "He looked awfully cheerful for someone who had been turned away, though."

Maeve had one foot on the steps when she stopped dead. "Wait a minute, did he look familiar to you?"

Sarah glanced in the direction he'd gone but he was out of sight now. "I don't think so."

"Could he have been at Bing's funeral?"

Sarah tried to remember. "Possibly. He might work at the shop, although I don't remember seeing him there. That could explain why he was at the front door, though. Maybe he had a message from Will Warren or something."

"Do you think Will Warren sends his men to deliver love notes to Pearl?" Maeve scoffed.

"I said a message, not a love note," Sarah said. "If you're really interested, I guess we can ask Mrs. Bing."

Maeve smiled knowingly. "Before or after you ask her if Carrie is carrying Bing's baby?"

Sarah rolled her eyes and shooed Maeve on up the front steps, where Maeve halted again. This time her expression stopped Sarah, too. "Could that have been Tom Yingling?"

Sarah frowned at that disturbing thought. "Why would he have been here?"

"Delivering love notes to Carrie?" Maeve guessed.

"Tom thinks she murdered her stepfather rather than submit to him," Sarah reminded her. "Is it likely he'd be pursuing her?"

"Men can be awfully stupid sometimes," Maeve said.

She had a point, but Sarah didn't want to argue

it on the Bings' front stoop. "Just knock on the door, will you?"

Maeve shrugged and did as she was told. When the maid answered the door, she asked them to wait in the hall while she carried Sarah's card up to Mrs. Bing.

"She never blinked when you called Ethel 'Mrs. Bing,' so I guess the servants don't know Bing was a bigamist," Maeve said.

"Servants know everything," Sarah reminded her. "They wouldn't dare call her anything else, though, unless instructed to do so."

The maid returned shortly and escorted them to the formal parlor, where Ethel met them. She looked a bit flustered. "Do you have any news?"

"About Nora's death, you mean?" Sarah asked. "No, I'm afraid not. It's much too soon."

"That police detective talked to the servants. I don't know what they told him, and he left without telling me what he found out."

"The police won't tell you what they learned."

Ethel rubbed her forehead as if she was suffering from a headache. "I'm sorry, please sit down. Can I offer you some tea or coffee?"

"No, thank you," Sarah said, not daring to meet Maeve's eye. The thought that Ethel would actually try to poison them would probably make her snicker.

"I'm sure you're wondering why we're here," Sarah said when they were seated.

Ethel smiled weakly. "I did wonder, since you don't seem to have anything to tell me."

Sarah opened her mouth to begin the speech she had carefully prepared while lying sleepless the night before, but Carrie burst into the room.

"Mother, where is— What are you doing here?" Then she noticed Maeve and added, "And why are *you* with *her?*"

"Carrie, that's very rude," Ethel chided.

"It's very rude for somebody to ask you a lot of questions when you don't know they're working for a detective," Carrie said, glaring at Maeve.

"I was just making conversation," Maeve said.

Ethel's puzzled gaze darted back and forth between Carrie and Maeve. "What are you talking about?"

"Nothing," Carrie said. "What do they want? You don't have to talk to them, Mother."

"They are guests in our home, Carrie, and you're being less than gracious."

"I'm feeling less than gracious. They aren't really guests either, not if they work for you, and if you hired them, then they work for you."

Ethel rubbed her head again and closed her eyes, as if she was praying silently.

"See, you're upsetting my mother," Carrie informed Sarah and Maeve. "You should leave."

"Carrie, that's enough," Ethel said sharply.

"It's all right, Mrs. Bing," Sarah said, using the name most likely to annoy Carrie. "I'm sure

Carrie doesn't intend to be rude. Perhaps it's just her time of the month and it's made her irritable."

"It's not my time of the month," Carrie snapped, even angrier at being patronized. "I haven't had a period in three months, and I hope I never have another."

Maeve gasped, but Ethel was apparently too horrified to notice. She turned her alarmed gaze on Carrie. "That is hardly a topic for discussion in public, Carrie. Go to your room until you remember how a proper young lady behaves."

Carrie's derisive sniff indicated that was a lesson she preferred never to remember, but she did as she had been bid and left the room.

Ethel's face had gone white, but she tried to put on a brave front. "I don't know what gets into her. Ever since her father died, she's been . . . difficult."

"Mrs. Bing—"

"Please don't call me that. I wasn't married to him, not really. Call me Mrs. Lane."

"Mrs. Lane," Sarah began again, "I came here today because I suspected that Carrie might be with child."

For a second, Sarah thought Ethel might faint as every last drop of color left her face, but she finally drew a breath and let it out in a tremulous sigh. "Why would you think something like that?"

Not the outrage one would have expected from

the mother of a young girl, which meant it wasn't a surprise to her. "I'm a midwife," Sarah said. "Or at least I was for a long time before I married Mr. Malloy. When she complained about having heartburn, I began to suspect . . ."

"Everyone gets heartburn now and then," Ethel said a little too desperately.

"And when I began to suspect," Sarah continued as if she hadn't spoken, "a lot of other things began to make sense."

"And didn't Carrie just confirm it herself?" Maeve asked, earning an impatient glance from Sarah.

"I . . . I don't know what you're talking about. Carrie is only fifteen and—"

"Mrs. Lane," Sarah said sharply, making even Maeve jump. "Mr. Malloy thought it odd that you refused to tell him why you so desperately wanted to divorce Mr. Bing. That told him the reason was something you couldn't bring yourself to discuss. Then I began to suspect Carrie was in a family way, and we've since learned some other things that made us think Mr. Bing was responsible."

Ethel was shaking her head, although Sarah couldn't tell if she was denying Sarah's assertions or simply trying to convince herself they weren't true. "You can't tell anyone," she finally said in a broken whisper.

Sarah's stomach knotted at the confirmation. She'd actually been hoping her suspicions weren't true. "We have no intention of spreading gossip, Mrs. Lane. We're simply trying to find out who killed Mr. Bing, which is what you hired my husband to do."

"I did it," Ethel said so softly Sarah almost didn't hear her. "I killed him."

Sarah glanced at Maeve to make sure she'd also heard the confession. Her shocked expression confirmed it.

"*You* killed him?" Sarah asked, incredulous.

"Is that so difficult to understand? You know what he did to Carrie. He even . . . That is, I think he even killed Kenneth. Kenneth was my husband."

She hadn't said her *first* husband. "Why do you think that?" Sarah said carefully.

"I found out he was there when it happened, when Kenneth died. He . . . he actually told me himself. Alvin, I mean. After we were married, and he knew I couldn't do anything about it. Not right away, you understand. He waited until Carrie was completely under his spell. Then he told me he was there."

"Did he actually admit that he did it?" Maeve marveled.

"Not in so many words, but I could see how proud he was of his plan and how it had worked out and he'd gotten rid of Ken. I thought . . . Well, at first, I thought he wanted *me,* although I couldn't figure out why. He certainly never acted like he cared about me. I didn't mind his indifference, you understand. I was still grieving Ken, and he was so kind to Carrie and so generous . . ." Her voice broke and she pulled a handkerchief from her sleeve to dab at her eyes.

"When did you start to suspect he was being more than kind to Carrie?" Sarah asked gently.

Ethel looked up with eyes so full of pain, Sarah could hardly bear to look at her. "Just a few weeks ago, a month or so, I guess. She said some things about how Alvin should have married her instead of me. I thought it was just silly-young-girl talk. No one could blame her for being enamored with him. He gave her everything she wanted. But then the maid mentioned to me that she hadn't had her monthly visitor for a while. She was . . . *warning* me, I think."

Sarah glanced at Maeve, who whispered, "Servants know everything."

Servants made the beds and washed the sheets, too. They would have known what was going on long since.

Ethel dabbed at her eyes again. "I went to see an attorney about getting a divorce. I knew it was too late to save Carrie, but I had to get her away from him at least. When I found out divorce was impossible, I knew I had only one choice."

Sarah's mind was racing. What would Malloy ask Ethel? "Why did you choose that particular day?"

317

Ethel looked up in surprise, and she chewed her lip for a long moment. "I . . . When Carrie came home early, I saw my chance. She said she was going to go back to get Alvin that night, after the show closed. I told her it was too late for her to be out alone and that I would go instead."

Sarah nodded. It made perfect sense, and Ethel certainly had good reason for killing Bing. "What did you do then?"

"I . . . I drove Carrie's auto down to Madison Square. I waited until he came out and then . . . then I drove the auto into him and ran over him."

"You must have hated him," Maeve said.

"Yes. I . . . I hated him so much, you see. I couldn't let him keep after Carrie. I had to stop him."

"But why kill Nora?" Maeve asked. Sarah was glad. She was so unnerved she might have forgotten.

Ethel's eyes widened in surprise. "I didn't kill her."

Both Sarah and Maeve simply stared at her in response.

"I . . . I didn't have any reason to kill Nora," Ethel insisted. "She never did anyone any harm. I . . . She must have killed herself, don't you think? I mean, she couldn't get revenge on Alvin, and Pearl hated her . . ." She gestured helplessly.

"Did Pearl really hate her?" Sarah asked.

"She wasn't happy to have her here," Ethel

said. "At least not at first. I know Nora was miserable. Her drinking proves that, doesn't it?"

Sarah wasn't sure of that, so she didn't reply. She was too busy trying to figure something out. "Mrs. Lane, if you killed Alvin Bing yourself, why did you hire Mr. Malloy to find the killer?"

The question seemed to surprise her, but she pulled herself up straighter in her chair and lifted her chin defiantly. "I thought it was the best way to divert suspicion from myself."

Sarah could think of several objections to such a plan, but she chose to mention only one. "Didn't you think Malloy would eventually figure it out?"

She smiled wanly. "No, I didn't, and I was obviously right. You were going to blame Carrie, weren't you?"

Sarah wanted to deny it, but they *had* been ready to blame Carrie. "She certainly had a good reason."

"Except that she loved Alvin," Ethel said as if the words left a sour taste in her mouth. "She loves him still, and she's furious that he's dead."

"So, you decided to confess to protect her," Sarah said.

"I couldn't let her take the blame for my sins, could I? Not my own child."

Sarah had no answer for that.

Ethel sighed again. "What are you going to do now?"

"I don't know," Sarah said quite honestly.

Ethel was obviously surprised. "Aren't you going to report me to the police?"

"I'll have to discuss this with my husband. He . . . he isn't obligated to do anything except what he was hired to do. You hired him to find Mr. Bing's killer, and . . ." Sarah sighed wearily. "I'll let him decide what he thinks is best."

"Do you mean he might not report me?" Ethel asked in surprise.

"It's possible. But if you killed Nora—"

"I didn't, I swear! You must believe me. I felt sorry for her, but I would never . . . I couldn't possibly hurt her."

As much as it galled her to admit it, Sarah believed her, although she also couldn't imagine the feisty woman she had known Nora to be committing suicide. "We should go, Maeve."

Sarah rose and Maeve followed suit, but Ethel jumped to her feet.

"Wait, you said you are a midwife . . ."

"Yes?"

"Is there . . . ? Can something be done for Carrie? She's so young, and . . ." She made a pleading gesture.

"I think you know there is, but I don't do that sort of thing. I can't help you."

"But you must know someone who can," Ethel insisted.

"It's very dangerous," Sarah warned her.

"More dangerous than bearing a bastard conceived in incest?" Ethel asked bitterly.

What a horrible place the world was when a young girl was reduced to such choices. "I'm sorry, but I make a point of not knowing the people who do that sort of thing. I can't help you."

They didn't wait to be shown out but found their own way to the front door.

"How awful," Maeve said when they were outside again. "Carrie is a brat, but no one deserves what happened to her."

"I hope her mother is wrong about her still loving Alvin Bing," Sarah said. "What a monster he was to take advantage of a girl's innocence and convince her it was out of love."

"It makes you wonder, doesn't it?" Maeve mused.

"Wonder what?"

Maeve looked up with knowing eyes. "If Bing did the same thing to Pearl."

Frank was grateful that Sarah hadn't wanted him to go with her to the Bing house. He certainly had no desire to discuss Carrie Lane's delicate condition or to deal with Ethel Lane's hysterics when Sarah raised the subject. When he considered where he might have spent the morning, a trip to the morgue actually sounded appealing.

At least he wasn't going to Bellevue this time. He'd convinced Doyle to send Nora Bing's flask and the whiskey bottle to his friend Titus Wesley. Technically, Wesley was an undertaker who made his living embalming the dead and preparing them for burial, but he was also, as Frank had discovered, a skilled coroner and chemist who had more than proven his worth in previous cases. He also knew exactly how to test for arsenic poisoning.

His place of business was a plain storefront where he displayed some coffins of various quality. He came out from his workroom to greet Frank.

"Doyle said you'd stop by," Wesley said when they'd exchanged pleasantries. "I figured you'd be early, too, so I did the tests last night."

"Arsenic, right?"

"Why do you need me if you already know the answer?" Wesley said with feigned outrage.

"To make it official."

Wesley grinned. "Then officially, Nora Bing died of arsenic poisoning."

"Was it the same compound as what Doyle found in the kitchen?"

"Yes. Whoever did it wasn't very clever about it either, except they put in enough arsenic to kill a horse and a cow on top of it."

Frank nodded. "You could see some clumped in the bottom of the whiskey bottle."

"Which is another thing that doesn't make sense," Wesley said with a frown. "I guess I can see the woman filling her flask from the bottle. She'd want to be discreet and carrying around a whole whiskey bottle is not discreet. But if she wanted to kill herself, why put arsenic in the bottle? Just put it in the flask or directly into a glass."

"She was in her bedroom, though, so maybe she just poured it directly from the bottle," Frank said.

But Wesley shook his head. "There was arsenic in the flask, too. So, she—or someone—put arsenic into the bottle and filled the flask from it."

"Then you're saying it should be in one or the other but not in both."

"Exactly, at least if she did it herself. But if it was somebody else, they could've put it in the bottle, and she could've filled the flask from it, not knowing it was poisoned."

"You're a good detective, Wesley."

He shrugged modestly. "I get a lot of poisonings. It's usually pretty easy to figure out if it's on purpose or an accident."

"How does somebody poison themselves accidentally?" Frank asked in amazement.

"Easily, I'm sorry to say. For example, a man uses a spoon to spread arsenic along the baseboards to kill rats. Then he uses the same spoon to eat his dinner but doesn't bother to wash it in between."

Frank winced. "I see it now."

"Yes. Mankind isn't always blessed with intelligence."

"Would it be safe to say that in your professional opinion someone poisoned Mrs. Bing?"

"Yes, it would," Wesley said. "You don't seem happy to hear it."

"I'm not. If somebody poisoned her, then I should turn them in to the police, and I'm not sure I'll want to do that."

Gino shouldn't have suggested that Maeve accompany Mrs. Malloy to visit the Bing house. If he hadn't, he would have Maeve for company at the office instead of being stuck here by himself and bored to death because no clients were calling and he didn't have anything to do.

Just when he was considering a nap, he heard the office door open, and suddenly he didn't feel the need for a nap at all. Maybe it was a new case. He jumped up from his desk and went out to the reception area, to find Pearl Bing looking around expectantly.

"Good morning, Miss Bing," he said in what he hoped were professional tones. She really was a pretty young lady, which tended to be distracting.

"Where is the girl who works here?" she asked, not bothering with any courtesies.

Gino couldn't help smiling at the irony of it. "She went with Mrs. Malloy to visit your stepmother."

Pearl scowled at him. She was pretty even when she scowled. "She's not my stepmother."

"Sorry. Mrs. Malloy went to visit your *house*."

"And the girl was with her," Pearl concluded.

"That's right. Her name is Miss Smith. But I'd be happy to help you."

She looked him up and down in a way she obviously intended to be an insult to his manhood. "I don't suppose you know why they went to see Ethel, do you?"

Gino later excused his callousness by reminding himself of the look she had just given him, although he knew it wasn't really an excuse. He was just being rude in return. "Mrs. Malloy thinks Carrie is going to have a baby."

Plainly, she'd had no idea. The color drained from her face, and she actually swayed. Gino rushed to catch her, taking her arm and leading her to one of the chairs they kept for clients to wait in, although that rarely happened. "Are you all right? Can I get you something?"

This time her glare was half fury and half horror. "You made that up," she accused.

"No, I didn't. She . . . I think she was going to see Mrs. Bing—Ethel—to make sure."

Pearl closed her eyes as if she could no longer bear to look at him and drew a shuddering breath.

"That bastard," she said so softly Gino could pretend he hadn't heard.

"Let me get you a glass of water," he said, snatching a glass from Maeve's desk and hurrying out to the washroom in the hallway. He almost expected her to be gone when he returned, but she was still there, as pale as a marble statue and staring into space.

He had to clear his throat to get her attention before she accepted the glass from him. She drank deeply and then handed it back, as if he were the butler or something.

"I'm, uh, sorry I shocked you," he tried. In truth, he was more than sorry.

"Are you?" she asked without much interest. "I actually thought I was beyond being shocked. It's rather comforting to learn that isn't true."

He waited, but she had nothing more to add. He tried again. "I would be happy to help you, if you tell me why you came."

"I came to talk to that girl," she repeated. "Unless you're a girl, too, you can't help me."

Gino wasn't about to admit defeat, especially not to Pearl Bing. "I can take you to her." He pulled out his pocket watch to check the time. "They might be home by now, and if not, we can wait for them."

The color had returned to her face, and she gave him another of her dismissive looks. "Are you planning to abduct and seduce me?" she asked, astonishing him even though she didn't look particularly disturbed by the thought.

"I wouldn't dream of it." Well, he might dream of it, but he'd certainly never do it.

"Well, then, I have my auto. I can drive us there." She rose and headed for the door.

"I need to lock up," he called after her.

She didn't wait for him, but he found her sitting in her auto, which she'd parked at the curb near the entrance to their office building.

"I'd be happy to drive," he said, thinking how much he'd love to give the snappy little vehicle a try.

"Absolutely not," she informed him. "If you can't bear to be driven by a female, you can run alongside."

"I have no objections," he said, climbing into the passenger seat. "That's a nasty dent you have there," he added, indicating the one he'd noticed the day of Bing's funeral when he and Tom Yingling had inspected her and Carrie's autos.

"Carrie drove my auto once when she forgot to charge her own," Pearl said, her annoyance clear. So much for getting a confession to Bing's murder. "Where are we going?"

He gave her the directions to the Malloy home on Bank Street, and she started out. Gino marveled at how easily the auto moved. He hadn't even realized the motor was running. He'd been saving his money for a long time, intending to use it when he finally got married, but now he was thinking he should spend it on an electric instead, since his marriage didn't seem to be on the schedule yet.

"Why do you need to speak with Maeve in particular?" Gino asked to see if he could get her talking.

"Is that the girl's name?"

"Yes. Maeve Smith."

She made a huffing sound of derision.

Gino tried again. "Is it because you only want to speak with another female?"

She didn't even glance at him, but she swerved so abruptly to avoid a pushcart that Gino had to grab the side of the auto to keep from being thrown.

"You're nosy, aren't you?" she said when they were clear of the pushcart.

"I'm a detective," he corrected her.

"Not a very good one if you haven't figured out who killed my parents yet."

"Who says we haven't?"

Pearl hazarded a glance at him before turning her attention back to the traffic. "Nobody has been arrested yet."

She had him there. "We're just finishing things up."

"Are you? Should I expect the police to come for me at any moment?"

"Why should they come for you?" he asked to test her.

"I don't think your Mr. Malloy believed me when I said Will and I were together the night Father was killed."

"Warren did deny it," Gino reminded her.

"He was just trying to be a gentleman."

"He also seems to care for you very much."

"Which I suppose means he'd lie to protect me. That's what you think, isn't it?"

"I suppose it is, but did he lie to protect your reputation by saying you *weren't* together, or will he lie to give you an alibi by saying you *were* together?"

"It must be very confusing being a detective," she said with sly grin.

"Yes, especially when people lie."

"Which I suppose they often do," she said, still amused.

"Yes, they do. Like the way you lied when you said you have no intention of marrying Will Warren when you actually sneak out all the time to visit him."

She was no longer amused. "That wasn't a lie."

Gino frowned. "Then maybe you'll explain to me why a young woman in your position would do a thing like that."

"Did you believe her?" Maeve asked Sarah when they were finally back home and could speak freely. They had retired to the parlor to wait for Malloy to return from his visit to Titus Wesley.

"I'm not sure. Her story didn't exactly match Tom Yingling's version, did it?"

"But Yingling might be lying," Maeve said.

"Why would he lie?"

Maeve shrugged. "Lots of reasons. Some people lie to make themselves look better or to protect somebody else or maybe just because they can."

"Who would he be protecting?" Sarah scoffed.

"Well, maybe not that. I don't think Yingling cares about anybody else enough to protect them. But it was dark, so maybe he didn't really see what happened, and he made up a story to make himself look important."

"And to get back at Carrie, if he thought she rejected him," Sarah added.

Maeve sighed. "Even if Ethel killed Bing, I believed her when she said she didn't kill Nora."

"So did I, but you're the expert, so your opinion counts more. But if she didn't kill Nora, that ruins everything. It's difficult to believe that two people—a married couple even though they hadn't lived together for a long time—were murdered by different people."

"Unless Nora really did kill herself."

"Ethel did make a good case for why she might have," Sarah allowed.

"It must have been a horrible shock for her to finally find her daughter and then realize her daughter didn't want anything to do with her."

"And yet Pearl invited her to live in the house with her and planned to keep her there," Sarah reminded her. "And Ethel herself told me they had seemed to reconcile during Nora's last days."

"But if Bing interfered with Pearl the way he did with Carrie . . ." Maeve said ominously.

"Why would that make Nora more inclined to take her own life?"

"Maybe she felt like she'd failed Pearl somehow because she wasn't there to protect her."

Sarah shook her head. "I don't believe that. Nora wasn't the kind to blame herself. She'd know whom to blame, and he was already dead."

Maeve sat up straighter. "Maybe Nora killed him, and the guilt got to her, so she killed herself."

Before Sarah could point out that Ethel would hardly have confessed if Nora was the guilty party, someone rang the front doorbell.

XIV

Sarah was hoping it wasn't Mrs. Ellsworth, since she really didn't think she could focus on a social call, but their maid, Hattie, came in a few minutes later to announce that Miss Bing and Mr. Donatelli had come to call.

"Gino?" Maeve marveled when Hattie left to escort them into the parlor.

Sarah shrugged her own confusion. Fortunately, they didn't have long to wait.

Sarah and Maeve rose when their guests came in. Before they could say anything, however, Gino said, "Miss Bing came to the office to speak with Maeve. She wouldn't tell me what it was about, so I brought her here." His smile told them he knew he had done exactly the right thing.

"Thank you, Gino," Sarah said, managing not to show her amusement at his conceit. The situation was far from funny, and she didn't want Pearl to get the idea they were laughing at her. "Would you like to speak with Maeve privately or would it be all right if I sit in?"

Pearl gave Gino a meaningful and dismissive glance, which he easily interpreted. "I'll see if Mr. Malloy's motorcar needs any attention." He closed the parlor door carefully behind him.

"You'll have to tell me how you do that," Maeve

said, earning a begrudging smile from Pearl.

"You may stay, Mrs. Malloy," Pearl said. "When you hear what I have to say, you'll understand why I didn't want to discuss it with that man."

"Of course. Please sit down. Can I get you something? Some tea, perhaps?"

"Tea would be nice." She looked as if she could do with something stronger, but Sarah couldn't possibly offer it to a respectable young lady.

Sarah rang for Hattie, who appeared instantly, being the perfect maid that she was. When Hattie had been dispatched for the tea and the women were seated, Sarah folded her hands in her lap and simply stared at Pearl expectantly. Maeve followed her lead, leaving the silence for Pearl to fill.

Pearl held herself perfectly erect, as if bracing for what was to come. She seemed reluctant to begin, looking from Maeve to Sarah and back again. Finally, she said, "That man told me you suspect that Carrie is in a family way."

Sarah managed not to wince. Why on earth had Gino told her such a thing? She'd speak to him later, but meanwhile she'd deal with Pearl. "Yes, and her mother has confirmed it."

Pearl closed her eyes and drew a shaky breath, but when she opened her eyes again, she seemed in complete control of her emotions. "Do you know who the father is?"

Was it possible she didn't know? Sarah thought not. She was probably just testing them. "Ethel has reason to believe it is Mr. Bing."

Pearl nodded, although whether to confirm or just to acknowledge the information, Sarah couldn't be sure. "That stupid girl," Pearl said. "I warned her."

"Then you knew?" Maeve said, sounding a bit too judgmental for Sarah's taste.

Pearl smiled then, a ghastly parody of joy that was painful to behold. "Oh yes. I knew exactly what he was up to with his gifts and his favors and his little attentions."

"Because you'd seen it before," Sarah guessed.

Pearl looked at her sharply. "Yes, I'd seen it before. It starts out so innocently. He tells you that you're beautiful and that he loves you more than anyone else. He brings you gifts, lovely things that you treasure because he chose them especially for you. Then he kisses you and holds you in his lap and tells you that you are more precious to him than any wife could be."

Her eyes glistened with unshed tears, and Sarah said, "Pearl, you don't have to—"

"Yes, I do," Pearl said angrily. "I need to make you understand. Because at first you don't even know it's wrong. It's just because he loves you so much, you see, and by the time you understand, it's too late, and then one day he doesn't want you because you aren't young and innocent anymore and there's a new girl who will believe his lies and do whatever he wants."

Pearl was seated alone on the love seat, and Sarah jumped up from her chair and went to her. She slipped an arm around her shoulders, but Pearl resisted her embrace.

"I don't need your pity," she said defiantly.

"Why would I pity you?" Sarah asked, blinking at tears of her own. "You are a strong young woman to have survived."

"Am I?" she asked bitterly. "I don't feel strong."

"But you are. You're stronger than you know. You tried to warn Carrie, didn't you?"

"She's such a stupid girl," Pearl said in disgust. "She said I was just jealous. She said . . ." She shuddered.

"You don't have to tell us if you don't want to," Maeve said. It was almost a plea, and Sarah was sorry that Maeve had witnessed Pearl's anguish.

But Pearl didn't seem to hear Maeve. Her gaze was fixed on Sarah now, her eyes begging her to understand. "She said he was going to marry her when she was old enough. He'd promised to divorce her mother and marry her."

"What a scoundrel," Sarah said, wishing she weren't a lady so she could say what she was really thinking.

"He used to tell me the same thing," Pearl said, "when I was a stupid girl, too. I didn't know it was impossible for a father to marry his daughter. I didn't know that he would lie to me like that. And then I was older, and he said he was done with me. I didn't realize why at first. I thought it must have something to do with Ethel, but I didn't understand why he'd married her at all. He said I needed a mother. I'm twenty years old! Why would I need a mother after all these years?"

"But it was Carrie he wanted," Sarah said.

"How could I not have known that?" she cried. "How could I not have seen what he was doing?"

"But you finally did see, didn't you?" Sarah prodded. "And you warned her."

Pearl smiled that hideous smile again. "I even tried to win him back. I used Will to make him jealous."

At last her visits to Will made sense. "Did it work?" Sarah asked, already knowing the answer.

"Of course not. I told you, he didn't want me anymore. He told me I should marry Will. Can you imagine? After raising me on the lie that I would be his wife, he wants to pass me off to the first man who comes along."

"He was going to pass Carrie off to another man as well," Maeve said, making Sarah wince. This probably wasn't the best time to mention that.

Pearl straightened in surprise. "Who told you that?"

Maeve gave Sarah a desperate glance, obviously sorry to have raised the subject.

"The man himself told us," Sarah said. "He was blackmailing your father, and he found out you were *visiting* Mr. Warren, so he decided that he should have the same, uh, privileges."

"Was it Will?" Pearl demanded.

"No, it wasn't Will."

Pearl's shoulders slumped with relief. Perhaps she cared more for Will Warren than she had claimed. "But Father was going to give Carrie to someone else to . . . use?"

"Yes," Sarah said, wondering if she should be telling Pearl all this. But it was too late now. "He may have told her the day he was killed, in fact."

Pearl seemed shocked. She stared at nothing for a long moment until Maeve finally said, "Carrie must have been very angry."

Pearl turned to her. "No, she would have been hurt. She honestly believed he loved her. She believed all of his lies."

"But what a terrible betrayal," Maeve said.

Pearl frowned. "You think she killed him, don't you?"

Maeve and Sarah exchanged a glance, and Sarah said, "Ethel has already confessed."

"Ethel?" Pearl said as if she'd never considered her father's bigamous second wife as a possible killer. "Did she know about Father's plan to . . . to . . . His plan for Carrie?" She obviously couldn't bring herself to say it.

"I don't think so. She said she had discovered

that Carrie was with child, and she wanted to get Carrie away from him." Sarah decided it wouldn't hurt to tell her everything now. "She originally tried to get a divorce from Mr. Bing."

"A divorce?" Pearl echoed as if she'd never heard the word. "Then why didn't she just divorce him? It would certainly have been easier than murdering him."

"Not really," Maeve said, earning a black look from Sarah and a puzzled one from Pearl.

"She was unable to get a divorce," Sarah explained. "Adultery is the only reason New York State will grant a divorce."

Pearl's ghastly smile bloomed again. "But he was committing adultery with Carrie."

"I'm sure you can understand why Ethel would not want that information made public."

Pearl sighed and rubbed her forehead as if it ached. It probably did. "Oh, Father, what an evil man you were." She dropped her hand and looked up. "But you said Ethel confessed to killing him. Does that mean you're going to turn her over to the police?"

Sarah bit her lip, wondering how to answer her. Maeve beat her to it. "Do you really think we should?"

Now it was Pearl's turn to hesitate, and she did, but at last she said, "He might have deserved it, but my mother didn't."

"Do you think Ethel killed your mother?" Sarah asked.

"Who else could have done it?" she challenged.

Maeve and Sarah exchanged another glance and Sarah nodded, giving Maeve permission to voice their theory. "Ethel swears she didn't harm Nora. She thinks Nora was, uh, despondent because her husband had married another woman and you had rejected her."

"*Rejected* her?" Pearl scoffed. "I didn't reject her. We were going to move out of Ethel's house and get an apartment together. I couldn't believe I'd found her again after all those years of thinking she was dead."

Ethel had even said as much.

"You didn't act like you were glad to see her again," Maeve remarked.

Pearl scowled at her. "Exactly how was I supposed to act?"

Maeve had no answer for her.

Sarah tried to smooth things over. "You did seem a bit impatient with her at the funeral."

"I was impatient with everyone at the funeral. It was a difficult day." She shook her head at the memory. "I didn't know whether to laugh or to cry. I'd lost the father I had once dearly loved who had abused me in unspeakable ways and then discarded me for another girl. Every time someone said they were sorry, I wanted to scream."

Sarah's first instinct was also to say she was sorry, too, but she bit it back. Aside from being inappropriate, what comfort could mere words offer to a young woman who had lost so much?

"I can't imagine how you must have felt that day," Maeve said, somehow finding the words Sarah couldn't. "I'm glad you were at least able to be reunited with your mother, even for so short a time."

Pearl's eyes glistened again, although she still refused to cry. "I couldn't believe she was still alive. Well, I suppose what I really couldn't believe was that my father had lied to me about it. I hated him so much then . . . But I had my mother back, and he couldn't separate us again. That was the important thing. But now . . ." She blinked, dislodging one tear that she angrily brushed away.

"And you believe Ethel killed her?" Sarah asked.

Pearl gave her an impatient look. "If she's the one who killed Father, then of course she did. How many killers do you think we have in our little family group, Mrs. Malloy?"

"But *why* would Ethel have killed her?" Maeve asked.

"Because . . ." But plainly she had no answer. She gestured helplessly. "The money, I guess."

"But Mr. Bing left Ethel and Carrie almost everything. Killing Nora would have gained them nothing," Sarah reminded her.

"She also didn't have to kill Nora to get rid of her," Maeve said. "All she had to do was ask her to leave the house that she now owns."

"And you said yourself that the two of you were planning to leave anyway," Sarah said.

Pearl frowned. "But that was before we knew about the will. I guess I just assumed I'd get some of Father's money when he died, and Mother and I could use it to live on. When I found out I'd get nothing, we knew we had no choice but to stay with Ethel. Since Ethel could only keep the house if she allowed me to live with her, I would insist that Mother stay, too. If Ethel refused, I could simply complain to the attorney that Ethel was throwing me out and we'd all be homeless. So if Ethel really objected to having Mother there, I suppose that would give her a good reason to want Mother dead."

That was certainly a reason they hadn't thought of before. "Ethel believes that Nora may have, uh, killed herself."

"Killed herself?" Pearl echoed sarcastically. She turned to Maeve. "Is that what you meant when you said Mother was *despondent?* That's ridiculous! She would never dream of such a thing."

"We can't know what someone else is going through," Sarah said gently.

"I know what my mother could endure, though," Pearl said. "She spent almost six years looking for me all over the country. She worked at any job she could find and went hungry when she couldn't find one and slept in the streets when she had to, and she never gave up. Do you think a woman like that would kill herself when she had finally found me?"

Before Sarah could even begin to think of an answer, the parlor door opened. The three women looked up to see Malloy in the doorway. His expression was grim. "Miss Bing," he said in surprise.

Pearl was on her feet. She hadn't wanted a man present at this discussion for obvious reasons, but Sarah knew he'd come from seeing the coroner.

"Did you learn anything from Mr. Wesley?" Sarah asked, rising as well.

He glanced meaningfully at Pearl, silently asking if he should speak about her mother's death in front of her.

"Miss Bing was just explaining to us why her mother couldn't possibly have committed suicide," Sarah said.

He nodded once, acknowledging that she had given him permission to speak openly.

"Miss Bing is right. According to the coroner, Mrs. Bing was murdered."

Hattie had used Frank's intrusion as an excuse to deliver the tea tray, and he had to sidle out of her way so she could get through the parlor door.

"Come in, come in," Sarah urged Frank. "Tell us everything you found out."

He made his way to the empty chair next to Maeve and across from where Sarah and Pearl Bing sat on the love seat. Pearl looked about ready to explode from either fury or outrage, maybe both.

The moment Hattie closed the parlor door behind herself, Frank said, "I'm surprised to see you here, Miss Bing."

"She went to the office first," Maeve explained. "She wanted to speak to me, so Gino brought her here."

Frank hadn't missed the note of pride in Maeve's voice when she said Pearl had wanted to speak to her. "I see," he said, although he didn't, not really.

"Miss Bing wanted to speak with a female. She was just confirming the things we suspected about Mr. Bing," Sarah said.

Since he knew how sensitive those things were, he also didn't bother to ask for clarification. No sense in causing Miss Bing discomfort when he still needed some answers from her.

"We were also telling Miss Bing that Ethel confessed to killing Mr. Bing," Sarah continued.

Frank couldn't conceal his surprise, although something in Sarah's tone warned him that she didn't really believe it. "She confessed?" he echoed in amazement.

"Yes," Sarah confirmed, still sending him some kind of silent message about the truthfulness of this confession. "But she insists she didn't kill Nora. She believes Nora committed suicide."

"But you just said she was murdered," Pearl reminded him. She was leaning forward in her seat and ignoring the teacup Sarah was trying to hand her. "How do you know?"

"I went to see the undertaker," he said. "The one I suggested you send your mother to. Thank you for that, by the way."

She waved away his thanks with an impatient flick of her wrist. "What did he say?"

"He explained to me how he determines if someone was poisoned accidentally or on purpose." He briefly recounted Titus Wesley's observations about the poison being in both the flask and the whiskey bottle and what that probably meant.

Pearl no longer looked merely upset. She looked deadly serious. "Anyone could have sneaked into Mother's room and put arsenic into the whiskey bottle."

"I gather that your mother was in the habit of carrying the flask with her," Sarah said in that gentle voice she used when she was saying something terrible but didn't want to give offense. Frank was always amazed at how well it worked, and this time was no exception.

"I won't apologize for her," Pearl said apologetically.

"You don't need to. She had a very difficult time of it after your father deserted her," Sarah said. "Ethel saw her pouring from it more than once, so I assume anyone else might have seen the same thing."

Plainly, Pearl hated to admit it, but she said, "Yes. She said it helped her forget the bad things, and everyone in the house knew she used it."

"How did she fill the flask?" Sarah asked, using that soft voice again.

Pearl winced but she said, "She would take a bottle from Father's liquor cabinet up to her room. He had a nice supply."

"So, somebody could have gone in her room and poisoned the bottle," Frank said, "knowing that she would fill her flask from it."

"What about the arsenic itself?" Maeve said. "Who had access to it?"

"Everyone," Pearl said. "It was in the pantry where anyone might find it. The only question is, Who hated my mother enough to use it?"

No one spoke for a long moment and finally Maeve said, "I know you think she had a good reason, but Ethel swears she didn't do it."

"Well, she would, wouldn't she?" Pearl said bitterly. "You might forgive her for killing my father when you know what kind of a man he was, but not for killing my mother, who never harmed anyone at all."

"Wait," Frank said, suddenly confused. He turned to Pearl. "What reason do you have for thinking Ethel killed your mother?"

"Because of the house. Ethel had to allow me to live there or she would lose it, and I insisted that Mother be allowed to stay. The only way to get rid of my mother was to kill her."

"That seems like a rather weak reason to kill someone, but if it wasn't Ethel, who is left?" Sarah said. "Carrie might have had a reason for killing Mr. Bing, but not for killing Nora."

Pearl made a moaning sound. "So it probably *was* Ethel, but it doesn't really matter who it was. I know it wasn't me, and now I'm afraid to eat or drink anything in that house."

"Then you can stay here," Sarah said.

Pearl looked up in surprise. "I couldn't possibly do that."

"Why not? We have plenty of room, and it's just until we figure this out. Once we do, you'll be perfectly safe."

"But I don't have any clothes and—"

"We'll send someone for your things and to tell Ethel where you are," Sarah said.

"I'll go," Maeve said. "Gino can take me in Mr. Malloy's motor."

Pearl took a long moment to consider the offer. "I . . . Thank you. You're very kind."

Kindness had little to do with it. Frank knew Sarah wouldn't want another death if she could prevent it.

"We're happy to help," Sarah said.

"But I can't let someone else collect my things," Pearl said. "I have my auto. I'll just go back and tell Ethel what I've decided and pack for myself."

"Will you be able to fit everything in your auto?" Maeve asked. Frank had been wondering the same thing. Pearl's auto was awfully small.

"I'll just need enough clothes for a few days. I can collect the rest later."

"And maybe we'll clear all this up by then and you'll feel safe enough to go home," Sarah said.

Pearl didn't look like she believed that, but she nodded. "I should go now."

"There's no rush," Sarah said, "and luncheon is almost ready. Stay and eat with us first."

"And then you won't be tempted to eat anything poisonous there," Maeve added with a sly grin.

Pearl returned it with a wan smile. "I suppose you're right."

"Is Gino still here?" Frank asked.

"Yes. He's probably out in the garage," Sarah said.

"I'll tell him what's going on and invite him to lunch, too," Frank said, glad for the opportunity to escape.

He found Gino in the garage, fiddling with the motorcar. He looked up and grinned when he saw

Frank. "Did Wesley give you anything useful?"

Frank told him Wesley's theory about the poisoning.

"Mrs. Frank was sure Nora didn't kill herself," Gino reminded him.

"Pearl Bing is sure, too. She even thinks she knows the reason Nora was murdered."

"Do tell," Gino said with a grin.

"Remember, Bing's will left the house to Ethel as long as she let Pearl live with her until she married, but Pearl wanted Nora to live there with her, so Pearl thinks Ethel murdered Nora to get rid of an unwelcome houseguest."

Gino closed the engine cover with a bang and shook his head. "That seems a little extreme."

"I thought so, too, but it seems that Ethel has already confessed to killing Bing."

"When did that happen?" Gino asked in amazement.

"When Sarah and Maeve visited her this morning. I haven't had a chance to discuss it with Sarah yet, but I got the impression she didn't believe Ethel's confession, and Ethel denies killing Nora. She insists Nora killed herself."

"But she didn't kill herself."

"Exactly," Frank said with a sigh. "Why confess to one murder and not the other? And now Pearl is afraid to stay in that house, and who can blame her, so Sarah offered to let her come here for the time being."

"That makes sense, I guess."

"Pearl is going to drive herself back to the house to pack up after we eat lunch. You're invited to eat with us."

Gino grinned at that. "Thanks. I wonder if Miss Bing would like someone to drive her. That auto of hers is a dream."

"But awfully cold in winter, as Sarah would remind you."

"The one she was driving at Warren's shop was enclosed," Gino remembered.

Frank decided not to respond to that. "Come on in and eat. You can try talking Pearl into letting you drive her auto."

Lunch was a quiet affair. Pearl seemed sunk in gloom, probably wondering what was to become of her with no inheritance unless she married and no place to live where she felt safe. Sarah tried to make small talk but discussing the weather didn't take much time and no one else seemed able to think of another topic that wouldn't recall Pearl's predicament.

When they had eaten, Sarah took Pearl upstairs to choose a guest room, then she saw Pearl off on her errand. Maeve offered to go with her, but Pearl insisted on facing Ethel alone. Gino had lingered until Pearl was gone, probably still hoping Pearl would let him drive her. Then he and Maeve left for the office.

In the meantime, Frank had sat down in the

parlor to enjoy a few minutes of peace and quiet when he could consider all they knew about the Bing murders and see if he could make sense of it.

Sarah found him there. "Poor Pearl," she said, sinking down into the chair beside his. "I don't think she has slept well since her father died, and her mother's death has been quite a shock. She doesn't even know if she should have a funeral since hardly anyone in the city even knew her."

"Somehow I can't picture Ethel and Carrie helping her mourn either."

Sarah shook her head. "It's so sad. I wish she did love Will Warren. At least he could offer her some sort of a life, and if she married, she would get the dowry her father left her."

"Which reminds me, I don't think anyone ever checked to see if she really was with Warren the night her father was killed."

"That's right, we didn't," she said. "I think we were so sure of it that when she finally admitted they were together, we simply believed her."

"But even if they were together, they still could have killed him."

"Do you think Pearl drove Carrie's auto and that Will just—I don't know—stood by and watched while Pearl ran over Mr. Bing?" Sarah said with a wry grin.

"Well, maybe not. There's also the matter of Ethel confessing to killing Bing, and now we know that Ethel had a reason for wanting Nora out of the way, even if it doesn't make sense to us."

"I just wish I believed she did it," Sarah said.

Frank grinned. "I knew you didn't believe it. Why not?"

Sarah sighed. "No real reason except Maeve and I both thought she was telling the truth when she said she didn't kill Nora."

"I might question your judgment on that, but Maeve is somewhat of an expert on lying, isn't she?"

"Yes, she is. It's a dubious talent but a useful one. The trouble is, we both also aren't sure she was telling the truth about killing Mr. Bing."

Frank winced. "I can see why that would be a problem."

Sarah seemed oblivious to his dismay. "I can understand why Ethel would deny killing Nora, especially if she didn't do it, but why confess to killing Mr. Bing?"

Frank decided to play along. "To protect someone else. That's the usual reason, but who is she protecting?"

"The obvious answer is Carrie, but that brings us back to Carrie having no reason to kill Nora at all."

"Which brings us back to Ethel," Frank said. "Nora's death has really ruined all our theories. If what Tom Yingling told Gino is true about Bing's death—"

"Wait, I almost forgot," Sarah said. "What does Tom Yingling look like?"

Frank tried to remember. "I only saw him at the funeral. You probably did, too."

"I didn't really pay that much attention. What do you remember about him?"

"He's young," Frank recalled. "Kind of homely, if he's the one I'm thinking of."

"Freckles? Protruding front teeth?" Sarah asked.

"I think so. Why do you care?"

"Maeve and I saw a young man leaving the Bing house when we arrived there this morning. He was wearing work clothes, like the men in Will Warren's shop, and I wondered if it could have been him."

"Why would he have been at the Bing house?"

"That's what I would like to know. I wondered if he was bringing a message from Will Warren or something."

"A message to Pearl, you think?"

"I don't know. I guess we'll need to ask her when she gets back. Whatever his reason for being there, he looked awfully pleased with himself when he left."

Maeve and Gino walked to the office since they had no excuse for needing the motorcar. Gino offered her his arm, and after a moment's consideration, she took it. He rewarded her with a satisfied grin that almost made her regret her decision, but being close to him was too nice, so she left her hand where it was.

They weren't able to discuss the case while they were out in public, which gave Maeve a chance to think through what they knew.

She'd been reviewing everything Ethel had told them when she confessed to killing Mr. Bing. She apparently hadn't known Bing was going to force Carrie to submit to Tom Yingling to protect himself from a charge of murdering Carrie's father. That would have given Ethel another reason to want the man dead, but the one they already knew about was reason enough.

But had Bing told Ethel his plans for Carrie that night when he'd gone over to speak to the woman in the auto? Bing had assumed it would be Carrie, and Tom Yingling had, too, but Ethel hadn't allowed Carrie out that night.

Or so she said.

One detail kept bothering Maeve, though. If Ethel was indeed the woman in the auto that had killed Bing, what had they been arguing about? Tom Yingling said that Bing had spent some time talking to the woman before starting back for him. If the driver had been Ethel, what would they have been talking about? Bing might have been angry that Carrie wasn't there, because that ruined his plans, but after berating Ethel for coming in Carrie's place, what would they have had to discuss? She might have been berating him for trading away Carrie's virtue, but she didn't seem to know even now that he'd done that.

Then again, she was assuming Tom Yingling had told the truth. On that thought, they had reached the office, and Gino unlocked the door and held it for her.

"What does Tom Yingling look like?" she asked Gino.

Gino gave her a puzzled look as he closed the office door behind them. "Why do you want to know?"

"Because Mrs. Malloy and I saw a young man leaving the Bing house this morning. He was dressed like somebody who should have gone to the kitchen door, but he was coming out the front door."

Gino frowned as he considered her question. "Yingling is about my age. Kind of gangly. Lots of freckles and his front teeth stick out."

"It was him, then. But what would Tom Yingling be doing at the Bing house?" Maeve mused.

"No reason I can think of," Gino said.

Maeve slipped off her coat and hung it on the coat tree before taking her seat behind her desk. Gino pulled one of the client chairs over and sat down in front of her desk, plainly intending to continue their discussion. "But he must have had a reason or he wouldn't have been there," she said.

Gino lifted his feet and propped them on her desk, ignoring her frown of disapproval. Then he gazed up at the ceiling as if he was thinking or maybe looking for divine intervention. "Let's see what it could have been. Was he delivering something?"

"Something for one of the autos?" Maeve said. "But wouldn't he have gone to the garage for that?"

"And to the back door," Gino agreed, leaning back in his chair so it balanced on the two rear legs. "Maybe it was a message."

"Who would he be delivering a message for?" When she thought of who lived in the house, she shuddered. "Ew, you don't think he was trying to see Carrie, do you?"

Gino frowned his distaste. "Only if he was an idiot."

Maeve nodded. "He still might have wanted to collect on his blackmail threat, but with Bing dead, there was no one to force Carrie to comply."

Gino considered this for a moment, and then his eyes grew wide, and he jerked his feet off her desk and his chair came back down onto all four legs with a thump. "Unless he thought he had a new way to blackmail her."

"What do you mean?"

"I mean, he thought the woman in Carrie's auto—the one that ran over Bing—was Carrie. That would make Carrie a murderer. After he saw

Bing kill Lane, Tom had decided to blackmail Bing into giving him Carrie, so if it worked on one murderer, why wouldn't it work on another one?"

"Oh, Gino, that makes my skin crawl, but how could he blackmail Carrie if he already told you she was the killer?"

"You'll have to ask him, but I think he just may not be very smart."

"Evidently not, but I think you may be right about him blackmailing her. You should have seen the expression on his face when he left the Bing house. He was actually whistling!"

"Which means he must have been successful in whatever his business had been at the house this morning," Gino said.

"Do you think they would have let him see Carrie? I mean, rich people are so proper and the servants don't let just anybody in."

"He worked at Warren's shop. Maybe he said he was there on business or something."

"Business with Carrie?" Maeve scoffed.

"I don't know. I'm just guessing." He looked awfully cute when he was defensive.

"And so am I, but if he saw Carrie and he was hoping to blackmail her the same way he was blackmailing Bing . . ."

"And he left with a smile on his face . . ." Gino added.

"Then Carrie was the woman in the auto."

"And she's the one who killed Bing."

XV

Waiting for Pearl's return became somewhat of an ordeal. Sarah and Malloy had gone round and round after Maeve and Gino left, trying to decide if wanting to keep a house was enough of a reason for Ethel Lane to have murdered Nora Bing. Malloy thought it might be—people had been murdered for far less—but Sarah still believed Ethel's claim of innocence.

Eventually, Mother Malloy and Brian returned from his school. Mother Malloy volunteered there, mainly so she could get lessons in American Sign Language but also so she had something worthwhile to do with herself now that Brian was in school all day. Brian had many things to tell them, and then Maeve and Gino brought Catherine home from Miss Spence's School and she also had many things to tell them, giving Sarah little time to wonder why Gino had returned with them.

When the children finally calmed down, Maeve ushered them upstairs to the nursery with a wistful smile for Sarah. "Gino has something to tell you," she confided as the children clattered up the stairs. "Something I figured out."

Sarah couldn't help her grin. Of course Maeve would want credit. Her duties with the children often prevented her from helping as much with investigations as she would like.

"What have you two been up to?" Sarah asked Gino as she led the two men into the parlor.

"Have they been up to something?" Malloy asked with interest.

"Maeve said she figured something out," Sarah said provocatively, and as expected, Gino responded with feigned outrage.

"We both figured it out," he said, waiting until Sarah seated herself on the love seat before plopping down in one of the comfortable overstuffed chairs across from it. "Carrie killed Bing, just like Tom Yingling said."

"But Ethel already confessed to killing Bing," Sarah reminded him.

"She's just trying to protect Carrie."

Malloy obviously wasn't convinced. "Can we assume you have an actual reason to believe it was Carrie?"

Gino grinned and leaned forward in his chair. "Yes, we do, as a matter of fact. Do you remember seeing Tom Yingling at the Bing house this morning?" he asked Sarah.

"I remember seeing a young man that I think was Mr. Yingling," she said.

"Maeve remembers him, too, and from the description, I think we can be fairly sure it was him. Did you think he looked happy?"

Sarah frowned at his cocky attitude, but she said, "He did seem to be."

"Maeve said he was whistling."

"I do believe he was. And he was grinning, too, if that means anything."

"What could have made him so happy, do you think?"

"This isn't a parlor game, Gino," Malloy said irritably. "What are you getting at?"

Gino straightened in his chair, but he didn't bother to wipe the smug grin from his face while he briefly explained his and Maeve's theory that Tom Yingling had decided to blackmail Carrie for her favors just as he had done with Bing.

"Oh dear," Sarah said. "That poor girl."

"That *poor girl* is a murderer," Gino reminded her.

"But only if your theory is right," Malloy cautioned. "She could also be protecting her mother, who is the real killer."

"Do you really think Carrie would agree to something so vile to protect someone else, though?" Sarah asked, thinking of the rude, selfish girl she knew Carrie to be.

"And we still can't think of a reason Carrie would want to kill Nora Bing," Malloy said.

"Maybe Pearl can think of one," Gino said. "Is she back yet?"

Sarah frowned. "No, she's not. I'm starting to worry about her."

"She probably had a lot of things to pack," Gino said.

"She was only going to bring enough clothes for a few days," Sarah said. "It shouldn't have taken her this long."

"She'll be back in time for supper," Malloy said. "We know she won't eat anything in that house."

But Pearl didn't return in time for supper. They'd set a place for her at the table, but she didn't arrive. Sarah could hardly eat for wondering what could have kept her.

"If only they were on the telephone," she said more than once.

"We'll go over to the Bing house as soon as we're finished here," Malloy finally told her.

They couldn't speak freely in front of the children at the dinner table, but Sarah couldn't help thinking that Pearl had returned to a house where someone had already murdered two people. Whether that person was Carrie or Ethel, they might well kill Pearl, too.

"Do you want me to drive you?" Gino asked hopefully when Maeve had taken the children back to the nursery after dinner.

Sarah entertained the disloyal thought that they'd get to the Bing house faster if Gino drove the motorcar—he thought nothing of exceeding the city's five-mile-per-hour speed limit, while Malloy faithfully observed it—but she decided not to mention it. Malloy apparently agreed, however, and he told Gino to bring the motor around to the front door.

When they were suitably garbed in their dusters and goggles, Gino drove them to the Bing house. Sarah tried not to imagine all the terrible things that might have happened to Pearl in the meantime. Perhaps there was a perfectly good reason that didn't involve murder for why she hadn't returned to the Malloy house this afternoon.

Gino pulled up in front of the Bing house, and they hurried up the front steps without even bothering to remove their dusters.

The maid who answered the door was surprised to see three people looming on the front stoop in their ghostly garb, but she recognized Sarah from her previous visit.

"Is Miss Pearl Bing here?" Sarah demanded.

"No, ma'am, she isn't home," the maid said, her eyes still wide with amazement at their appearance.

"Then we need to speak with Mrs. Bing immediately," Sarah said, using the tone she had perfected when she'd been the daughter of an old New York society family.

The maid actually bobbed a curtsy but left them standing in the hall while she scurried off to find her mistress.

"I think you scared her," Malloy remarked, and

Gino coughed, probably so he wouldn't laugh. Nothing about this was funny.

The maid shortly reappeared and took them up to the parlor, where Ethel Lane waited. She also looked alarmed.

"Mrs. Malloy," Ethel said, "And Mr. Malloy and . . ."

"Gino Donatelli," he supplied helpfully.

"Have you . . . Have you come to arrest me?" Ethel asked.

No wonder she looked alarmed.

"We aren't the police," Malloy assured her. "We can't arrest anyone."

"Then what . . . ?" She gestured helplessly.

"We're looking for Pearl, Mrs. Lane," Sarah said.

"She isn't here," Ethel said. She was wringing her hands now, which alarmed Sarah as much as their visit had alarmed Ethel.

"Where is she, then?" Sarah asked, hearing the edge in her own voice but unable to do anything about it.

"I don't know. Pearl doesn't confide in me, I'm afraid."

"But she *was* here earlier today, wasn't she?" Malloy asked, equally as impatient.

"What? Oh yes, she came home and . . . She packed a bag and then she left again."

Which meant Ethel knew Pearl was leaving the house. Had she been afraid Pearl would move out and cost Ethel her home? If that was the reason for Nora's murder . . .

"Didn't she tell you where she was going?" Malloy asked.

"As I said, she doesn't confide in me," Ethel said, her nervous gaze flicking back and forth between Sarah and Malloy. "I did ask her, but she . . ." Ethel sighed wearily. "She said she would feel safer if I didn't know where she was."

Sarah winced at that, but Pearl was certainly justified to feel that way. "Pearl had come to our house to tell us, uh, some things we didn't know. She said she was afraid to eat or drink anything in this house after what happened to her mother."

Ethel gazed back at Sarah in despair. "I'm so sorry she feels that way, but I don't suppose anyone could blame her. No one here would harm her, though. I promise you that."

Sarah had no idea how Ethel could make promises on anyone else's behalf, but she said, "We invited her to stay with us until we get everything figured out. She was supposed to return to our house, but she never arrived."

"But she left hours ago," Ethel said, wringing her hands again. "Where could she be?"

"Are you sure you don't know?" Gino asked a little too harshly, Sarah thought.

Ethel's eyes widened in alarm. "You don't think I did something to her, do you? I would never harm her."

"Someone harmed her mother and her father," Sarah reminded her more gently. "Did Carrie see her when she was here?"

The color drained from Ethel's face, but she lifted her chin in a poor parody of defiance. "She and Pearl had a few words, but then Carrie went to her room to pout and Pearl left. I swear to you, Pearl was perfectly well then. I . . ." Ethel covered her face with her hands, and Sarah immediately went to her side.

"Here, sit down," Sarah said, directing her to the nearest chair.

"I should have asked all of you to sit down," Ethel murmured. "I'm so sorry . . ."

"Don't worry about that now," Sarah said sharply to get her attention. "We need to find Pearl and make sure she's all right."

Ethel lowered her hands and gazed up at Sarah in dismay. "I didn't hurt her and neither did Carrie. We didn't do anything to her. She was fine when she left here, just like I said, and she didn't say where she was going."

Sarah was inclined to believe her, but they still needed to make sure. "If she didn't feel safe here, where else would she go?" Sarah asked. "What about her friends? Is there someone she could turn to?"

"She didn't have any friends," Ethel said. "Mr. Bing never allowed her to meet anyone. He never allowed any of us to see anyone socially."

What a dreary life for the three females, although Bing probably needed to keep the girls isolated so they'd never realize how oddly perverse their family really was.

"Where would she go, then?" Malloy said. "You must have some idea."

"A hotel?" Ethel tried. But they all knew that no respectable hotel would admit a woman alone.

"Did she have any money?" Malloy asked, always practical.

Ethel's expression of dismay became distress. "I don't think so."

Then she couldn't have gone to a hotel. "There must be someone she could go to," Sarah said. "Otherwise, she would have returned to our house."

They all realized the answer at the same time.

"Warren," Malloy said for all of them.

She might not be in love with him, but he would protect her. "Do you know where he lives?" Sarah asked Ethel.

"I . . . I think I have his address in my book. I had to write to thank him for the flowers he sent to Mr. Bing's funeral."

Sarah hustled Ethel to the family parlor where she had her desk, and Ethel located her diary. Sure enough, she had an address for Warren.

"You'll let me know that Pearl is all right, won't you?" Ethel said as they prepared to leave.

Malloy and Gino both looked astonished, but

Sarah said, "Of course we will, and if we don't find her, we'll be back to see if you can think of any other place she could be."

Gino shook his head as they crossed the sidewalk and began to climb into the motorcar. "We thought she might've killed Pearl, but now she's worried Pearl might be in danger."

"She is pretty softhearted to be a cold-blooded killer," Malloy remarked.

Gino pulled the crank from the trunk and started for the front of the vehicle. "She would've killed Bing in hot blood, don't you think?"

"If she did kill him," Sarah said. "But we can worry about that after we find Pearl."

Night had fallen over the city, and the motorcar's acetylene lamps provided little assistance. Only the main streets of the city had electric lights, and the gaslights on the side streets were far less effective. Still, they were finally able to locate the address Ethel had given them. The house was a newer brownstone and Sarah could readily understand why people would question Will Warren's need for such a magnificent dwelling. A light burned in the front window, and they wasted no time in climbing the front steps. Malloy pounded on the door, probably figuring that would be more likely to be answered than a polite rap or ringing the doorbell.

After only a few minutes the door opened

and Will Warren himself stood there. Sarah remembered that he had claimed not to have any servants who could serve as his alibi for the night Alvin Bing died.

"What on earth . . . ?" he said in amazement at the sight of them before Malloy pushed his way inside.

"Where is Miss Bing?" Malloy demanded, sounding more like an outraged father than a private detective.

"I'm right here," she said from a nearby doorway.

Sarah pushed past Warren and Malloy and went to her. "Are you all right?"

Pearl stared at her as if she thought her insane. "I'm fine. What on earth are you doing here? How did you find me?"

"We were alarmed when you didn't return," Sarah said, thinking she really shouldn't have to explain this, "so we went to find you. Ethel said you had been there and gone."

Pearl was still amazed. "Did you think they'd murdered me?"

"The thought did cross our minds," Gino said from where he stood in the front doorway.

Will Warren muttered something that might have been a curse. "Miss Bing is perfectly safe here. We . . . We're going to be married," he added with a bit less certainty and a nervous glance at Pearl.

She did not contradict him. "I suppose I should have told you where I was going," she said to Sarah.

"That would have been helpful."

"I didn't think it was anyone's business but my own," Pearl said, amused now that she had all the facts. "I had no idea you would care so much."

"Perhaps you just aren't used to people caring about you," Sarah said.

"It is a rather new experience."

Sarah glanced at Mr. Warren, who was frowning at this exchange, probably because he didn't quite understand what was going on. "I care about you," he said.

She gave him a sad smile. "Yes, I know."

"You don't need to make any hasty decisions," Sarah said, wondering if Pearl would choose to marry Will Warren if she thought she had another choice.

"I'm not making a hasty decision," Pearl said. "Please don't tell Ethel where you found me."

"I'm afraid she is the one who gave us Mr. Warren's address, so she already suspects," Sarah said. "And she asked us to let her know you are all right, so that's one more person who cares about you."

"Do you really think so?" Pearl asked with bemusement. "Well, she's not the one I'm worried about, in any case. I don't suppose there's any way to keep it from Carrie, is there?"

"We'll figure something out," Malloy said, surprising Sarah.

"She's the one, you know," Pearl said. "She killed Father, and she killed my mother, too. You should have seen the look she gave me when she saw me packing my clothes. It could have drawn blood. I may not know why she did it, but I'm sure she did."

"If we could figure out why, we would have a much better chance of doing something about it," Malloy lamented.

"I don't really blame her for killing Father. He deserved it after what he did to her. To *us*," she added sadly. "But I'll never forgive her for killing Mother."

"Just stay here until . . . until we contact you," Sarah said.

"And don't let Carrie in," Gino advised Will Warren, who answered him with a glare.

As they made their way back to the motorcar, Sarah said, "That was a relief."

"To know she's safe, yes," Malloy said, "but what are we going to do about Ethel and Carrie? One of them is a killer, and we can't let that killer get away with it."

"Ethel did ask us to let her know Pearl was all right," Sarah said. "Let's also ask her again about killing Mr. and Mrs. Bing so you can judge for yourself if she's telling the truth."

They had little opportunity for conversation on

the drive back to the Bing house, but they also had little need for it. Their mission was clear. They needed to determine once and for all who had killed Alvin and Nora Bing.

This time they removed their dusters before seeking admittance, and the maid took them right up, informing them that Mrs. Bing had been awaiting their return.

Ethel was on her feet the moment they entered. "Is Pearl all right?"

"Yes, she's fine," Sarah assured her.

Ethel literally sagged with relief. "Thank heaven." She looked as if she might collapse completely and Sarah hurried to her side, just in case.

"Please sit down," Ethel said with a weary wave of her hand as she did so herself, probably because her legs couldn't hold her anymore.

Sarah moved to the chair nearest her, leaving Malloy and Gino to their own devices. "Are you well?" she asked Ethel, who didn't look well at all.

"I'm just worried. About Pearl, that is. Was she with Mr. Warren as we thought?"

"Yes," Sarah said, earning a frown from Malloy, who was probably remembering Pearl's entreaty not to tell anyone.

Ethel sighed. "That's good. Mr. Warren will protect her."

"Protect her from what?" Malloy asked before

Sarah could. He'd taken a seat on the sofa and now he leaned forward expectantly.

Ethel seemed disturbed by the question. "Oh, from . . . from everything, I suppose. Life can be difficult for a woman alone."

Which was certainly true but probably not what she had originally meant. "Mrs. Lane, Nora Bing did not take her own life," Sarah said.

Ethel looked up in alarm. "What . . . ? How can you possibly know that?"

"The coroner told us," Malloy said. "He could tell by the way she was poisoned."

Which was a stretching of the truth, but it had the desired effect on Ethel. She looked as if she might faint, and Sarah was glad she was sitting down.

"Our only question is who might have put the arsenic into the whiskey bottle," Sarah said gently.

"That's how it was done, then?" Ethel asked in a hoarse whisper.

Sarah nodded.

"I did it," Ethel said. "I put the arsenic into the whiskey bottle. We all knew she drank. All of us. Everyone in the house," she added almost desperately.

"Then Carrie would have known," Malloy said with a gentleness that impressed Sarah.

Ethel's eyes widened but her face was already bloodless, so she couldn't turn any whiter. "*All* of us knew," she said weakly.

"We know why Carrie killed Mr. Bing," Sarah said, drawing Ethel's terrified gaze back to her.

"But she doesn't know about the baby. She doesn't know that she's . . . she's with child. She's too young and she doesn't know anything about . . . about that sort of thing," Ethel said.

"And you haven't told her," Sarah guessed.

"Not yet. I didn't . . . With everything else, I didn't want to upset her. There's plenty of time . . ."

"And I don't suppose she told you Mr. Bing's plans for her, did she?" Sarah asked.

A spasm of pain flickered across Ethel's face. "She told me he had promised to marry her."

"But there was more," Sarah said, sure now that Ethel hadn't known everything. "You suspected that Mr. Bing had killed your husband, but Tom Yingling actually saw him do it."

"Who is Tom Yingling?" Ethel asked, genuinely confused.

"He works in Will Warren's shop. He's one of the mechanics," Malloy said.

"Are you telling me he saw Mr. Bing kill Kenneth and he did nothing?" Ethel cried in horror.

"He did do something," Malloy said. "He started blackmailing Bing."

Ethel began to rub her temples with her fingertips, and she squeezed her eyes closed, as if she could block out the awful truth of it. Then she suddenly sat up straight and dropped her hands.

"That's it, isn't it? Tom Yingling killed Alvin," she said.

"Blackmailers don't kill their victims," Malloy said reasonably. "That would be foolish. No, blackmailers usually get greedier, and that's what happened. Tom decided he wanted more."

"More money?" Ethel asked.

"No," Sarah said, sending Malloy a glance so he would allow her to break this news. "He wanted Carrie."

"He wanted to marry her?" Ethel asked, obviously confused again.

"We don't think he had marriage in mind," Sarah said tactfully.

Ethel closed her eyes again and a shudder shook her. "My poor little girl."

"He told her that day," Malloy said. "Bing did, the day he died. He told her either earlier in the day, which may be why she went home in the afternoon, or he told her when she came to fetch him later when the show was over. Either way, she was angry, Mrs. Lane, and who could blame her? She was so angry that she ran over him with her auto."

Ethel was weeping silently now, large tears running unchecked down her pale cheeks. "How could he do such a thing to her? She's just a baby."

No one had an answer for her.

"You weren't driving Carrie's auto that night, were you, Mrs. Lane?" Sarah said. "You had no idea Mr. Bing was planning to let Tom Yingling have his way with Carrie that night. You hadn't even thought about murdering Mr. Bing because you aren't the kind of woman who thinks of things like murder, are you?"

"I did want him to die," Ethel insisted. "It was the only way I could see of being free of him, of getting Carrie free of him."

"But you'd never do it yourself, would you?"

"Yes! Yes, I would," Ethel insisted, but she fooled no one.

"Why don't we ask Carrie what she thought of Mr. Bing's plans to give her to Tom Yingling," Sarah said.

"She's just a child," Ethel said. "She would never . . ."

But Sarah had already risen and pulled the bell cord that would summon the maid.

She came almost at once, making Sarah suspect she had been listening outside the door to find out what these strange visitors had wanted. "Yes, ma'am?" she said with a questioning look at Ethel.

"Would you ask Miss Carrie to join us?" Sarah said.

The girl's gaze darted to Sarah and then back to her mistress again. "Miss Carrie isn't here, ma'am."

Ethel jumped to her feet. "What do you mean, she's not here?"

"She went out, ma'am." The maid glanced

374

around at the four people gaping at her now. "She . . . I think she took her automobile, ma'am."

"Gino, go check the garage," Malloy said.

Gino hurried out.

"Did she say where she was going?" Sarah asked in her commanding voice.

"No, ma'am. She never tells us anything."

"Where could she have gone?" Ethel wailed, wringing her hands.

"I don't suppose she has any friends she would visit," Sarah said.

"No. She . . . she used to have friends, at school, but Mr. Bing decided she didn't need to go to school anymore. She hasn't seen anyone since . . . since we came here to live."

"Could she have gone to find Pearl?" Malloy asked.

That had been Sarah's first thought, but when she asked herself why Carrie might sneak out at night, she thought of Pearl's late-night visits to Will Warren, and . . . "Did Tom Yingling call here this morning?"

"That young man who was . . . ?" Ethel glanced at the maid and decided not to finish that sentence. "Why would he have called on us?"

But Sarah turned to the maid who still stood in the doorway, watching the conversation with avid interest. "Did a young man call here this morning, just before I arrived to visit Mrs. Lane?"

The girl nodded quickly. "Yes, ma'am. I tried to send him around to the back, but he said he needed to speak to Miss Carrie."

"Why didn't you tell me this?" Ethel demanded.

The girl winced but she said, "He said it was about her automobile. I know how much store she sets by that machine, so I went to ask if she'd see him, and she did."

"She actually spoke with him?" Sarah asked, to clarify.

"Yes, ma'am. She sent me away, so I didn't hear what they said, but he was here for a few minutes, and then he left."

Sarah turned to Malloy, who was frowning.

"What?" Ethel demanded, seeing their expressions. "What is it?"

Sarah sent the maid away before replying and made sure the parlor door was securely closed. The servants already had enough to gossip about. When she turned back, she said, "Mrs. Lane, you should sit down."

Ethel sank obediently back into her chair, all resistance gone as she braced herself for whatever additional bad news Sarah had to deliver. "Tom Yingling saw Carrie run over Mr. Bing the night he was killed."

Ethel's eyes were so full of anguish, Sarah could hardly bear to meet her gaze. She even seemed to have forgotten she had claimed to be the one who killed Alvin Bing. "How could that be?"

"He had come to the show that night because Bing was going to send Carrie off with him when she arrived to take Bing home," Malloy said.

"He saw Carrie drive up in her auto, and he watched as Mr. Bing went over to tell her she'd be going home with Tom," Sarah said. "Then he saw her run over Mr. Bing."

"With Bing dead," Malloy continued when Ethel couldn't seem to summon any reply, "we think that Yingling decided to blackmail Carrie instead. Her, uh, favors in exchange for his silence."

"That may have been why he came to the house this morning," Sarah said, "to inform her of his demands."

"But she would never . . ." Ethel said faintly, shaking her head in silent denial. "She would have told me. Surely, she would have. I'm her mother. I could've helped her."

The parlor door opened, startling them all, and Gino slipped in, his expression grave. "Her motorcar is gone."

Ethel's gaze touched each of them. "Do you think she's gone to him? If she did, we have to stop her. We can't let her . . ." Her voice broke on a sob, and she covered her face with her hands.

Sarah could see that they all were thinking that it might well be too late to prevent Carrie from being raped, but they could certainly go and get her and bring her home again.

"I know where Yingling lives," Gino said.

Ethel was on her feet again. "Then you must take me to her."

"Let us go instead," Sarah said. "I'm a nurse in case . . . And Mr. Malloy and Gino will manage Mr. Yingling. You stay here in the event she returns home before we find her. She might have gone someplace else entirely, you know."

It was a lie of kindness and Ethel didn't believe it for a moment, but she clung to it just the same. "Take care of her and bring her back to me."

"I will," Sarah promised.

When they were out on the street again, Gino said, "Yingling's landlady doesn't allow female visitors. Maybe she caught Carrie and sent her away."

"We can hope," Sarah said.

They quickly slipped into their dusters and goggles and Gino cranked the engine to life. The trip through the darkened city went quickly since the hour was growing late and most people were safely tucked into their houses by now. Gino steered expertly through the sparse traffic, passing plodding draft horses pulling rickety wagons and the occasional hansom cab. At last they reached the ramshackle house where Yingling roomed.

This time Gino went first. The landlady opened the door a crack to peer out, and Gino smiled his most charming smile. "I'm sorry to bother you so late, but I need to see Tom Yingling right away."

"Come back in the morning," she told him, not charmed at all.

"We think he has sneaked a young lady into his room and her mother has sent us to rescue her," Gino said, slapping his hand on the wooden panel when she would have slammed the door in their faces.

The landlady opened the door a little wider. "I don't allow no young ladies to be sneaked upstairs in my house."

"He told me he often does it and that you never catch him," Gino said, apparently outraged to know such a thing.

She had to think this over for a few seconds, but she finally said, "I suppose you can check . . ."

Before she even finished the thought, Gino had carefully set her aside and strode into the house with Sarah and Malloy on his heels. Sarah gave the landlady an apologetic smile, noticing the woman was already in her nightclothes and that she had thrown a dressing gown over them to answer the door.

Gino wasted no time climbing the stairs to the second floor, and Sarah followed, with Malloy close behind. Gino tried the door, but it was locked. He pounded on it and shouted, "Open up, Yingling."

Oddly, there was no response.

Malloy turned to the landlady, who had followed them up the steps. "Are you sure he's here?"

"He came home right after work, and I never saw him leave."

Gino pounded and shouted again, and the only response was an odd, short cry that stopped as abruptly as it began. "Someone is in there." He raised his foot to kick in the door, but the landlady shoved him out of the way, almost knocking him down.

"I've got a key," she informed him. She fumbled with a ring of keys until she found the right one and the door opened at last.

Gino was the first inside, but he stopped after only a few steps. The smell hit them all at the same time, the nauseating odor of vomit. Malloy tried to hold Sarah back, but she shrugged off his hands and stepped around Gino to see what had stopped him. She needed a long moment to interpret the bizarre scene before her.

Tom Yingling lay on the floor in a pool of vomit. Carrie sat in a chair—the only one in the room—looking mildly surprised to see them. She was fully dressed and appeared as serene as if they had found her sitting in the park watching the pigeons.

Malloy went to Yingling and nudged him with his foot. "Yingling, get up."

"He can't," Carrie informed them smugly. "He's dead."

XVI

Sarah was a bit surprised when her maid told her Mrs. Willard Warren had come to see her. She needed only a minute to figure out who her visitor was, though, so she didn't show any surprise when Pearl Bing came into the parlor.

"Mrs. Warren," Sarah said by way of greeting. "I gather congratulations are in order."

"Yes, thank you. Will and I were married a few days ago."

Since it was a blustery day, Sarah asked her maid to bring them some tea, and she invited Pearl to sit with her by the fire.

"I must say I'm a little surprised to see you," Sarah admitted.

"I'm sure you are, but Will insisted I owed you a debt of gratitude that I should acknowledge, and I've come to realize he is right."

"We only did what we were hired to do," Sarah said.

Pearl smiled at that. She really was a lovely girl, and even lovelier now. Sarah realized she seemed softer somehow, probably because she was no longer angry at all the ways in which life had betrayed her. "I believe Ethel hired you to find out who killed my father, but you did far more than that. You even tried to rescue Carrie from a fate worse than death," she added with a small, ironic smile.

"Carrie obviously didn't need our assistance, though."

"Is it true she poisoned that fellow the same way she poisoned my mother?"

Sarah sighed. "Yes. It seems she took a bottle of Mr. Bing's whiskey with her to Mr. Yingling's rooming house. Sadly for him, he couldn't resist sampling it before taking advantage of Carrie."

"No one can blame her for that one, or for killing Father either, come to that. After what he did to her . . . to both of us . . ."

"Yes, you are a strong young woman to have survived."

"You've said that before, that you think I'm strong," Pearl said, a little surprised.

"Surely you can believe me now that you see how your father's abuse destroyed Carrie's mind."

Pearl frowned thoughtfully. "I guess you're right."

"Of course I am," Sarah said with a small smile to soften the words. "I just wish she hadn't killed your mother. I know how much pain that caused you, and I still don't understand why she did it."

"Don't you?" Pearl said. "I didn't either until Carrie told me, but I thought you might have figured it out by now."

"Carrie told you?" Sarah echoed in amazement. "Have you seen her?"

Pearl winced a little. "Yes. I really didn't want to, but it was the only way I could find out why she did it since there isn't going to be a trial."

"But if she really is insane . . ." Sarah said, thinking of all the times Carrie had lied in the past. How could they believe her now?

"She isn't insane, at least not in the way we normally think of people being insane. She isn't raving or talking nonsense. She's just very quiet and so very young, like a child who doesn't quite understand what's happening to her. If you could have seen her . . . I don't think she even understands how bad the things she did were."

"And did she tell you her reason for poisoning your mother?"

"Oh yes. She said she killed my mother because she thought Mother knew she'd killed Father."

Which would have been a perfectly understandable motive if it had been true. "Why did she think that?"

"Because of something Mother said one day when you were visiting. I wasn't there, but Ethel remembered when I asked her about it. You were visiting with Ethel, and Carrie was there. Mother came in and . . . Well, I suppose she was defending me. Carrie was trying to convince you that I murdered Father because I went out the night he was killed. By the way, you were right, I had gone to Will for comfort that night, although I was too proud to admit it when you suggested it. At any rate, during your visit, Mother said something about Carrie going out whenever she wanted to, too, so she could be guilty as well. That made Carrie think Mother knew the truth, although I'm sure she didn't even suspect. None of us did at that point."

"Oh dear," Sarah said, remembering. Nora actually had denied accusing Carrie of being the killer that day, but Sarah had silently disagreed. If only she had said something. Would it have made any difference? "I remember now, but I didn't realize . . ."

"It wasn't your fault. Ethel didn't remember it either until I asked her about it. I don't blame either of you."

"But of course you blame Carrie for killing your mother."

"I'm still angry, of course. I'm angry at losing Mother after finally finding her again after so many years, but Will helped me understand that Father is the one to blame. He's the one who turned Carrie into a killer, and he got what he deserved. Blaming Carrie is foolish, and Will says it will hurt me more than it will hurt her."

"He's right, and Carrie has already been punished for her sins."

Pearl nodded sadly. "Yes, she has. The sanitarium where Ethel put her is clean and the patients are well treated, but she will probably never be able to leave it."

"I know how difficult it was for Ethel to put her in that place, but if she had been tried, a jury of men might have taken pity on such a young girl and acquitted her. Even Ethel had to admit that it was too dangerous to allow her to go free. Heaven only knows whom she might have decided she needed to kill next."

"I've thanked Ethel for that, too, because she also saved me from the scandal a trial would have caused. Putting Carrie away quietly didn't even merit a story in the newspapers, and since she is expecting a child, the doctors can blame her delicate condition for her mental breakdown."

"Do you know what will happen to the baby?"

"Ethel plans to raise it."

"You've discussed it with her?" Sarah asked in surprise.

Pearl smiled sheepishly. "I've been to see her a few times. We have found that we have a lot in common, and I think she appreciates my support. I have Will, but Ethel is completely alone now."

"That's very kind of you. I hope you're happy with Mr. Warren," she added to see what Pearl would say.

To Sarah's surprise, Pearl smiled a genuine smile. "I never expected to be happy, but I've discovered that having someone adore you is rather pleasant."

"Yes, it is," Sarah said. "And you'll make sure Ethel never relents and has Carrie released?"

"I will do what I can, but I don't think Ethel will need much convincing. Carrie blames her mother for locking her up, and Ethel is terrified of her now."

"I suppose we should be thankful for that."

"I'm thankful for many things, Mrs. Malloy, and I owe some of them to your interference. Without you and Mr. Malloy and your associates, we might never have figured out what happened, and Carrie might have continued killing us one by one until she felt safe."

"Then I'm glad we were able to help, at least a little."

"It was more than a little, and I thank you for all of it."

Frank was grinning like a loon when he came into the house, and he knew he was giving himself away, but he couldn't seem to stop smiling. He found Sarah in the kitchen discussing menus with their cook, Velvet.

"What are you up to?" Sarah asked the moment she saw him. Even Velvet grinned.

He wasn't fooling anybody, but he didn't even care. "Mrs. Malloy, may I see you for a moment?"

Sarah exchanged a puzzled glance with Velvet, who said, "Ain't no hurry on this, Mrs. Frank."

Sarah shrugged. "Will it take long?" she asked, following him out of the kitchen.

"It might."

She gave him a suspicious look. "We're not going upstairs this time of day."

He actually laughed. "Now you've ruined my surprise."

"Malloy," she said in warning.

"We're not going upstairs," he said, "although you might want to reward me when you see my surprise."

"Now I really can't wait," she said, although she didn't sound like she meant it.

That didn't matter. She'd forgive him everything when she saw what he'd done.

She stopped dead when he started to open the front door. "I'm not dressed to go out."

"You won't be going far." He threw open the front door and waved his arm in the kind of flourish he'd seen doormen in fancy hotels use.

She obediently looked through the doorway and he eagerly watched the emotions flickering across her beautiful face. Confusion, then doubt, then joy. "Is it mine?" she cried, hurrying down the front stoop to where he'd parked the electric motorcar at the curb.

"Of course it is."

"Is this the one I saw at Will Warren's shop?" she asked, looking it over with what could only be called adoration.

"The very same one."

"Oh, Malloy, it's beautiful!"

"You'll need some lessons before you start driving it."

"Of course, of course. I'm sure Gino or Maeve would be happy to oblige."

"What about me?" he asked, feigning dismay.

"Somehow I don't think it's a good idea for a husband to teach his wife to drive."

She was probably right about that. "Now you'll be able to drive yourself to the maternity hospital whenever you need to go."

"I can drive myself *anywhere,*" she said, her eyes shining with pleasure. She turned to him, smiling provocatively. "And you were right, I do want to take you upstairs, but first, I want to take a ride in my new automobile."

Author's Note

I had a lot of fun researching this book. Learning about early automobiles was so fascinating! It is amazing how close we came to having electric cars be the vehicle of choice from the very first. In the beginning, electrics were the most popular, followed by steam-powered, with gasoline-powered being a distant third. How different our world would be had we not become dependent on fossil fuels, but even Thomas Edison wasn't able to create a lightweight battery that would last long enough for electric vehicles to be practical, although he and his staff worked hard on it.

I discovered that the early electrics worked very much like modern golf carts. Golf carts usually have keys, but the key locks the cart only to foil joyriding. The key doesn't actually start the engine the way it does in a gasoline-powered vehicle. The batteries were always "on" if they were charged, so simply moving the accelerator lever put the auto in motion, and they were as quiet as modern electrics are today. Because electrics didn't require cranking, which could be even more dangerous than I described (people were sometimes killed when the engine backfired, propelling the crank into the air with enough force to fracture a skull), ladies preferred them. Sadly, they gained a reputation of being a ladies' car, and men refused to drive them. Add to that the difficulty of keeping the battery charged on long trips at a time when most homes weren't yet wired for electricity, and the gasoline-powered vehicles soon dominated the market. When Henry Ford introduced an electric starter to the Model T, thus eliminating the need to crank the engine to life, he sounded the death knell of the electric auto for almost another century. And yes, they originally called it the "internal explosion" engine until someone with more marketing sense changed it to "internal combustion."

New York State did have very strict divorce laws in 1900, when this book is set, with adultery being the only grounds accepted, although couples might obtain a legal separation or an annulment in unusual cases. This situation lasted until the Divorce Reform Law in 1966. Prior to that, wealthy people could travel to one of the western states where the laws were more lenient, and this is how Reno, Nevada, became the divorce capital of the country for a time. In spite of all these obstacles, the United States still had the highest divorce rate in the world during this period.

I also mentioned some shady election practices, which were quite common in those days. Ward heelers did encourage men (only men could vote at this time) to vote in every precinct, and free drinks were often the lure. This is why, after Prohibition was repealed, many states made laws that required all bars to close on Election Day. That law is still in effect in seven states today. Voter registration laws now make it impossible for people to vote more than once so our elections are much more secure today.

I hope you enjoyed this book. You can follow me on Facebook at Victoria.Thompson.Author or on Twitter @GaslightVT. Check out my website for all my titles at www.VictoriaThompson.com and send me an e-mail to get on my mailing list so you'll always be notified when I have a new book coming out.

Center Point Large Print
600 Brooks Road / PO Box 1
Thorndike, ME 04986-0001 USA

(207) 568-3717

US & Canada:
1 800 929-9108
www.centerpointlargeprint.com